4/9/16

To Arthur & Mariluz —
two wonderful, long-time,
irreplaceable friends —
With love from Chicand

Ed

# THE PATRON MURDERS

## EDWIN WILSON

PROSPECTA PRESS

NEW YORK AND WESTPORT 2015

Prospecta Press

P.O. Box 3131

Westport, CT 06880

www.prospectapress.com

*Book and cover design by Barbara Aronica-Buck*

Hardcover ISBN 978-1-63226-042-0

eBook ISBN 978-1-63226-043-7

Manufactured in the United States of America

First Edition

To my wife, Catherine Wilson

With thanks to Sidney Offit
and my agent, Tom Wallace

# CHAPTER ONE

For an actor appearing in a new play, the most exciting time is the opening night, plus, if you are lucky, the day or two after, when the reviews and congratulations roll in. That's what everyone assumes. Wrong. The truly stimulating time is not end of the process but the beginning—the days and weeks leading up to the opening when you are in the rehearsal room and, after that, on a bare stage.

On the first day of rehearsal, you sit around a table with the director, the playwright, and the other creative people, reading through the script. Later, you get the play "on its feet," blocking scenes: how you enter and leave, when and where you move. Next, you memorize your lines and get "off book." All the time you're working on your character: Who is this person? What is he really like? How does he relate to the other characters in the play? For a performer this is what it's all about—creating a living, breathing stage character.

I'm an actor, Matt Johanssen, and at the time this story begins I was in just such a situation—rehearsing a play headed for Broadway. Entitled *The Unwitting Executor*, it was written by a young playwright, Elliot Webster, about a dysfunctional family—naturally. Ninety percent of the new plays in the post-millennium era were about family members at each other's throats, figuratively if not literally. Webster, however, was far better than most of the "emerging" playwrights, producing sharp, pungent dialogue that was often extremely funny. He also had a keen sense of character.

In *The Unwitting Executor*, a well-to-do uncle has died, and, since he has no children, he has left everything to his sister's family, which consists of a husband (a borderline alcoholic); the wife, who feels she was robbed of a singing career when she got pregnant and married her husband; and their three children, all in their late teens or early twenties. The uncle, who rarely saw the family but was aware of their problems, has not made specific bequests to individual family members, but rather has appointed an executor to his estate who is to visit the family, get to know them, and then decide who gets what. This uninvited executor, a long-time friend and colleague of the uncle's but not known to the family, is a sort of other-worldly figure brought in to uncover long-standing animosities and perhaps ameliorate them. Naturally, the family members vie frantically for his attention and favor. I was playing the role of the executor.

On our last day of rehearsals before we moved from the studio to the theatre, we put in a new scene, a good example of the kind of thing that happens when a new play is in rehearsal. Carol Saunders, the actress who plays the younger sister in *The Unwitting Executor*, was a promising young performer, talented as well as versatile. Twenty-two or -three, she looked younger and could easily play a convincing eighteen-year-old. For some time she had been saying that our main scene together, hers and mine, was too predictable, too static. Her concern coincided with a general feeling I had about my role: playing the part of a seemingly neutral, independent character, I felt there was the constant danger that I would emerge as two-dimensional, a stick figure without any emotional qualities or idiosyncrasies.

Elliot, the playwright, had taken all this to heart and revised the scene between the two of us to provide more give and take. When he emailed it to us, I was impressed with what he had done. The idea was that Carol and I would get to the theatre about forty-five minutes early on Friday and go over the scene. If it seemed to be working, we would put it in Friday night.

In the original version the impulsive, seemingly spontaneous actions of Carol's character appeared genuine, but, the way the scene was rewritten, this could have been playacting on the character's part as a means of manipulating my character. On my side, Elliott had me doing a bit of the same. In the new version, most of the time I seemed totally sincere and appeared to be taking this free-spirited young lady at face value, but then he introduced a twist, a note of skepticism that suggested I was on to her game and was simply playing along with it, perhaps to get more insight into who she really was and discover what game she was playing.

When I arrived at the rehearsal hall, Carol was there ahead of me, as were the director, Rowan, and Connie, the stage manager. We went through the new scene once, merely saying our lines while Rowan set the blocking. Just as the new version was less static than the old one, so the movement now was more fluid: we circled around each other more, playing cat and mouse. Having established the blocking, we went through the scene for real, and it was one of those moments of discovery you have every so often in the theatre. Three or four minutes into the new scene, we knew it was clicking. We were taking turns throwing each other off-balance; there was thrust and parry, and far more emotion as well as uncertainty. Everyone agreed that the new scene should go in that night. The rest of the cast, seeing the spontaneity of the scene, the ebb and flow, were inspired to inject a bit of the same into their scenes with me. Without changing the lines, the overall effect was a freshness, an excitement, we all shared.

• • •

*The Unwitting Executor* was a coproduction of Dorothy Tremayne and the Centre Theatre Group, known as CTG. Dorothy had discovered the play at a workshop reading in SoHo and brought it to CTG, headed by artistic director Ardith Wainwright and managing director Freddie Stamos. Though a nonprofit organization, CTG had a Broadway theatre, the Adelphi, on 49th Street between Seventh and Eighth Avenues. It was one of the smaller Broadway houses and ideal for new plays and small musicals.

Dorothy's great love was for new work, both plays and musicals. Mostly, she supported off-Broadway ventures, but she also helped bring several promising plays to Broadway, and *The Unwitting Executor* was one of those. Not a dilettante—one of those producers who teamed up with twenty other non-creative backers just so her name could be "above the title"—she either produced plays herself or, as in this case, with a nonprofit company.

Though Dorothy's passion was serious, worthwhile theatre, her interest did not exclude musicals, comedies, or even farce. But it was always theatre, never film or TV, and even with theatre she was wholeheartedly opposed to what she saw as the dumbing down of the art form, a good case in point being those Disney-type extravaganzas based on sophomoric films or cartoons. For her, the latter belonged in theme parks or Las Vegas, not in legitimate theatre.

When Dorothy first began to feel her way into producing, a character named Sybil Conway saw her as a "live one." A severe, smart-looking, ice queen type, Sybil was in the mode of those razor-sharp heroines of '30s and '40s movies. Her ash blonde hair was short and carefully styled to frame her face, in the Anna Wintour fashion. With penetrating amber eyes and a clearly defined nose and chin, she was supremely sure of herself, always aware of the effect she had on everyone, men and women.

Sybil had made a career of searching out would-be producers she pegged as neophytes and glomming on to them like a succubus. But she was extremely clever, as well as subtle. She never approached her targets with a frontal assault. At first she was all helpfulness and consideration, offering her services, her experience, and her knowledge of theatre, with no hint of an ulterior motive. Inevitably, however, once she had established herself as a partner, she slowly but relentlessly enlarged her share of the operation: an increase in the size of her billing on posters, a larger percentage of the royalties, and so forth. All this, of course, even though none of the money invested had been hers.

When Dorothy first took up with Sybil, people warned her of Sybil's reputation, but unknown to them Dorothy had her own agenda. She wanted to learn about producing as fast as she could, and she knew Sybil would give her a crash course. So, while everyone, including Sybil, thought that she was leading Dorothy down the garden path, Dorothy was doing exactly what she had set out to do: learn everything she could about the business as quickly as possible.

The crossroads, the tipping point, was a revival of *A Streetcar Named Desire*, being produced by the Triangle Company, the chief rival of CTG as a not-for-profit theatre operating on Broadway. Unlike CTG, which presented a number of new works, Triangle concentrated mainly on revivals of overlooked or difficult-to-produce classics. That wasn't the only difference between the two. Artemis D'Angelo, the artistic director of Triangle, was hot-tempered, whereas Ardith, the head of CTG, was cool.

For Triangle's production of *Streetcar*, Artemis had lured Cheryl Marshall, a star seemingly lost to Hollywood, back to the theatre. Cheryl had been nominated for three Oscars, had won one, and had also captured two Emmys, but in interviews she always claimed her first love was the stage. Each year, however, the prospect of her returning to the stage seemed less and less likely. Artemis had dangled the role of Blanche DuBois in front of her, with a director of her choice, and she had said yes.

Secretly, Artemis and Sybil had always wanted to join forces. In terms of personality and ambition, they were definitely on the same wavelength, and this seemed the ideal opportunity.

Dorothy had previously backed only new work, but Sybil had convinced her that bringing Cheryl back to Broadway would be a master stroke for live theatre, so Dorothy reluctantly went along. Rehearsals were about to begin when a film Cheryl had presumably finished insisted she had to return to re-shoot several key scenes. Under her theatre contract, she was allowed to bow out if that happened. Greatly underestimating Dorothy's inner strength, Sybil and Artemis were sure they could persuade her to go along with the production without Cheryl. But Dorothy, knowing that she had been manipulated, pulled out. Not only that: she told Sybil that this was the end of their partnership and suggested that Sybil vacate her office within three weeks. Dorothy, of course, had always paid for everything.

Once she had recovered from the shock, Sybil began pleading, saying that it was all a misunderstanding and that she herself had been misled by Artemis. She and Dorothy had always worked so well together and had had real success with virtually everything they had produced. When that argument failed, Sybil hurled a stream of invectives at Dorothy. She became so vehement that Dorothy called in the young man from her outer office, and asked him to call 911, whereupon Sybil walked out. Because Dorothy's enhancement funds had been the linchpin for the production, it had to be cancelled, much to the embarrassment of both Artemis and Sybil.

People were surprised by Dorothy's show of strength, but I wasn't. To me it had been coming on for some time—several months, in fact. I had first met Dorothy some ten or twelve years before when she was still married to Warren Tremayne, long before she had become a theatre producer. Warren was a successful mid-level hedge fund operator in the '90s and early 2000s with whom I had invested for a time and done quite well.

When Dorothy got divorced, four or five years ago, she got in touch with me, and we would meet once a month or so, and she would ask me about the workings of the theatre. In one of our recent meetings, before the *Streetcar* debacle, she confided to me that, more and more, she felt she should be her own person, stand on her own two feet, trust her instincts and not rely on others. I told her to go for it. "You don't need Sybil," I said. "You don't need anyone." I could tell she was ready, and she knew she was, too.

• • •

The day we put in the new scene between Carol and me was our last day working on *The Unwitting Executor* in the rehearsal studio. Although the whole process of putting on a new play is a challenge, the period we were in just now was particularly difficult. For several weeks we had been in the familiar confines of the rehearsal studio—a large, open rectangular space with only tape on the floor to indicate walls, doors, entrances, and exits. On Thursday, however, we would report to the Adelphi Theatre. Over the last few days, various crews had been moving in equipment: scenery, costumes, lighting, and sound gear. Our new schedule, Thursday through Saturday, would be rehearsals during the day and run-throughs each night. Technical rehearsals would begin on Monday. As we moved into this new environment, a lot of things had to come together; many things could go wrong. The plan was to have two days of technical rehearsals, then dress rehearsals before a small invited audience for the balance of the coming week. After that we would have a week of previews and then the opening.

Though we did not realize it at the time—nor did anyone else—on the same day we were putting in our new scene, something far more dramatic was occurring thirty blocks away at the Metropolitan Museum of Art.

# CHAPTER TWO

A stocky six feet one, Marcus Antonelli had worked at the Met Museum for twenty-seven years. With the cauliflower ears of a boxer, a wide, flat nose, and a buzz cut of salt-and-pepper hair, he looked more like someone's idea of a longshoreman or construction worker than a museum employee. He had begun at the Met as a janitor: cleaning bathrooms, picking up debris the morning after a gala at the Costume Institute, or fishing pennies out of the pool near the Temple of Dendur.

After a few months, though, there was a vacancy in Service and Shipping, so he was taken on there. Through the years he moved steadily up through the ranks. Despite his appearance, including a pair of ham-fisted hands, he proved slowly but surely to be so caring, so firm yet gentle in dealing with paintings and pieces of sculpture, especially masterpieces—a Rembrandt, for instance, or a priceless figure of Greek or Roman sculpture—that he eventually became head of Service and Shipping. Marcus was the person in charge of hanging special exhibitions, and of preparing irreplaceable paintings, maybe a Vermeer or a Rubens, when they were packed for shipping to the Louvre, the National Gallery in London, or the Kimball in Fort Worth. He had, as one former director put it, "soft hands." He was the first person to touch such an object when it left its customary space at the Met and the last person to touch it before it was sent on its way.

In the late 1980s, the Met began featuring installations out of doors, on its roof, from May to October. The type of exhibitions featured included, in 2008, Jeff Koons's balloon sculptures and, in 2010, the Starn brothers' bamboo jungle, a three-story-high maze of intertwining bamboo, cane shoots, and sticks. The most recent exhibit had been a work by a Frenchman, Alphonse Cartier called *Through the Air*, a construction made entirely of linear, wooden athletic objects: hockey sticks, baseball bats, old wooden skis and ski poles, pole-vaulting poles, javelins, arrows, wooden golf shafts. The exhibit, which drew large crowds and mixed reviews, closed on the first Sunday in October, and crews spent Monday and Tuesday dismantling it.

On Wednesday morning Marcus, as was his custom, went alone to the roof to see that everything had been cleaned up and put in order. Once out the door, he turned to the right, where a small snack bar was traditionally set up, and found it spotless except for a plastic fork lodged in the hedge. He walked carefully around the area and up a short flight of steps leading to the exit. At the top of the steps behind a low wall was a flat area, covered in tarpaper. Marcus glanced across the surface, expecting it to be empty, but was greeted with a ghastly sight he could never in his wildest dreams have expected to see. "My God," he exclaimed. "Oh, my God!" What he saw, lying along the hedge below the wall, was a man in a well-cut business suit, stretched on his back, with the point of a javelin buried deep in his chest and the staff sticking in the air.

After standing in shock—frozen in disbelief—for what seemed like minutes but was actually seconds, Marcus turned, hurtled down the three steps, and headed through the entry doors, as fast as he could run, toward the executive offices of the museum. Moving ever faster, he skirted down hallways through two outer offices straight into the office of the director. Gasping for breath, he ignored a curator who was in the office, and moved straight to the director, blurting out the word, "Come." Disbelieving the sight of the always-reserved Marcus standing before him issuing a command, the director asked, "Where?"

"The roof."

• • •

The victim turned out to be a man in his late sixties named Clifford Mulholland. Mulholland had been on the Board of Trustees at the Met for four years and had just recently been elected to the Finance Committee. There had been a meeting of the committee on Tuesday afternoon, which Mulholland had attended. Detectives surmised that, following the meeting, two men had somehow kidnapped the victim as he was leaving—assuming two men because it would have taken at least two to subdue Mulholland and get him to the roof unnoticed.

The murder investigation was under the direction of not one but two police precincts. The nearest precinct to the Met was the 22nd which served Central Park. But, because the museum faced 82nd Street, the men at the 22nd called in the

19th, located fifteen blocks south on 67th near Lex. In the heart of the Upper East Side, the 19th was accustomed to handling crime among the upscale residents of the area. Immediately it was decided that this would be a joint operation of the 19th and the 22nd, with the former taking the lead. Not surprisingly, both precincts put their best men and women on the case, all under the direction of Detective Vince Markham from the 19th. For the moment, however, law enforcement seemed not to have a clue as to why the crime was committed or who did it. All they were certain of was that it was a professional job. Also, the nature of the crime—the javelin from the exhibition, the site of the execution, and the identity of the victim— strongly suggested that the relationship between the museum, its art, and its trustees seemed to be at the heart of the matter.

Late Wednesday afternoon, the Met issued a statement decrying the heinous crime that took the life of an outstanding trustee who had contributed so much to the museum and the city. They singled out the particularly brutal nature of the murder with its gratuitous sensationalism. The museum praised the work of Mulholland, a tireless and stalwart trustee, they said, who had served the institution with distinction and devotion. They offered their heartfelt condolences to the widow and the family and stated that the museum would be closed the next day, Thursday, in memory of Mulholland. They expressed the hope that the perpetrator would be found forthwith and brought to justice. The statement closed by pointing out that the museum was a place of beauty and enlightenment, a repository of all things noble and inspiring in the long march of artistic achievements.

What the statement did not say was that the closing on Thursday would give both the museum and the police time to track down clues and evidence, unencumbered by a stream of visitors.

• • •

By five o'clock Wednesday, the media circus surrounding the murder at the Metropolitan was in full swing. Every TV channel in the city was camped out on the front steps of the museum. Large white vans, their dishes and antennas on top, were parked up and down Fifth Avenue for several blocks north and south of 82nd Street. Every side street off Fifth had become a solid lane of vehicles with press credentials on their license plates.

The fact that there was absolutely no news in the way of specifics did not deter the voracious appetites of either the local or national TV outlets. Because there were no actual photographs of the victim with the javelin in his chest, there were endless pictures of the front of the Met and file footage of the main lobby of the building, as well as images of the rooftop exhibit of sports items that had just closed. Reporters endlessly pointed out the sharp contrast between the serenity and dignity of the museum and the gruesome, grisly circumstances of the murder. They speculated wildly on the method, the perpetrator, and the purpose of this sensational crime. There seemed to be an inverse ratio between how little the reporters actually knew and how far afield they let their imaginations roam in attempting to fill the void.

On Thursday morning the tabloids weighed in. The *New York Post* turned the front and back pages sideways—something they did only twice a year or so. Across the full width of the back and front pages was a rendering of a man in a business suit, lying on his back with a javelin protruding from his chest. Inserts in the four corners featured a file photo of Mulholland, a picture of Marcus Antonelli, and photos of the façade of the museum and the recent roof exhibition. There were other photographs in the press and on TV of the exterior of the Mulhollands's apartment house as well as a shot of Mulholland and his wife at a recent black-tie gala.

There were wild conjectures in the press as to who might have done it: an embittered artist whose work was not included in the Met collection, a group of artists similarly excluded, a jealous philanthropist who was denied membership on the Met's Board of Trustees, perhaps a woman—a spurned mistress or disillusioned curator. The list went on and on. There were also detailed hypotheses of just how the perpetrator drove the javelin into the victim's chest, what might have been said as the blow was delivered, how the murderer had gotten away.

To cover the murder, the *New York Times* had assigned a team: Georgina Fleming, known to her friends as Gina, who was on the arts beat, and Andrew Considine from the financial desk, suggesting that the paper suspected the crime involved both art and finance. The first thing the two reported on was the actual cause of death, discovered at the postmortem: it was not the javelin thrust, but asphyxiation. Apparently the victim was first suffocated, perhaps by having a plastic bag held over his head, and then stabbed. This meant, of course, that the javelin thrust was primarily symbolic. The perpetrators were clearly crying out for attention.

It was pointed out in their first article that the Metropolitan Museum had been subject to very few art crimes—none, for instance, approached the large-scale thefts from the Isabella Stewart Gardner Museum in Boston in 1990. This clean record made the current episode that much more embarrassing. Certainly there had never been anything as lurid and melodramatic as the Mulholland murder.

The fact of the suffocation before the stabbing also suggested that the crime was probably a highly professional job, one that had been carefully thought out and planned. This was borne out by the fact that the lenses of all the surveillance cameras—in the elevators, the hallways, the underground areas, and a number of behind-the-scenes offices—had been sprayed with black paint to obliterate any images of the perpetrators. As for the galleries and main entrance hall, the hordes that crowded these spaces at any given moment would have made it virtually impossible to pick out a likely suspect from pictures on security video cameras. Someone could easily have mixed in with any gallery group and sauntered out unnoticed. One other fact: Mulholland's wife, Roxanne, who had lived in Chicago prior to marrying her husband, had been in Chicago at the time of the murder. Whether her trip was a coincidence or she had been lured there in some way was yet to be determined. Solving the crime was not going to be easy, to say the least.

In their later piece in the *Times* on Friday morning, the team of Fleming and Considine focused on Mulholland. If little was known about the person or persons responsible for the crime, Mulholland himself was both known and unknown. As for the known part, his recent history was well documented, which is what the *Times* writers focused on. Mulholland had followed a well-trodden path, making lots of money in the Midwest—his net worth was estimated to be between $2 and $3 billion—and then moving to New York to become a culture maven. The door was opened, as it almost always was, via philanthropy. One donated, and if one passed a few social tests, one was eventually invited to join a prestigious board. It didn't always work, but that was the fervent hope.

Among various boards, there were none headier than the Metropolitan Museum of Art. The Museum of Natural History, Lincoln Center, the Frick, the New York Philharmonic, the Museum of Modern Art were all plums, but the Metropolitan Opera was the only institution that truly rivaled the Met. There were a couple of criteria that bestowed on each of these two institutions the pride of place. One was the silent but unmistakable obeisance paid to them by such publications as the *Times* and *Vanity Fair*. The other was the matter of cold, hard cash: it was no secret that the minimum gift for an invitation to become a trustee at the Met was at least $10 to $15 million. That, however, was just for starters. There were also annual donations, the underwriting of special exhibits, and perhaps a gift large enough to have some nook or cranny in the museum bear the donor's name.

All this, of course, was just the kind of opening Mulholland had been looking for. Like so many before him, he had had an apparently insatiable desire to break into the magic circle—to have himself and his wife appear as often as possible in Bill Cunningham's gallery of the elite that was featured each Sunday in the style section of the *Times*. Besides the money and the desire, Mulholland had something else going for him: his wife, Roxanne. In traditional fashion—in his move from entrepreneur to connoisseur—he had shed his first wife, whom he had married just out of college, and married Roxanne. She, however, was no airhead or bimbo.

Mulholland had met her at a dinner party in Chicago. It turned out that she was a docent at the Art Institute there, with a master's degree in art history from Kansas. She was, in fact, the head docent, training others. Everyone agreed that she was sharp enough and accomplished enough to have been a curator, if she had not been the wife of a major player in the Second City. The meeting with Roxanne was indeed fortuitous for Mulholland, who had been hoping to soon begin his assault on the New York cultural scene.

A year and a half before Mulholland and Roxanne met, her husband, Zack Wineglass, had suffered an embolism on the golf course and died within a few hours. In a very short time Mulholland recognized that Roxanne was just the partner he was looking for. Tall, brunette, striking-looking, but independent-minded and obviously savvy, she came across as anything but the conventional trophy wife.

Mulholland was patient, recognizing that the last thing he should do was rush things. He had only recently moved to Chicago, and had bought a tasteful apartment on Lake Shore Drive. He was enjoying getting to know the city—the many theatres (he had discovered what a gold mine Chicago was for theatre) as well the museums. Despite his interest in dance, opera, and theatre, he let it be known that his real love was art. Slowly, steadily, he convinced Roxanne that he was a willing and observant pupil, eager to improve his knowledge and judgment when it came to appreciating art. Meanwhile, he quietly began his campaign for her not only to marry him but to come with him to New York. Finally, after a good many months, she agreed, acknowledging that Chicago had many good memories but also some painful ones, now that Zack was gone.

As for the murder itself, the *Times* coverage stated that, more and more, it appeared to have been a carefully planned, fully professional job. The Tuesday night on which it occurred, for example, was not only the night after an afternoon Finance Committee meeting but a rare night when the Museum itself was open. An enormously popular exhibit featuring the work of a French dress designer had drawn unprecedented crowds, crowds so large that the museum had extended the exhibition and added a few evening openings of which this particular Tuesday night had been one.

# CHAPTER THREE

As an actor, I was not only the first person in my family to be involved in the theatre—I was the only one. My family on both sides was what used to be called "well-to-do." Both my mother and my father came from "good families." Mother's father had been a professor and then a college administrator—first a dean at Brown and then president of Bowdoin College in Maine. My father, like his father before him, was a lawyer, a partner in the firm of Arnold, Beloit and Delaney, one of the top four or five law firms in Manhattan. My mother's brother had been a partner at Goldman Sachs and, two years after the firm went public, bowed out with a cool $48 million in his pocket. We spent the summers at the compound of my father's family in Little Compton, Rhode Island.

Surrounded by establishment achievers in law, education, and investment, it was assumed that I would surely go into one of those three fields. Actually, I tried. I graduated from Princeton and was all set to go to Yale Law. But two things happened. In June, I got married. Her name was Cindy Osborne, a gorgeous blonde, with pale blue eyes and a few freckles spread across flawless, creamy skin, who was also loads of fun. We had been dating for nearly two years, and she graduated from Mount Holyoke the same year I finished Princeton.

In terms of marriage practices at that time, it was a transition period. For years couples had gotten married in their early twenties, and almost never later than the mid-twenties. By the end of the twentieth century, young people were waiting longer—often living together, but postponing marriage for who knows how long. Cindy and I, however, were comfortable with the past. Besides, both our families were unreservedly for the union. So on a lovely day in late June, at a white clapboard church in New Canaan, Connecticut, we were married.

The other reason I didn't rush off to law school is that we had a chance to spend a year in London. I had a one-year fellowship at the London School of Economics, and a year long honeymoon abroad seemed too good to pass up. So in late summer, Cindy and I headed to England, found a small flat in Cheyne Walk, and had a terrific year abroad, mostly in London and nearby environs, which we explored avidly, but also with side trips to the Continent.

The next fall I was back in New Haven, at law school. That's when it began to happen. I lay awake nights, tossing and turning. Cindy thought I was worried about classes and the fierce competition at Yale. I was worried about classes, but what kept me awake was something entirely different. I began to think I wanted to be an actor. At Princeton I had been in the Triangle show every year and did some acting at the McCarter Theatre, playing the young man in a production of *Tea and Sympathy* and a similar role in *Dark at the Top of the Stairs*. Increasingly, that fall at Yale, I came to the conclusion that acting was what I wanted to do. By early December, I had made up my mind.

When I told Cindy, and later my family, not surprisingly, everyone was shocked. The reactions ranged from incredulity to dismay to outright anger; questions were even raised about my sanity. Everyone assumed this was something you did earlier on the curve—maybe your junior year in college, in a summer job, or the first year after college when you take time off to travel, just as Cindy and I had done. In my case I had had several summer jobs as well as the year in London, so it was assumed that I had gotten all the uncertainty "out of my system." But here I was, married, starting law school, and suddenly I wanted to take off to be in the theatre, of all things.

I tried to get into the Yale Drama School for the second semester, but was told I had to wait until the fall. Meantime, I had heard about a group in San Francisco called the American Conservatory Theatre, known as ACT. I had learned two things about it that I liked: their focus was on the actor, and they emphasized the classics. I took a long weekend in early December to fly out and audition for the company. I was accepted as an apprentice actor and, together with the person in charge of actor training, developed a two-year acting regimen that was the equivalent of what later became their Master of Fine Arts program.

For Cindy, more than for anyone else, this was a bolt out of the blue. I'm sure that, like my parents, her parents, and everyone else we knew, Cindy was certain this was a "phase" and would pass. But once she absorbed it, or rather, realized that I was going to go through with it, she was supportive. And so, in January, a somewhat frightened aspiring actor and his dazed young wife took off for San Francisco.

I knew from the start that this might mark the beginning of the end of my marriage. The Greenwich-Manhattan axis was in Cindy's DNA. In her world, no matter how far one strayed—a year in London, law school at Stanford, whatever—one always returned to that world. Like birds who fly south for the winter but return home in the spring, people who grew up in that world invariably came home to roost. Not surprisingly, then, by the fall we had separated, and six months after that, we were divorced. It was entirely amicable, especially since I assumed full and complete responsibility.

• • •

The summer after I finished my two-year training program at ACT, I got a job at a small theatre outside San Francisco; it was a holdover from the old summer stock syndrome, with a new show every two weeks. During the season, we put on two or three musicals mixed with straight plays, all of them familiar, either from the distant past or a recent Broadway run. I worked hard, appearing in two out of every three shows. What I remember most about that summer, however, was not the shows but Trixie Somers, the resident comedienne who saw it as a point of honor to bed any young leading man who came into the troupe. At ACT, I had been so focused on getting my degree that my sex life was intermittent at best. That summer I made up for lost time with Trixie. As an actress, Trixie was totally predictable, employing the same clichés and shtick week

23

after week, but in the sack she was endlessly inventive as well as tireless.

By the end of the summer, I was utterly exhausted and retreated to the family compound in Little Compton to rest and recharge my batteries. It was the end of the season, so I was pretty much alone there, and for three weeks was able to more or less collapse. After that, I girded up my loins and headed for Manhattan.

When I arrived in New York in the mid-seventies, the theatre was entering a period of fragmentation—a period, needless to say, that it has been enmeshed in ever since. Gone were the glory days of new plays every year by writers like Williams, Miller, and O'Neill; long gone also were the halcyon days of the American musical: the works of Rodgers and Hart, George Gershwin, Cole Porter, and Jerome Kern. Rather, the theatre was becoming a patchwork quilt of old and new, the solidly traditional and the wildly experimental, Beckett and Genet next to Neil Simon. It was a mélange of La Mama, Caffé Cinno, gay, lesbian, Latino, and African American offerings, a gumbo of Broadway, off-Broadway, and off-off-Broadway.

Amid all this I remained a traditionalist. I went to a great many avant-garde offerings and did my best to appreciate and understand them. Some had a spark of originality; some admirably shook up preconceptions about theatre, and life; some were quite amusing. But many were pretentious, not to say fatuous. The theatre I loved was what I saw as the timeless offerings stretching from the Greeks, through Shakespeare, Molière, Ibsen, and Chekhov, into the twentieth century. Also, this struggle between the tried-and-true and the experimental did not immediately impact me. I did what actors have been doing for decades, which is to say I attended auditions, morning, noon, and night. I began to get a few acting jobs, but to pay the rent I also managed a few guest appearances on soap operas: *One Life to Live*, *The Young and the Restless*, *All My Children*. Eventually, through a friend who was a writer for *As the World Turns*, I landed a continuing role on that timeless epic.

Through the years I was able to carve out a niche for myself as an actor, mostly in traditional roles, comic as well as serious. I had a decent speaking voice, and to improve that aspect of my work, one summer early on, I attended a three-month workshop at the Royal Academy of Dramatic Art (RADA) in London, returning home having mastered a more than passable British accent. In terms of looks, I do not have the matinee idol appeal of a Paul Newman or Robert Redford, but I come across as quite presentable: dark hair, an open face, and a reasonably trim physique.

In terms of stage movement, I'm no dancer (though I can do a mean soft shoe), but I learned to manage a convincing sword fight and to be adequately nimble in executing stairs, platforms, and the like. I was thus able to land a number of parts in British plays: *The Importance of Being Earnest*, the work of Noël Coward, and, of course, Shakespeare. The latter was important because the Bard is the most widely produced playwright in the United States. Among more recent British writers, I often landed parts in the plays of Tom Stoppard, and even Harold Pinter.

What I could not portray well, and frankly, was not the least interested in playing, were the profane, disaffected, and often low-life characters in plays by writers like Sam Shepard and David Mamet. Rather, in American works, I proved a natural for establishment middle- and upper-class figures in plays such as Pete Gurney's *The Dining Room* and *Love Letters*. Also, a few years ago I got some of the best reviews of my career playing the college professor, George, in a revival of Albee's *Who's Afraid of Virginia Woolf?*

I also had an acceptable singing voice, not of operatic quality certainly, but with a sure sense of pitch, and strong enough for most of the mainstream musicals. There was a two-year period, for example, when I played the lead in Stephen Sondheim's *Company* in a number of regional theatres across the country. *Hair* and other rock musicals, however, were not my cup of tea.

Once I had established a foothold as an actor, it became clearer to me what I could and could not do, as well as what I did and did not want to do. In the '70s and '80s, the non-profit theatres in many parts of the United States were in the ascendancy and proved to be a natural for me. I was fortunate that several of the best ones were nearby—New Haven, Hartford, Providence, Boston—but I found work in other first-rate regional theatres: Louisville, Chicago, Minneapolis, Los Angeles.

As for film work, it was not my first love. The work I did in the soaps on TV was mainly for financial support. As soon as my stage career took hold, I moved away from daytime television. I did, however, get into film a bit. In the '80s and '90s, more and more movies were being shot in New York. At that point I was represented by an eager agent who pushed for a film career. Early on, I had the second lead in a couple of feature films, whereupon my ambitious agent wanted me to move to Los Angeles and work chiefly in films—agents are always pushing their clients to go for the big bucks. It soon became clear that she and I were on different wavelengths, and we parted ways.

Thereafter, I found a new agent, Mollie Avery, who understood where I was coming from, and since then we have had a pleasant and productive relationship, stretching now over twenty years. I still appeared in the occasional feature film, and in its fourth season I got a continuing part in *Law & Order*, appearing every three or four episodes. My role was that of a psychiatrist called in periodically to analyze a person or situation. For the most part, however—ninety percent of the time—it has been the stage.

• • •

Monday night we were holding our first technical rehearsal for *The Unwitting Executor*. For an actor, tech rehearsals are the worst nights before a show opens. The actor might as well not be there, because such nights belong to the director, the stage manager, and the designers. It's the time to set light and sound cues, to work on scene shifts and costume changes. Instead of playing each scene, you start "at the top" and then go "cue to cue." An actor will deliver an opening line, "This is the most bizarre thing I ever heard of—" and the director will yell, "Cut." Then you skip to where the next light cue comes. The stage manager will read from the script, "Believe me, I don't like this any more than you do . . ." and the lights begin to change. And so it goes, from scene to scene, cue to cue, with the actors little more than marionettes with strings pulled by the director, in our case a man named Rowan Wilkinson.

We were halfway through the second act in our tech rehearsal when it happened: an ear splitting scream from somewhere offstage. Everyone froze. A clearly distraught gopher, Madeleine something, came running up to the stage manager. "It's Dorothy . . . on the floor in the lounge . . . she's . . . she's . . . dead."

• • •

The Adelphi theatre had a downstairs lounge with a bar where patrons gathered before a show and during intermission. The johns were also in this area, so it got a lot of traffic in the intermissions. During tech rehearsal no one was down there, but the gopher, Madeleine, had been sent down to get a supply of bottled water. There was only a dim light in the lounge, and when she turned on the switch, there was Dorothy on the floor. When the gopher blurted out what she had seen, the stage manager, Connie Hoffman, told her assistant to call 911, and then she and Rowan and a couple of actors, including me, headed downstairs.

When we got to the lounge, there she was, the vibrant, thoughtful, exceptional person I had admired and even loved, lying motionless on the carpet. She was on her back with her head slightly turned. Her face had turned faintly blue, and her eyes, still open, bulged slightly. One arm was flung awkwardly to the side, her hand limply lying open. I could not believe it. One never can in such circumstances. So much raced through my head, but then emotions overcame everything else. It was a mistake; it couldn't be real. But another part of me knew it was all too real.

Our ever-efficient stage manager bent over Dorothy's body, ready to administer CPR. When she realized there was no point, she headed upstairs to meet the police, while the director and I remained. In a moment, Rowan decided that he too should get back to the stage to calm the cast and crew, so he asked if I would stay and watch over Dorothy. When he was gone, I moved toward the body. She was wearing a yellow turtleneck sweater under a pale blue jacket, and a pair of smartly tailored gray slacks. There were no obvious knife or gunshot wounds, but there was something on the back of her head, a small gash that had been bleeding. I took out my handkerchief and carefully pulled down the neck of the sweater and saw the dark bruises that indicated she had been strangled, and rather brutally at that. I moved the sweater back under her chin and stepped away—just in time, actually, for the police at that moment came bounding down the steps and took over.

In rapid succession, police detectives, and a photographer arrived at the theatre, with the coroner following a bit later. Upstairs, still in shock and disbelief, we all gathered in the front rows of the theatre: actors, designers, crew, everyone. Rowan tried to bring some order to the general murmur and atmosphere of fright and sorrow. And in a moment, Ardith Wainwright, the artistic director of CTG, and Freddie Stamos, the managing director, arrived. Rowan gladly handed over the meeting to Ardith. A person of great presence, she was nevertheless clearly shaken, as was everyone else. Nothing like this had ever happened to CTG, she said, and in fact nothing this serious had happened to her in all her years of theatre. Freddie and Rowan nodded in agreement.

Naturally, tech rehearsal would be suspended, Ardith said. She and Freddie would decide later what to do, and we would hear by email from the stage manager. In the meantime, the police wanted everyone to stay. Ardith didn't think any of the people present would be suspects, because they had all been in the theatre for the past two or three hours, in sight of one another. This included not only the actors and designers, but also the crew. "Some of us were away for short periods of time, while we were not needed on stage," one of the actors said. "In the dressing rooms," she hastened to add. "True," said Ardith, "and I'm sure the police will want a statement from you about that."

Finally, we heard that the police, the photographers, and the coroner had finished, and the body had been taken away for the postmortem. We were taking a collective deep breath, waiting to be questioned, when Danny came bursting in. "Where is she? Where is my mother?" he screamed. Ardith, Freddie, and Rowan took him in hand and gently eased him off stage.

Danny was Dorothy's son, a blond-haired young man, almost pencil-thin, with a sharp nose, pointed chin, and eyebrows so blond they appeared almost white. Danny had recently graduated from Penn and was taking a year off to work in his mother's office before going for a master's in art history at NYU.

Danny was gay, which Dorothy, after taking some time to come to terms with it, had finally accepted. What she didn't accept was Danny's current partner, Mikey Wyskovski. Mikey was the type the somewhat effete Danny seemed attracted to. Dorothy had tolerated this with others, but Mikey was a different story. Spiked hair, often dyed two or three colors, stud rings in each ear, tattoos and T-shirts cut off above his biceps, he had all the earmarks of what has long been termed "rough trade." Just how rough, no one knew. Danny bore no obvious bruises or outward signs of mistreatment, but, seeing him with Mikey, no one would have been surprised if he had. In any case, Dorothy had drawn the line at Mikey, which had caused Danny great distress. Mikey, however, had not been dismayed. He was pissed off at Dorothy, and he had let everyone know it. This, of course, made Mikey a clear candidate as a possible perpetrator of the crime.

# CHAPTER FOUR

The night of Dorothy's murder, after the photographers and crime scene crew left, and the body was taken away, the cast and crew remained in the theatre to be questioned. The detective in charge was Kevin Monaghan, from the 18th precinct on West 54th Street, known as Midtown North. He assigned himself and two other officers to question the actors and the staff, and, in corners of the stage, and pockets around the auditorium, you saw little twosomes huddled together, speaking in hushed voices. I was interviewed by Detective Monaghan himself.

"You knew Mrs. Tremayne?"

"Yes."

"Intimately?"

"No. Professionally. But I had met her before."

"Oh?"

"Some years ago I made an investment in her husband's enterprise, the Joshua Fund, and I had seen both of them on occasions when he entertained his clients."

"Did this continue?"

"I withdrew my stake several years ago."

"When were Mr. and Mrs. Tremayne divorced?"

"Shortly after that. It will be a matter of record."

"Any idea who might have done this?"

"None whatsoever. Like everyone else, I'm stunned."

"She was well liked, was she?"

"No one more so—an amazing lady, a class act all the way."

"You admired her, then?"

"Everyone did."

"Any particular reason?"

"Intelligent, level-headed, incredible artistic taste, a person of total integrity—in a business not always known for that quality."

"You mean theatre producing?"

"Precisely."

"I understand her son—Danny, is it?—he's gay."

"Yes."

"And has a somewhat unsavory boyfriend."

"That's what people say."

"You know him?"

"I've seen him."

"You were one of the first to see the body?"

"After the intern had discovered her, the stage manager and I went downstairs."

"And you were alone with her for a time?"

"A very short time. The stage manager went upstairs before I did, but it was only a matter of seconds before the police arrived."

"You didn't by any chance touch the body?"

"Absolutely not."

· · ·

As we all suspected, no one at the tech rehearsal was a serious suspect: they had always been on stage, in the dressing rooms, or in the wings with someone. I took the subway to my loft apartment and on the way began to go over possible suspects. Aside from Danny's friend Wyskovski, I ticked them off in my head. Early candidates seemed to be Sybil Conway, Artemis D'Angelo, Alistair Hargrave, and, despite his emotional outburst, perhaps even Danny himself.

· · ·

My loft took up the entire fifth floor of a building on Broome Street in SoHo, the area so called because it is South of Houston Street (in Manhattan, pronounced "how," not, as in the Texas city, "hew"). Except for the large thoroughfares—Houston and Canal—Broome is the widest cross street in that part of town, meaning the Village, SoHo, and Tribeca. Compared to most streets in the area, there is something stately and quiet about Broome. It has fewer brownstones than the Village but quite a number of four- and five-story buildings that are handsome, as well as substantial. Most were once small industrial buildings—garment manufacturing, paint factories, storage facilities. Also, Broome is less modernized—almost none of the glass-and-chrome motels or small apartments that have sprung up in other parts of that area. My building had apparently once been a small manufacturing plant making zippers, buttons, and fasteners of all kinds for the garment district. In the 1980s, the building had been converted into condos.

A young couple, riding the dot–com bubble, had bought the place and completely renovated it: new bathrooms, new kitchen, new lighting—the works. When the bubble burst, they had to sell in a hurry, and I got a bargain. Like most loft apartments, it consists of one large open area, with a dining section in one corner and, in the opposite corner, an office, with bookshelves, a desk, and a computer. In a third corner was a space for viewing TV. In the middle was the so-called living room space with a couch, easy chairs, and a coffee table made out of an old mahogany door rescued by a friend from a home in Vermont. A hand-woven rug of green, yellow, and light brown defined the living section. Against an outside wall was one of those Swedish open stoves—my fireplace, I called it—that I had found in Minnesota while playing in a show at the Guthrie Theatre in Minneapolis.

A wall along the side separated the open space from a large master bedroom and bath, next to a smaller guest room and bath. The wall enclosing this section was covered with art: a fair number of originals, a few choice theatre posters, and prints of two oil paintings. Agnes Scheinman, a good friend who owned a small, first-rate gallery in Chelsea, had helped me choose the original art and had been in charge of arranging everything—oils, posters, reprints—into what I thought of as a quite pleasing wall of colors, shapes, and figures.

When I returned home on the night of the murder, I rode the creaky, metal, open-sided elevator to my floor, opened the three locks on the door, and headed for the fridge, where I poured a glass of Sauvignon Blanc. It had been an awful night.

The tech rehearsal was a terrible bore, but the murder was horrific. Who could have done this, and how did they do it? I drank a few sips of wine, took a series of deep breaths, and settled in an armchair. I decided to save the "how" for later and focus on the "who," knowing that nearly everyone I had gone over in my mind—Artemis, Alistair, Danny—was a long shot. But perhaps not Sybil.

• • •

Tuesday: horrible morning. I awoke—which is wrong to begin with because I had hardly slept. Images of Dorothy, dead and alive, had intruded on my consciousness all night long. Still, I had to face the day. I turned on the coffeemaker and, after a shower and shave, sat at the computer. As I had suspected, there was an email from Connie, the stage manager. At 2 p.m. we were to meet at the theatre to finish the tech rehearsal interrupted the night before. Tonight we would have another, then probably two or three dress rehearsals. The first preview would be pushed back to next week. Of necessity, things remained fluid. Dorothy's funeral might be Thursday but most probably Friday. I was deleting spam from my computer when I noticed an email from Audrey, the assistant stage manager. She had remembered something. It might not be important, but then again it might be. Before she told anyone else, she wanted to talk to me. Could we meet after the tech rehearsal today away from the theatre, perhaps at Wade's Coffee Shop on Eighth Avenue, around the corner from the theatre? I emailed her back saying of course we could meet.

• • •

I then decided to try to reach Dorothy's children, Annie and Danny. When she was younger, Annie had had a wild streak. In college she experimented with pot as well as with men. But after a year of backpacking, she settled down and proved to have her mother's DNA. She had friends in the craft world who made sweaters, scarves, and the like. She hit on the idea of selling these things for her friends on the Internet and started a business called *sweatersforyou.com*, which was thriving. A year ago she had married Curtis Strong, who was at the Harvard Business School, and moved to Boston. When I called, the phone rang a number of times, then her answering machine came on. While the voice spoke, I was having one of those internal debates: should I leave a message or not? On such an emotional and sad subject, I was inclined not to. Then, before the recorded voice ran out, she answered.

"Annie, it's Matt Johanssen."

"Matt, I still can't take it in."

"Neither can I, and I was right there. Annie, there's no way to tell you how I feel."

"It's horrible, the worst thing that ever happened to me."

"I know."

"Do they have any idea . . . ?"

"About who did this?"

"Or why?"

"No. But the detective on the case, Monaghan, seems like a good man. For what it's worth, I'm going to keep after him."

"I hope you do. That would be some comfort."

"I wish there was more I could do. If you think of anything more you would like me to do, let me know. When are you coming down?'

"Curtis and I are catching the train in about an hour."

"Good. It's important for you to be here. Again, if there's anything—"

"Thanks, Matt. Staying in touch is very important right now."

When I hung up, I steeled myself to call Danny, but, before I could dial, the phone rang and it was Danny, so all-to-pieces he could barely get the words out. I tried as many reassuring and soothing words as I could manage, and eventually he was able to say that he wanted to see me as soon as possible. I told him we could meet for an early supper, between the tech rehearsal in the afternoon and the run-through in the evening. I suggested Carafini, a low-key but quite decent restaurant on 48th Street between Eighth and Ninth, and we agreed to meet at 5:45.

• • •

I wanted to find out about Sybil, where she was last night. I thought it was unlikely that she was responsible, and, even if she was, she would not have been directly involved: she would have lined up someone else to take care of things. Still, it wouldn't hurt to make an inquiry or two. I called Hector Rawlings, a publicist I had known for many years; considering his profession, he was the soul of discretion. When I heard his voice on the answering machine, I left a message asking him to call.

I next phoned Alistair Hargrave. Even less than Sybil did I think he was implicated, but I thought I might learn something from him. After Dorothy divorced Warren and moved to New York, Alistair began escorting her to openings, dinner parties, charity events. This went on for two or three years, until about four months ago when Dorothy had suddenly broken off the relationship. She wanted to remain friends, she told him, but the time had come to end their arrangement. Alistair, it was reported, was devastated.

When I reached him, understandably, he was extremely distraught. We commiserated with one another about our terrible, irreplaceable loss. Then he began to speculate about who might have done it.

"Surely it must be one of those theatre types," he said. "They're so volatile, so unpredictable."

"It's early days," I said. "As far as I know, the police have no idea who it was." I suggested, though, that the two of us have lunch. Perhaps after the funeral. Thursday if that was the day, but probably Friday. Friday was the day he had heard.

"How about the University Club?" I asked. "Only a block from the church."

"I understand the family may be going there. Why don't you be my guest at the Savile Club?"

"Fine. We'll confirm between now and then."

"You're on. I need someone to commiserate with."

• • •

After Alistair hung up, the phone rang: Hector returning my call. After we exchanged expressions of shock and sorrow, I told him that I would like to find out where Sybil was the night before.

"You don't suspect her, do you?"

"No, but I would still like to know if she had any inkling of this."

"I rather doubt it."

"You're probably right."

"Do the police have any leads? They must find out who did this."

"I agree. Not only is it a great personal loss for her friends, it's a tremendous loss for the theatre in general."

"You're telling me. The theatre has changed so much since you and I began working in it. Producers nowadays don't know Arthur Miller from I. Miller shoes; their only thought is to throw money at a production, hoping it will purchase them a spot onstage at the Tony Awards. What is today's theatre? Productions of timeworn plays whose only claim to fame is a film or TV star who can't tell 'upstage' from 'downstage' and audiences arriving in fleets of tour buses, with a man wearing a necktie nowhere in sight. Sorry. I don't mean to get carried away, but every Dorothy we have is precious to us. We can't lose a single one."

"You'll try to find out about Sybil then?"

"I'll do my best."

• • •

The finish of the tech rehearsal that afternoon was a depressing affair. I've already said that techs are dreary, but that particular afternoon no one could focus even on the most mundane changes. The one good thing was that the rehearsal was short; we had gone through a good part of the play the night before and had less than the final third to cover. Even so, everyone was thinking of what had happened, and a theatre rehearsal seemed supremely irrelevant. One way or another, we got through it and were told we had a call for 6:30 that evening.

I had forty-five minutes before I met Audrey. While everyone else was upstairs, I sneaked down to the lounge. I wanted to see exactly what the layout was: Were there ways in and out? Doors back to the storage areas? Where did passages go after that? There were two entrances from the upstairs lobby, one on each side, but there had to be other entrances and exits. There was a dim light on, and I had my cell phone flashlight.

On the basement level below the theatre, the bar and lounge were in the front. On the opposite side, toward the back, were the restrooms, and beyond them a utility room: heat, air conditioning, electrical, a storeroom for supplies. I returned to the bar area and discovered, in the wall on the west, a door leading to a narrow alley that ran the length of the theatre. Walking down the alley to the back I saw another door coming off the supply room. Neither door had a handle on the outside, which meant that, to get back in, you'd have to prop it open.

At the front end of the alley were steps that led up to the sidewalk fronting the entrance to the theatre. At the top was an iron gate secured by an industrial-strength padlock. Going in the opposite direction, I took a right turn at the end of the alley at the back and found more steps behind the theatre leading to another iron gate. It opened onto another small alley running from the back of the theatre to the street on the north. The heavy lock on this gate, I saw, had been cut through and cleverly closed again to make it look as if it was still secure. In other words, someone had made sure that you could have access to the alley alongside the basement by entering this way.

It was almost time to meet Audrey, but I had found what I was looking for: there were ways from the outside to get in and out of the lounge. I knew the official investigators had no doubt figured this out as well, but I also learned long ago that, though you might not get ahead of law enforcement, you should never fall behind.

• • •

Wade's Coffee Shop was not busy in midafternoon. I found a booth in the back and ordered a decaf cappuccino. The waitress was about to leave when Audrey appeared, ordered a cup of herbal tea, and sat down. After we talked about Dorothy and had been served our tea and coffee, she spoke. "It's about Dorothy. I was so upset I didn't remember at first. Then it came to me in the middle of the night. I couldn't go back to sleep. I don't know how important it is or who to talk to, but I heard that you know something about these things." She paused.

"What is it, Audrey?"

"It was five or six weeks ago, about two weeks before we began rehearsals. From time to time I did odd jobs for Dorothy: putting material on a computer, running errands, picking up scripts. This was early one evening, 7:30 or 8. I was bringing scripts from Kinko's back to her office. I had just entered the outer office when I heard voices, loud voices. I froze. I didn't know what to do, but I couldn't help hearing. There was the voice of a young man talking to Dorothy. He obviously knew her, and he wanted money. 'For drugs, I assume,' Dorothy said. 'Never mind what for,' he said. At first he was pleading. 'For old time's sake,' he said. Then Dorothy said, 'You know Paul and Marge would be embarrassed beyond words if they knew you were doing this.' 'Leave my parents out of it,' he answered. When the pleading didn't work, he started threatening. He knew things about her daughter. He had a video of her with a man, the two of them in all kinds of sexual and compromising activities, and if Dorothy didn't give him money, he would make it public."

Audrey continued. "I heard Dorothy say, 'Roger, that was six years ago—more than that.' 'Even worse now that she's married,' he told her. She told this Roger person that Annie had told her about the video. Dorothy said, 'She even said you might have taken pictures.' Then he asked her, 'What about Curtis?' and she said she was sure that, before they got married, Annie had told Curtis as well. She said, 'After all, Roger, you were a loose cannon. She didn't know what you might do. If you release those tapes, it will be unpleasant, but the people who will really suffer are Paul and Marge.' Then there was a pause, and Dorothy said, 'Everyone told me when you came out of rehab that you were doing so well,' to which Roger yelled, 'Fuck everybody!' and started out the door. I barely had time to jump into the closet," Audrey finished up. "But I think he was so angry he wouldn't have seen me, even if I'd been in plain sight."

"A desperate young man," I said.

"Putting it mildly. What should I do, Matt?"

"Paul and Marge Morehead are two of Warren and Dorothy Tremayne's oldest friends, and their son, the same age as Annie, has been a problem for years. Like Dorothy, I heard he had been in rehab and was doing okay, but obviously he's fallen off the wagon."

"Do I say anything?"

"You've got to tell Detective Monaghan exactly what you told me. And, when you talk to him, tell him it's important to keep you out of it."

# CHAPTER FIVE

Press coverage of Dorothy's death began Tuesday morning. TV immediately tied it to the Mulholland murder of the week before. The tabloids joined in, and it was one of the latter that coined the phrase "The Patron Murders." The circumstances were markedly different, of course. One was a dramatic, even sensational, and very public affair. The other took place out of sight, in the basement lounge of a small Broadway theatre. This distinction did not stop either the TV reporters or the tabloids. Both murders involved figures in the art world, and that was enough for them.

It was left to the *Times* reporters to point out the unmistakable differences between the two victims. Dorothy, they made clear, was not a patron but a producer, an active producer—not a trustee, board member, donor, or anything of the kind. Rather, she was a creative person who chose a play or musical and not only invested in it but nursed it along every step of the way, from early birth pangs to full production. It did her an injustice to confuse the two.

An array of file photographs of Dorothy was used by TV and the press—pictures of her with the playwright and director of our show, giving a talk on theatre at the Cosmopolitan Club, accepting an Obie Award, and so on. Needless to say, none of these photos did her justice. Dorothy was not tall, about five feet seven, with a slim yet full figure. A natural brunette, she had hazel eyes and an almond-shaped face with a rounded chin. Her skin was amazingly clear, almost pure white, with soft traces of pink. On her left cheek, near her ear, she had a small mole she had never bothered to have taken off. As with many people, it was no single feature but the way they all fit together—the overall effect—that gave her a classic but natural beauty. Neither glamorous nor overly aristocratic, Dorothy had projected a simple, straightforward look that was both genuine and attractive.

• • •

Carafini, where I was to meet Danny before the evening run-through, was a favorite of mine: the food classic Italian, the ambiance pleasant, and the owner and maître-d', Francesco, friendly and accommodating. The pale green walls were trimmed in yellow, with black-and-white photographs of scenes of Italy and Italian film stars. I was on the early side, so I asked Francesco for a booth in the back and told him I was expecting a young man.

"He's already here," Francesco said. "He wanted to be out of sight, so I put him back there." He indicated a booth behind a post in the rear. When Danny saw me, he jumped out of the booth, grabbed me, and hung on for dear life. I patted his shoulder.

"I know, Danny. It's devastating."

"I'm not sure I can go on."

"You have to, not only for Dorothy, but for lots of others."

"But why? Why?"

"Why did it happen, especially to someone as vital as Dorothy, in the prime of life?" I maneuvered him into the booth and sat down opposite him. "People have been asking that kind of question since the world began. I certainly can't answer it."

A waiter appeared and handed us menus. Danny ordered a Heineken and I ordered a glass of Pinot Grigio. When the waiter left, Danny asked, "Do you have any ideas about who it was?"

"Not yet."

"That guy Moheegan."

"Monaghan."

"He seems to suspect Mikey."

"Oh?"

"I can tell."

"I don't think he's far enough along to have zeroed in on anyone."

"Mikey has an alibi, you know."

"Good."

"He was at a bar in Tribeca. He told me earlier he was going there."

"Then he's got nothing to worry about."

"Mother hated Mikey."

"Let's face it, Danny. He's not the most lovable character around."

"You hate him, too."

"I didn't say that. I really don't know him." I paused for a moment. "What are the plans, Danny?" I wanted to get him away from his grief and self-pity, and on to something concrete.

"What plans?"

"For the visitation, the funeral?"

"Sis and Curtis got here a little while ago; they're staying in mother's apartment. I'm going over as soon as I leave here."

"Good. You should all be together now."

"The visitation will be tomorrow afternoon at the apartment. I'm not sure the exact time."

"And the funeral?"

"It depends on the police. We'd like it to be Thursday, but they may ask us to wait until Friday."

"Where?"

"At St. Thomas's."

"At 11:00 a.m.?"

"I imagine."

"Danny, what time did you get to the theatre last night?"

"9:30. That's the time mother told me she wanted me to meet her there. In the downstairs lobby, she said."

"Did she say why?"

"No. I assumed it was about Mikey, but maybe it was something about Dad."

"I'm trying to get an idea of a timeline here. 9:30 was about twenty minutes after we learned what had happened. And she wasn't in the lobby upstairs, but the one downstairs. Did she say she would be at the theatre earlier?"

"No. She said she wanted to check on the tech rehearsal but wanted to see me first."

"So obviously her plans changed. For some reason she

arrived earlier, at least thirty minutes earlier. Maybe more."

"What does that mean?"

"I don't know, but I intend to find out."

• • •

As might be expected, the run-through that night was a decided downer, even more difficult than the afternoon tech had been. It helped that we had no one in the audience, not even good friends who were often at dress rehearsals. We knew we had to press on, but no one had the heart for it. What we did, essentially, was go through the motions. An occasional mis-cue or mishap that had to be corrected took our minds off what had happened the night before. At odd moments someone would forget a line and have to be cued by the stage manager. In the end, we got through the evening, and the moment it was over everyone scattered as quickly as possible.

• • •

An email Wednesday morning confirmed that the family visitation would be that afternoon at Dorothy's apartment. A dress rehearsal had been set for that night at 8:00, with the actors' call at 7:15. The actors in one short scene that had had problems the night before were called for forty-five minutes ear-lier, but fortunately I was not in that scene. There was also an email from Gina Fleming, of the *Times* team: "Can we meet? Today, if possible." I emailed back that perhaps we could meet in the late morning or the middle of the day. She suggested noon at Dean & DeLuca on the corner of the *Times* building. We could pick up a sandwich and go up to a conference room.

The phone rang; it was Hector. "Sybil was supposed to be at a performance of *Mamma Maybe,* that sequel to *Mamma Mia!* at the Erlanger."

"Supposed to be? Was she?"

"As far as I know."

"Thanks, Hector—this is a big help."

"All I ask in return is that you keep me informed of what you learn about who did this."

"That's a promise."

• • •

I put in a call to Justin Salisbury, an old friend who worked at Teletix, a firm organized by a group of theatre owners that sold tickets by phone and online. If someone bought a ticket through them, they had a record of the name, address, and seat number. Justin had come to my aid before. When he answered, I asked him to check up on the Monday evening performance of *Mamma Maybe* for a single ticket sold to Sybil Conway, and the name of anyone sitting next to her. He asked me to hold while he looked it up.

When he came back, he told me I was in luck. Sybil had been sitting in R 109, and next to her in R 110 and R 111 were a couple from Passaic, New Jersey, Mr. and Mrs. Harold Dobson. What's more, he had their phone number. I thanked Justin profusely and, the moment after hanging up, rang the Dobsons. The wife answered, and I told her I was with the producing office of *Mamma Maybe*; we were doing a survey of people who had been at the show. She and her husband were there Monday night—correct? When she answered yes, I went on to ask how she and her husband liked the show. They loved it, she said, not as much as *Mamma Mia!* But then nothing could be as good as that.

After a few more questions, I slipped one in about those sitting near her.

"There was a single lady sitting next to you, I believe?"

"Yes, next to me."

"Do you think she enjoyed the show?"

"It's funny. She only stayed a short time—maybe fifteen minutes—then left. I wondered if she was coming back, but she didn't, so I put my husband's briefcase and raincoat on her seat."

"Do you know where she went?"

"No, the theatre was dark, and I never saw her again."

I thanked her and hung up. Interesting.

• • •

After Justin, I called Arnold Jameson, a friend who lived in Darien, Connecticut, and had a law office in Stamford. He represented many of the high-level investment people there. Arnie and I had been roommates our last two years at Princeton and had kept in touch. He had gone on to law school at Penn, and while there had married a gal who graduated from Bryn Mawr. After working at a law firm in Philly, he'd had a chance to get in on the ground floor with a young law firm in Stamford, and he and Deirdre moved to Connecticut, where they'd lived ever since. One reason we all kept in touch was that both of them loved the theatre, particularly Deirdre. They had come to almost every show I appeared in, and I was often able to get them tickets to other shows, hits to which I could obtain house seats.

Arnie's secretary said he was on a call, but she thought he would be finished soon. Would I care to hold? Absolutely. In less than five minutes, he was on the phone. "Matt, it's Arnie. We heard about Dorothy Tremayne. Terrible! Worst thing I ever heard of."

"I agree. I was there."

"Where?"

"At the rehearsal. It happened in the lounge while we were upstairs rehearsing."

"Awful. Must have been a real shock."

"About as bad as it can get."

"So, Matt, what can I do for you?"

"I was wondering about Warren. I've lost track of him. Someone told me he had started a new investment business, with a young partner. Have you heard anything about it?"

"Vaguely."

"I have to find out more about it."

"Is Warren a suspect?"

"Not really, and this may be a wild-goose chase, but I can be doing this while the police move ahead down here."

"So, what can I do?"

"I was thinking if you were available I might come up tomorrow. I've checked the schedule; I could catch the 11:50 Metro-North train and be there by 12:35. Any chance we could have lunch together?"

"I have a lunch date with Charlie Mayfield, but I can easily change that. I'll meet you at the station."

"You don't have to do that."

"It's easy."

"Great. In the meantime, Arnie, could you dig around a little and see what you can find out about this new firm and the young partner?"

"Righty-o. See you at 12:35."

# CHAPTER SIX

Later that Wednesday morning, just before noon, I arrived at the *New York Times* building to meet Fleming and Considine. Why, I wondered, had the two of them gotten in touch with me? I guessed that someone had told them I had known Dorothy and Warren for some time before Dorothy was killed, and they were hoping to get some background information. For my part, I welcomed the opportunity to learn what they knew about the Metropolitan Museum murder as well as Dorothy's. Besides, it would be interesting to learn what these two were like.

The new *Times* building stretches from 40th to 41st Streets on Eighth Avenue. A high-tech affair, especially compared to their old quarters just off Times Square, it is a fifty-two-story steel-framed building with New-Age ceramic horizontal bars from the street level to the top. The bars, by the way, proved to be an irresistible temptation for daredevil climbers, not a few of whom have scaled the building all the way up.

Dean & Deluca occupies the corner of 40th and Eighth Avenue. I was perusing pastries in a glass case when someone behind me said, "Mr. Johanssen?" I turned, and there they were,

Fleming and Considine: a striking visual contrast if ever there was one. Fleming was petite, about five feet four, with short, dark hair cut in a bob across her forehead with square sides that formed a perfect frame for her round, Kewpie-doll face. Riding on her pug nose, and covering much of her face, was a pair of the largest round glasses with black frames I'd ever seen.

Considine, on the other hand, was tall and angular, about six feet two or three, with arms akimbo and legs with a life of their own. On top was a thatch of straw-colored hair that wanted to go in several directions at once. With sunken cheeks and a sharp, thin nose, he had the air of a walking scarecrow.

"It's Georgina and Andrew—correct?" I said to them.

"Actually, it's Gina and Drew," she said.

"Both of you are enders."

"What do you mean?" asked Drew.

"Your names. One would think it might be Georgie and Andy, but with you two it's not the start of the names but the end." A joke that fell flat.

Gina changed the subject: "Why don't we get a sandwich or something and head up to a conference room?"

I chose a Black Forest ham and brie on dark bread and a cappuccino in a paper cup; Gina got a salad and Drew a chicken sandwich. The main doors of Dean & Deluca are on 40th and Eighth, but a side door opens directly into the *Times* building lobby. That door is ordinarily locked, but Gina and Drew had arranged for it to be open, so I was ushered through and whisked past security to the elevator.

We alighted on the third floor and walked briskly to a small conference room. Inside was a table with six chairs grouped around one end where we sat, with me in the middle at the head. As we began eating our lunch, Gina spoke: "Peter Patch, the theatre writer, told us three things about you."

"Oh?"

"First, he said you were a reliable, solid actor."

"Not exciting or mesmerizing?"

"I'm quoting directly."

"Good thing Peter is a theatre reporter and not a critic."

"Two, that you have a reputation as a clever amateur detective. And three, that you inherited a great deal of money and have an independent income."

"Sorry, but Peter has just blown it as a reporter."

"No independent income?" asked Drew.

"When I was in my late twenties, I received two modest inheritances: one from a grandmother on one side, one from a grandfather on the other. Neither of a size you could live on."

"But you do have the reputation of being well-off."

"When I decided to go into the theatre, I was focused on one thing: becoming a stage actor in New York, not film or television. That meant I had to have some reliable source of income to see me through when I was 'between engagements.' Early on, I began to teach myself about investing and, fortunately, found I had a knack for it."

"It takes more than that, and you know it," remarked Drew.

"Agreed. I studied assiduously, not just the markets and various funds, but the psychology of those who invested. I discovered that if you are inquisitive and alert enough, as well as detached and skeptical enough, you can do all right. In any case, within fifteen or twenty years I had enough capital so that I could get by on the income. Then, when my father died, I did inherit more money. Not a great deal, but enough to put my toe in the water with a hedge fund. That's when I crossed paths with Warren and Dorothy."

"And that worked out well?" Drew asked.

"In those days Warren was a whiz—not an overnight wonder, but a man who researched everything within an inch of its life. He would go to Idaho to visit a company with a new process for making plastic pipe, or to Silicon Valley to visit promising start-up tech firms. He was all over the place: infinitely perceptive and sharp, but also careful. His minimum investment was $500,000, and the inheritance from my father had given me just enough to join. Over the next six years, I increased my stake at a rate of nearly 20 percent a year. Every year Warren had a black-tie event for his investors, at the Frick, the Temple of Dendur, or some such place. It was at those affairs that I got to know Dorothy. Even then, she was interested in theatre, and several times she arranged for us to sit next to each other at dinner so she could talk about plays, actors, and producing.

"After I had been with the fund for about six years, I decided it was time to cash out. Nothing startling that I could point to, but I had the sense that Warren wasn't on top of things the way he had been, and that funds like his might be in for a reversal. So, following my cautious approach, I got out. Warren couldn't understand why. I told him it was because I was buying a loft on Broome Street. It was shortly after I pulled out that Warren divorced Dorothy. The other woman wasn't his secretary or some twenty-eight-year-old trophy wife, but a research analyst at his firm, a purposeful-looking gal, with dark hair, an upturned nose, and a firm chin. She wore rimless glasses that made her look like a serious academic, though I'm sure she looked a good deal less serious when she was alone with Warren and took the glasses off.

"Being the savvy person she was, Dorothy walked away with $28 million and the New York apartment. Moreover, she made certain that none of the money was invested with Warren's fund. She joined up with Charlie Winthrop, a top-of-the-line financial advisor to a select group of well-to-do clients. Devilishly astute but levelheaded and cautious, he husbanded his clients' assets while making them grow impressively. As someone said, he 'made rich people that much richer,' which is what he did for Dorothy. Warren was not so lucky. Two years later his fund went belly-up, even before the 2008 meltdown. I don't know what happened to his dark-haired research analyst."

"So, where is he today?"

"I don't know, but I mean to find out. I'm seeing some people tomorrow who may be able to help."

"And will you let us know what you learn?" Gina asked.

"About him or anyone else connected to this case," Drew added.

"I'll make you a deal. I'll tell you about Warren—and Dorothy—if you will tell me all you are allowed to about Mulholland."

"We can't promise . . ."

"I know. But I'm not interested in a one-sided affair."

"Understood," Drew assured me.

"I did want to thank you for making a sharp distinction between Mulholland and Dorothy. She was no dilettante, no one who bought her way in. She knew the difference, if anyone did, between the original and the synthetic."

"You admired her?"

"Enormously. But tell me, where do things stand with the Mulholland deal?"

"Precious little on the case itself."

"There must be something, some small clue: a discarded glove, a fingerprint, something."

"So far, not the slightest break at the museum itself."

"It can't be that airtight."

"The police say they've never seen one more so."

"People keep saying that it was a professional job, but they can't mean professional in the usual sense. This was not a mob operation, some hit man from New Jersey or a Russian assassin from Brooklyn."

They looked at each other. "We've reached the same conclusion," said Gina.

"Yes," Drew agreed, "there's something weird about all this. You've got this not-too-well-known trustee, this outrageously symbolic murder, and this airtight crime."

"True," I said. "So far the pieces don't add up." I added, "What about Mulholland the man?"

"Before we get to that, do you know someone," Gina looked at a note pad, "named Lucius Beaufort?"

"Sonny?"

"I think it's the same person."

"Absolutely. He was two years behind me at Princeton. We

knew each other in the Triangle Club. Why do you ask? No one's trying to connect him with this, are they?"

"It came up that he has been concerned with financial fat cats and Johnny-come-latelies buying their way into arts establishments."

"So?"

"You can see why his name surfaced."

"No, I can't. And neither could anyone else who knows Sonny."

"It's helpful to have your input on this."

"Now what about Mulholland?"

The two looked at each other. "Ah," Gina said.

"You're onto something there?" I asked.

"Let's just say he seems to be two different men: the one before Chicago and the one after Chicago," said Drew.

"And you're learning about the one before?"

"We have a long way to go, but it's already very interesting."

"When will the rest of us hear about this?"

"We're working on an article that will be out Friday or Saturday."

"Not sooner?"

"A few more stones we have to turn over—also, the legal department wants to vet the material."

"Intriguing, to say the least."

"Sorry we can't say more."

I looked at my watch. "I've got to be on my way." We exchanged cell phone numbers and promised to be in touch.

It had been raining off and on all Wednesday morning, the day of the visitation. The rain stopped a half-hour before I arrived at Dorothy's apartment, but the sky was still overcast. Her apartment, in the East 70s between Park and Madison, was a spacious, extremely tasteful space with a couple of Aubusson carpets, lovely draperies, and a nice mix of antique and modern furniture. The library was especially inviting, the scene of a number of play readings I had attended. Bookshelves covered two walls, with an impressive collection not only of theatre volumes but also modern classics. On a third wall was a small, wood-burning fireplace framed by two leather armchairs on one side and a short sofa on the other. On the wall opposite the fireplace was an antique table desk, with a computer to the side—obviously Dorothy's office at home.

When I arrived, someone took my raincoat and umbrella, and I signed the visitors' book. Moving into the living room, I thought to myself that only in a place like Manhattan would you find the variety of people assembled here: upscale couples from the suburbs; people from high finance in the city; and a mixture of actors, designers, directors, and writers from the theatre. It was relatively easy to spot the types even if you didn't know them individually. Old friends from Greenwich, New Canaan, Darien—predominantly WASPs, well-groomed, in appropriately somber outfits. Then there were the Manhattanites, the business types—lawyers, bankers, advertising executives—with their wives, a few of whom were slightly more colorful in their dress. Added to that were the younger ones, friends of Annie, Curtis, and Danny, the men in their tailored suits from Paul Stuart or Peter Elliot, and the women in subdued designer dresses from shops on Madison Avenue. The theatre folk came in two categories: those in the producing or business side, mostly dressed like the business types but often with a slightly flamboyant touch—a handkerchief spilling out of a jacket pocket, a wide-striped shirt, a more adventurous tie, even the occasional boutonniere—and the other theatre category, the artists. They, of course, were more unconventional: a tweed jacket over a turtleneck, a black shirt with a black tie under a checked jacket, a purple shirt and yellow bow tie, even one instance of a pair of baggy corduroy trousers below a loose-fitting, shapeless jacket.

Despite the rainbow coalition in dress, the entire group was bound together in its disbelief and dismay that this could have happened, that Dorothy, so universally loved and admired, could have been killed in the prime of life, and that the killing was so brutal. I made my way through the group, nodding here and there, but anxious to speak first to Annie, Curtis, and Danny. I found them in the back corner of the living room, surrounded by several young people their age. I went to Annie first and embraced her. Neither of us was anxious to speak, so for a moment we simply held one another.

Finally, I said, "Annie, I can't tell you."

"I know."

"I know this is hard for you—all of you." I included Curtis and Danny in the words. "I don't know whether it's harder being alone or surrounded by a crowd like this."

"It's not easy either way," said Annie.

In a moment, I broke from Annie and shook hands with Curtis and Danny. I suspected that Annie had taken a tranquilizer, and it was obvious from his subdued state that the excitable Danny had taken more than one. Despite that, he made it clear he wanted to talk to me.

"Can we go back to the bedroom for a moment?" he asked.

"Danny, you have to stay here and see people."

"When can we talk?"

"I have a run-through tonight."

"After that?"

"All right."

"At your loft?"

"I'll check with the stage manager to learn when we finish and let you know the time."

"Thanks."

I went back to Annie and Curtis and spoke to her. "Annie, if there's anything I can do . . ."

"Thanks, Matt. I think everything's in hand. People are being very kind. There is one thing, though."

"Which is?"

"Solving this thing."

"I'm working on it night and day, believe me. In my own way, of course."

"Any leads?" asked Curtis.

"A few, but so far nothing definite."

"Anyway, we all feel better with you involved."

Others were anxious to talk to the three of them, so I moved on, speaking briefly to the people I knew: Paul and Marge Morehead, the parents of Roger, the one who had threatened Dorothy in her office; Lance Middlecoff and others I recognized from the Joshua Fund days. Many of the theatre people spoke not only of how terrible it was, but how it must be particularly difficult for those, like me, about to open in a show she was involved in.

Sybil and Artemis showed up separately but not that far apart, which made me think they had probably come together but didn't want people to know it. Sybil was unusually subdued, wearing a gray-striped outfit over a white blouse and a minimum of jewelry. Artemis wore a blazer, blue shirt, and striped tie—extremely straight-arrow for him. I spoke to both of them; it was a decidedly formal greeting on their part, bordering on chilly—behavior that was not unexpected.

It was getting late. A number of people had come and gone, and I was beginning my exit, when Warren, Dorothy's ex-husband, appeared. I felt he should have come earlier, but better late than never, I thought. Then I noticed it: something about his manner was a shade off. Nothing you could put your finger on, but he seemed strangely detached, not quite connecting with the occasion or the people around him. He and I spoke, and if anything he was overly cordial. I decided he had either been drinking or was on some kind of medication. Watching him, I decided it was probably the latter. After bidding farewell to him and a few others, I made my exit.

• • •

I went home to change before going to the theatre for the run-through. In the meantime I called Seymour Pascall. Seymour worked at the coroner's office, and I first met him when he was much younger and we were filming a scene from

*Law & Order.* I was playing the part of an older brother asked to identify the body. When we were about to shoot the scene, the actor playing the pathologist suddenly became quite ill—a case of food poisoning, it turned out. The director was about to cancel the shoot when I intervened and said that, rather than wasting valuable time, we should try to use the actual pathologist. "I've been talking to him," I said, "and I'm sure he can handle it. We can take care of the union details later."

And that's what we did, with the result that Seymour appeared on national TV. We remained in fairly close touch, partly because I liked him, but also because I thought it was a good idea to have a friend in the coroner's office.

"Seymour," I said. "I would really like to know what they found with the autopsy on Dorothy Tremayne."

"The producer?"

"Yes."

"Are you connected to the show she was producing?"

"I'm in it. I was there when it happened."

"Oh, my God."

"You don't know the half of it."

"You know asking this is highly irregular."

"We both know that."

"I'll see what I can do."

"I appreciate it more than I can say."

# CHAPTER SEVEN

Wednesday night, I got to the theatre fifteen minutes before we were supposed to report. I wanted to check on the alley that I thought exited to the north of the theatre. I paced off the distance from the iron gate by the front of the theatre and then walked off the same number of feet on the street to the north. There it was: another alley, but with no gate at the entryway, only a random assortment of trash cans. I went past those to the end of the alley, at the back of the theatre, and found the iron gate I had seen before with the lock appearing as if it were intact and had never been tampered with.

The decision had been made that on Wednesday and Thursday we would continue running through the play on stage, with full lights, costumes, and the rest, but without an audience of any kind. Then on Friday and Saturday we would have the usual small invited audience, only the closest friends of those involved in the production and none of the fringe people who sometimes attended these early run-throughs.

I was in my dressing room getting into my costume when Audrey called, "Fifteen minutes." I went into the wings, stage left, to wait for the run-through to begin. Rowan, the director, had taken his place in the auditorium, along with the designers; Connie, the stage manager, was on the verge of saying, "Curtain," when the three young actors in the cast, whose names in real life were Francesca, Austin, and Carol, came down to the apron and spoke to Rowan.

Francesca, the oldest, said, "Rowan?"

"What is it?"

"We—" Francesca was speaking for the group. "We . . . before we begin, could we just talk a moment?"

"About what, Francesca?"

Austin spoke up, "To remember Dorothy."

"Well, uh . . ." Rowan looked at his watch. "We have a schedule here."

The youngest of the three, Carol, began crying softly. Francesca continued, "You older people have more experience than we do. You've learned to put things aside and get on with it, but it's not so easy for us. Nothing like this has ever happened to us."

Austin spoke up, "We find it difficult to pretend that nothing has happened, the way all of you seem to."

"We're not indifferent," Rowan said. "We feel it, too."

I decided to become part of the discussion. I walked on stage and spoke: "Rowan, I think these three have a point. They believe that people like you and me, people who have been around a while, must have encountered things like this before, but we haven't. At least, I haven't, and I'm probably the oldest one here. Things do happen—a heart attack in the audience, an actor falling off a platform—but this is beyond those."

"So what do you suggest, Matt?"

"Why don't we all gather up here before we begin? Bring some chairs on stage and take time to talk for a few minutes."

"Group therapy, you mean?"

"If you like."

"Would that suit you?" Rowan asked, looking at the three young actors.

"I think it would help," said Austin.

So that's what we did. I think what prompted this was the visitation. All of us had been there; we saw the wide range of people who were affected by Dorothy's death and were paying their respects to her. It brought home in a very visceral way what a traumatic event this had been.

After we had settled in our chairs, Austin spoke. "Who wants to go first?" I said I would, and so I began by talking about grieving. I noted that people always seemed to deal with grief in one of two ways: either to withdraw into a shell, to mourn quietly and alone, or to become perhaps overactive, as busy as possible. Our group didn't have much choice: we had an ongoing project that to some extent took us out of ourselves, whether we wanted it to or not.

"But in doing this," said Beatrice, the actress playing the mother, "maybe we haven't acknowledged that other part—the personal grieving."

"From all we hear," said Carol, "she was an amazing person."

"She was," I said.

The whole thing took little more than fifteen minutes, but I think it was something we had all subconsciously longed for. When we began the run-through, the performance, while not overly animated, seemed more heartfelt and honest than it had been before. Incidentally, the main plot device of the play—the appearance of the unwanted executor—turned out to be working much better than we had anticipated. For one thing, each character in the family had to play on several levels. There was the anger that members of the family already felt for each other. Then there was the suppressed anger, actually aimed at the uncle who had done this but, since he was no longer here, directed toward my character, the executor, whose name was Cecil. At the same time, the family members were hoping not to offend Cecil, while trying desperately to please and impress him.

• • •

After the run-through, when I arrived at my building, Danny was pacing the sidewalk out front.

"Have you been here long?"

"Ten, fifteen minutes."

"Come on up."

After we were settled in the apartment, Danny with a beer, me with a glass of wine, I said, "The visitation was an incredible tribute to your mother."

"I didn't expect so many people."

"I did. Did they stay long?"

"Some lingered for quite a while."

"I assume the family ate together afterwards?"

"A caterer brought in dinner."

"Something else happened, Danny—at the theatre— something I've never seen before. Just as we were beginning the run-through, the actors asked Rowan, the director, if we could take a few minutes to remember Dorothy. And we did. It was very moving."

"I'm glad you told me. Mother would have been happy about that." Then Danny turned to what was really on his mind. "They took him to the police station."

"Who?"

"Mikey. They think he did it—killed Mother."

"I imagine they took him in just for questioning, not to arrest him."

"But why would they take him in at all?"

"I assume they need information."

"Is he a suspect?"

"I wouldn't know."

"But he has an alibi. He was at a bar—the Purple Parrot."

"Have you talked to the detectives?"

"I spoke with an assistant to that fellow Monaghan."

"And what did he say?"

"He claims that they checked with the owner, and with the bartender. He says both seem to know Mikey well, and both swore he was not there Monday night. But that's impossible."

"Have you talked to Mikey?"

"I haven't been able to reach him." Danny held out a cell phone. "I lost my iPhone."

"When?"

"About a week ago. I've looked high and low. I can't find it anywhere. This is a new cell."

"So you haven't talked to Mikey in the last two days?"

"No. I've tried. I went round to his place, but he wasn't there."

"The police seem to have found him."

"I need to see him."

"Danny, why would he say he was at the Purple Parrot? Maybe he was with someone else and didn't want you to know."

"I won't believe it until I hear it from him." He paused briefly, then continued, "People have it in for Mikey."

"People like your mother?"

"She didn't like Mikey."

"And he didn't like her."

"Because of the way she felt about him."

"Is that the only reason?"

"What do you mean?"

"Did Mikey ever ask you for money?"

"Personally?"

"For any reason."

"Investments, yes."

"What kind of investments?"

"Different things."

"Such as?"

"He had an idea for catering."

"Yes?"

"For opening-night parties at Chelsea art galleries and off-Broadway openings—things like that."

"Even if you landed all of those, it could hardly support a business."

"That wasn't all. He had an idea called 'Harley Holidays'—planning excursions, trips for bikers."

"My impression is most motorcycle groups know where they want to go. They seem very well organized."

"There were other ideas."

"Some would call them schemes."

"He wants to make his own way."

"With other people's money."

"You're like all the others."

"Danny, Mikey is an operator, a con man. I'm not saying he doesn't like you for who you are, but he also knows you come from a wealthy family."

"I don't have any money of my own."

"That doesn't mean you don't have access to it, and he knows that. Put yourself in Monaghan's shoes. Here's a hustler, an opportunist, and here you are: someone who likes him and trusts him. You say you recently lost your cell phone. Let's just say that Mikey took your phone, thinking it might come in handy some time. Then he learns you are supposed to meet your mother Monday night at the theatre, and he knows the time. He texts her on your cell to meet thirty or forty minutes earlier, and he's there waiting for her."

"To kill her?"

"Probably not—maybe just to shake her up. Try to convince her to let you have money to invest in one of his schemes. And then, as so often happens, things didn't go as planned."

"You're saying this is what happened?"

"No. It's purely hypothetical, but not impossible. Your mother was not the only one who thought that Mikey was not good for you, that you were better than he is—not socially or financially, but in your character, your integrity."

"You don't know him."

"Yes, I do. Not personally, but living where I have all these years, and doing what I do, I've known lots of Mikeys."

Danny put his head in his hands, broke down, and wept. Through his tears he said, "Mikey was the one I was holding on to."

"Let me suggest something else. I don't know what's in your mother's will. I'm sure one day you will inherit a lot of money, but it's just possible, given your age and attachment to Mikey, that she might have made provisions in recent months that your share would go into a trust, to be administered by a conservator, and that you would get generous living expenses but not much more until you're, say, thirty or thirty-five. If she did, just imagine how Mikey will react when he learns you are not going to be able to invest in his schemes or support him in the manner to which he feels entitled. My guess is he'll be out the door faster than you can say Harley Davidson."

Danny was weeping openly now, racked with sobs. "Everything's happening at once," he said. "Mother killed, Mikey lying to me. I have nowhere to turn."

"Yes, you do."

"Where?"

"I'm going to say this one thing, and then I think we should both go to bed. I want you to stay here tonight, in the guest bedroom. You're too strung out to go anywhere else." I paused for a moment, then continued, "Your mother left you and Annie a lot of money, which you will receive at some point if not right now. But she left you with something even more valuable."

"What do you mean?"

"An example. You're gay, Danny, and there's nothing wrong with that. But there is something wrong with being a perpetual victim, with playing the role of a self-pitying pigeon, someone always being taken advantage of. Your mother was an extraordinary woman, and in the last months of her life she became an amazingly strong woman. When she broke with Sybil, it was her Emancipation Proclamation. She had come to realize she did not need to lean on others, but could be her own person. More and more she became comfortable in her own skin. That's her example, what you can learn from her, and what you need to strive for. And I'm certain you can do it."

Danny started to speak, but I interrupted him and said, "No, don't say anything right now when you're so overwhelmed, but put this in the back of your mind. Think of how she achieved this, and then how you can, too. Not on anyone else's terms, but on yours." After a moment, I continued, "Now, I'm going to get you a pair of pajamas and a sleeping pill. There's a new, unopened toothbrush in the guest bath. Sleep as late as you can tomorrow."

# CHAPTER EIGHT

Thursday morning I had just stepped out of the shower, dripping wet, when the phone rang. I ran to answer, not wanting to wake Danny, and a no-nonsense voice spoke: "Johanssen?"

"Monaghan?"

"I'd like for you to be in my office one hour from now."

I looked at the clock. "It's 8:00 in the morning. No one calls actors at this hour."

"I do."

"Actors work nights."

"So do detectives."

"I just got out of the shower."

"When can you make it?"

I thought a moment. "9:30."

"Don't be late." He hung up.

I went to the guest room door and listened. Danny was still asleep. I could hear him snoring. I dressed in a coat and tie, as I was meeting Lance Middlecoff at 10:30 and heading for Stamford on Metro-North at 11:50. Then I checked my emails, paid a few bills, and went downstairs. I stopped by Anton's coffee shop on the corner, had a quick cup of coffee and a cheese Danish, and headed for the subway.

On the ride uptown, I went over why I thought Monaghan had been so brusque, almost rude, on the phone: he had found out about my history with the NYPD. Going back fifteen years or so, I had helped solve several crimes, always working unobtrusively and out of sight. The cases included a costume designer who was stabbed in his studio; a second-tier actor with AIDS who, out of sheer malevolence, deliberately infected an ex-partner with HIV; and a rather sensational crime called the "Mezzanine Murder," where a very angry bipolar director shot a rival at a performance and then disappeared. The director was found, but not his weapon, which I assumed now resided at the bottom of the Hudson River.

And then there was the case involving Saved On Stage, better known as SOS. A real estate magnate, Alan Wycoff, had made a fortune on low-income housing in the five boroughs. Along the way, he was constantly accused of being a racist for the way he treated blacks, Hispanics, and other minorities in his ventures. In the hope of counteracting the drumbeat of criticism, he consulted a high-powered public relations firm to help him burnish his image. The scheme the firm came up with was SOS, a plan to set up in three areas—Harlem, the Bronx, and Staten Island—a program using theatre people (actors, directors, playwrights) who, in community halls, churches, and schools, would engage underprivileged kids in theatrical activities. For out-of-work actors and starving playwrights, the stipend they received was most welcome, plus there was the satisfaction of doing something worthwhile.

The project was a smashing success, largely, it was thought, because the PR firm had found a charismatic black man, Brian Barrow, to run it. He turned out to be not only extremely personable but a whiz at organization. The success of the program added to the consternation of Wycoff's rivals in the real estate world, who knew that, in addition to being a bigot, Wycoff was thoroughly dishonest. He was bound, they were certain, to take advantage of SOS monetarily, probably to launder ill-gotten gains, a practice he had engaged in before. Someone I knew at the NYPD asked me if I could identify three or four young theatre people working in SOS who might serve as undercover operatives to get at the facts. I interviewed the young people I thought most likely, recommended them, and they came up with the goods, sending Wycoff away for a decent stretch at a federal pen.

• • •

Leaving the subway, I walked to the Midtown North police station on West 54th Street, the precinct that handles the theatre district, and was ushered into Monaghan's office. It looked like a set from a 1950s movie: a scarred wooden desk with three drawers on each side of the kneehole, a series of battered metal chairs with faded green plastic seats, two old-style metal file cabinets in the corner. There were pictures on one wall of Monaghan: one as a cadet, another being promoted to lieutenant, a third when he was made a detective. Family pictures were on a scarred credenza behind his desk.

"Sit down," he commanded.

I continued to stand. "I feel as if I've been summoned to an execution."

"I'm pissed off," he said, waving a dossier of four or five pages in the air. "Your history with the NYPD." He pointed to the document: "Six, seven, eight, God knows how many cases you've been involved in. Why didn't you tell me about this?"

"It was some time ago."

"Not that long." He pointed again to the dossier. "You should have told me. Working in secret, investigating on your own. I can't have people going behind my back, especially people involved."

"What do you mean 'involved'?"

"You were there when it happened, you knew the victim, you know her family and friends."

I finally sat down. "Look, I haven't . . ."

"Don't tell me you haven't done some investigating—a lot of investigating."

"I admit I've been trying to find out about Warren."

"And . . . ? I don't believe that's all there is. I have no idea where you're snooping around, who you've talked to, who you're tracking down. If this were not a special situation, I would order you to quit forthwith. If I have any inkling whatsoever that you are a rogue investigator, out on your own, I won't hesitate to arrest you and throw you into a cell."

"What do you mean 'special situation'?"

"Your history with these people in the theatre, in Warren's business, in the family. Under those circumstances I'd rather have you inside the tent than outside, but if I'm going to do that, we have to have some ground rules. First, I want you to tell me what you've done so far. Second, I want to be clear about what you can and cannot do going forward."

I was not about to tell Monaghan of my ventures in the lounge and basement of the theatre or about the walkway that connects to the alley leading to 50th Street. Nor would I mention my pursuit of Sybil's activities or my exchanges with Gina and Drew at the *Times*. But I could talk about Warren. "I've been focused almost exclusively on Warren, who seems quite elusive right now. Also, no one appears to have a handle on what shape he's in these days."

"We finally found him. It took some doing, but we discovered he has some kind of financial company in Stamford, although he lives in Greenwich." Monaghan consulted a piece of paper. "He's living in the carriage house of a friend, on Round Hill Road. We finally talked to him at his office this morning. He says he and his young partner, Stuart Ross, were working late that night, until 8:30, in their office in Stamford. We checked with the young man, and he supports the story."

"My first update under your rules. I was planning on going to Stamford this afternoon to check with a friend of mine. Is that all right?"

"As long as you report to me everything you find out."

"In the meantime, is there any news about Danny's friend Mikey?"

"The most slippery one of all. Danny insists Mikey was at some gay bar in Tribeca that night."

"And?"

"We checked the bar. They know Mikey well, and he wasn't there that night."

"Do we know where he was?"

"We're working on it. One thing seems sure: Mikey wanted Danny boy to *think* he was at the bar. Originally, Mikey said he had a buddy who would vouch for him, but so far the buddy is nowhere in sight. Until the buddy appears, Mikey is near the top of the list."

"Speaking of Danny, I saw him last night just before rehearsal. He says he was supposed to meet his mother at the theatre at 9:30. They had exchanged text messages, it seems."

"And the murder was discovered fifteen or twenty minutes before that. Which means it would have taken place, say, ten to thirty minutes before that."

"Exactly."

"So she came earlier than her appointment with Danny, and either someone knew she was coming earlier or they arranged it so that she *would* come earlier."

"Looks like it. And Roger Morehead, the hophead—any news on him?"

"It took a while, but yes. Danny gave us a lead, and we found Morehead in the apartment of a friend near Columbia, a student there."

"And?"

"He doesn't have much of an alibi. Also, he's a very angry young man. He probably is off-the-wall enough and mad enough to consider something like this. But we decided he's so unstrung he would have trouble planning it, let alone executing it."

"If it's okay, I might try to contact him. I know the parents."

"I'm not sure it's worth it, but be my guest." Monaghan handed me a paper with Roger's address and cell phone number and continued, "But I want to throw out another idea. I've been thinking. This could have been someone else, you know, even an outsider."

"Oh?"

"Those rehearsals were going on for several days."

"At the theatre, yes, and before that at a rehearsal hall."

"I'm only interested in what was happening at the theatre. Usually, I understand, only the stage door offers access to backstage, but for a few days the front doors were open so crew members could easily get out to the street to have a smoke or take a break. Is that so?"

"Yes, now that you mention it."

"So someone—either connected with the show or someone completely from the outside, a person looking to score in some way—could see all this, drift in with the group, hide somewhere, and when they saw a mark come in, a well-dressed lady like Mrs. Tremayne, go after her. They manage to get her off alone, grab her, silence her, drag her downstairs, try to rob her or get something from her, and it goes bad. Or, maybe someone slipped inside and went down to the lounge to hide. When she came in and went downstairs to the ladies' room, the person hiding had a perfect target. As I say, this person could be someone who knew her, or someone who had never seen her before. That sort of thing happens all the time. And whoever it is ends up throttling her."

"There are a lot of 'ifs' in there."

"When you've been in this business as long as I have, you realize you can never rule out coincidence: a man goes into a house in Queens to kill his ex-wife and her boyfriend; a moment later, a neighbor from three doors down drops by to return a bottle of olive oil and is killed too. A man in the Bronx plans to rob a 7-Eleven, goes inside, and runs into an off-duty cop buying donuts. I've asked my people to go back to the actors and technical personnel to ask if they saw anyone strange or unfamiliar coming in or out of the lobby or hanging around. That doesn't mean I'm not doing everything to keep on top of all the people you gave us."

"You're right, of course, to follow those other leads."

"I have to."

"Meanwhile, I won't go off the reservation. I'll stick to the people we've talked about, and I'll keep you fully informed."

"You'd better."

• • •

From Monaghan's office I headed for my meeting with Lance Middlecoff. He had been the CEO and major stockholder in a large insurance company that dealt not in auto, home, and theft but in the more rarefied stuff: corporations, investment banks, and manufacturers, insuring them against the occasional catastrophe. At a certain point in the late 1990s, he sold the company to AIG and walked away with a cool $130 million or so. He had always been interested in the theatre, from the days when he was active in Mask and Wig, the undergraduate theatre group at Penn. Even before he retired from business, he had invested in theatre productions. Lance was discerning, with a clear preference for and keen appreciation of quality. He never wanted to be what is known as the "lead producer" who initiated a Broadway production. Usually he invested in a production that had been successful abroad, in London's West End for instance, or was being put together by a producer he trusted.

About six feet two, broad-shouldered, and fairly heavyset, Lance was built like a tight end on a college football team. His full head of dark hair was graying at the temples, and he had a flat nose above a square chin. He could easily have been in TV ads for products aimed at middle-aged achievers. His office, interestingly enough, was in the high forties on Sixth Avenue: a strategic as well as symbolic location, roughly halfway between the legal offices on Park and the theatre district in the West 40s. When I ran into him at the visitation for Dorothy, I asked if he would mind seeing me. He knew Dorothy and Warren well, but also Sybil Conway. Shortly after he had sold his insurance business—when he first opened his current office—Sybil, not surprisingly, offered to introduce him to the theatre business. This, of course, was before she had become involved with Dorothy. She tried, some said desperately, to get Lance to join her in forming a production company. He was the ideal candidate—lots of money, a love of theatre, and almost no practical experience. He talked to her about it, but eventually declined.

Lance's office was on the twelfth floor: a small reception area with a secretary, who was probably an administrative assistant, and after that, Lance's office itself. A comfortable, male office: plain dark orange carpet, walls painted a greenish gray, framed posters of plays, but also a framed picture of a *Fortune* magazine cover that featured Lance. A side table with family photos in silver frames: his wife and three children, two boys and a girl, when they were young, and now with their spouses and small children.

I told him first of all that I wanted to get caught up on Warren. "Ah, Warren," he said. "Haven't seen him lately, but from what I hear, he's not in good shape."

"Financially or emotionally?"

"Both, I gather. After his fund went under, he walked away with a good deal of money he had salted away separately. But, when the derivative and credit default swap fever started in 2005, '06, and '07, he couldn't resist jumping in the pool with the young Turks, and in the summer and fall of '08 he went down hard. Ever hear of Arthur Ross?"

"Doesn't ring a bell."

"No reason it should. From St. Louis. Runs a manufacturing plant: batteries. One of the companies Warren had in his original fund. Unlike others, it's been a steady earner, and now, with the whole green thing, it's better than ever. He has a son, must be thirty by now, who's been a problem for years. Last year Arthur's son got into deep trouble with a young woman out there, so Arthur wanted to get him out of town. He asked Warren if he would take the kid under his wing: Arthur would put up a fair amount of capital to underwrite a modest fund that Warren and his son would run. I don't think Arthur had any idea how things were with Warren. Not surprisingly, Warren jumped at the chance. They've got offices in Stamford, I understand."

"In the meantime, I wanted to ask you about Sybil."

"Ah, yes. The sinister siren. Is she a suspect in the case?"

"Not really."

"What's happening with the case, by the way? Any progress? Any leads?"

"Very slow going so far, but it's still early in the investigation."

"You mentioned Sybil."

"I've always wondered: What's her story? Where did she come from?"

"Originally from Cincinnati, she went to the University of Ohio, where she was a beauty queen: Miss Buckeye. Her last year in college she married the university's reigning playboy, Clyde somebody. Apparently she thought this would be her meal ticket out of her humdrum, lower-class life, because Clyde's family had megabucks. But Clyde let her down by up and dying three years out of college—too much drugs and booze. She got a small cash settlement and with that began a residential real estate business in Cincinnati. She became a paragon of small business and active in social causes. One was the local theatre. She became the treasurer of the board and found out she had a feel for how to handle their budgets. A few years later, a larger real estate company bought out her firm, and she took off for New York to begin her producing career here."

"How did you learn all this?"

"When she began pressing me, I thought I'd look into things, so I called a friend, head of one of our affiliates in Cincinnati. By the way, I understand she has a new target."

"I heard something about that: Wilbur? Willard?"

"Wilfred Covington, from Tulsa. His grandfather was a key developer of the Andarko oil basin in the panhandle, and

Wilfred hasn't had to work a day in his life. He and his wife recently bought a penthouse somewhere in the East Sixties. He likes big, brassy musicals, and, as you know, Sybil can swing either way, so she's helping him get into that."

"Another notch in the belt."

"Right. But I also hear the wife keeps Wilfred on a short leash."

"A good challenge for Sybil."

"Right."

As I was leaving, I thanked Lance, and he asked me to keep him posted on progress in the investigation; I promised I would.

"See you at the funeral," he said.

• • •

From Lance's office I rushed to Grand Central and bought a ticket for the 11:50 to Stamford. Once on the train, I began to go over what I did and didn't know, or, in the parlance of my bridge-playing friends, to "review the bidding." The more I thought about it, the more I realized that Monaghan had every reason to investigate individuals who might have wandered in or out during tech rehearsals. I had been so fixated on the cast of characters I knew about—in theatre and in finance—that I had blocked out other possibilities, but he had a real point.

Before the advent of computerized tickets, there used to be a group known as "second acters": students, young professionals, impoverished theatre enthusiasts. They knew exactly when the intermission of each Broadway show occurred and would arrive in front of the theatre at just the right moment to mingle with audience members gathering on the sidewalk. Unobtrusively, just before the second act, they would wander into the theatre and spot a few unoccupied seats, easily identified by the lack of programs or rain coats. When everyone returned from intermission and the lights began to dim, they quietly slipped into a vacant seat and enjoyed the rest of the show free of charge.

More to the point, during a production like *The Unwitting Executor*, there is a great deal of back and forth during the tech period. I don't go out often because I don't smoke, but I do go outside to get a breath of fresh air or maybe just sneak down the block to buy a coffee. So, yes, people were coming and going that night, and they weren't dressed up—certainly not the designers and the techies. And a vagrant or someone with mischief on his mind could easily have blended in with the group.

Looking at it from a different angle, the theatre world is a small world, a highly competitive one, with a fair quotient of paranoia. There are only so many slots in a theatre's schedule during a season, only so many parts in a play, and only so many productions for which a director or designer can be chosen. It's not difficult for someone who missed out repeatedly to believe that another person got a break because of favoritism, nepotism, or whatever. Under this scenario the disgruntled individual, knowing about our tech rehearsals, could have mingled with the group out front, been assumed to be a friend of someone in the cast or crew, and drifted into the theatre without undue suspicion. Dorothy would have been a natural target, not necessarily as the one who committed the presumed offense but as someone who could exert pressure, maybe in the future if not right now. Perhaps the person never expected her to put up resistance, and she surprised him.

I was suddenly roused from these thoughts by the fact that the train had stopped. Looking out the window, I saw that we were already in Stamford. I barely managed to get off before it was moving once again, on its way to Bridgeport.

# CHAPTER NINE

Down the platform in Stamford, Arnie was waving at me. We shook hands, and I thanked him profusely for seeing me on such short notice. "We're in luck," he said. "Oh?"

"Palmer Randolph is joining us for lunch. He's a partner at Loeb, Sims, and Whiteside, a conservative bond fund, but he has his finger on the pulse of everything and everyone in Stamford. He's meeting us at the Downtown Club."

The Stamford Downtown Club was on the top floor of one of the office buildings that dot the city center. When you get off the elevator, you leave behind the chrome, glass, and stainless steel of the floors below and enter the world of a men's business club, based, no doubt, on English models but found throughout corporate America: leather chairs with brass studs, prints on the walls, a bar well-stocked with single malt Scotch, and a view of the city below. I quickly discovered there was a club crest or coat of arms with SDC embossed on a shield above crossed, old-fashioned wooden golf clubs. It was emblazoned not only on the waiters' white jackets but also on the fancy paper napkins at each place at the table.

Palmer turned out to be on the short side, about five feet seven, with a round face, a reddish nose, and jowly cheeks. Bald on top, he made up for it with bushy hair sticking out on the sides, thick eyebrows, and a nice bristly crop of hair protruding from each ear. He and I were introduced, and the three of us were shown to a table by a window, fortunately out of earshot of nearby tables. Once we were seated, one of those white-coated waiters appeared and took our drink order. Arnie ordered a glass of Pinot Noir, Palmer had a glass of iced tea, and I asked for a nonalcoholic beer.

After Palmer expressed his shock and sadness about Dorothy, I explained to him briefly my involvement with Warren and how I had invested in the Joshua Fund, which was when I had gotten to know both Warren and Dorothy. I added that I had done quite well with Warren's fund but had gotten out a few years back because I wanted to invest in other things. "You were lucky," Palmer said.

"In hindsight," I said, "very lucky. But after that I lost touch with Warren. Dorothy, of course, I saw a lot of because of our common interest in the theatre. But Warren I haven't spoken to in I don't know how long, and I wanted to get caught up on what's been happening to him."

"It's not been good, I'm afraid," Palmer said. He explained that, somewhere along the line, just before the 2008–09 crash, Warren's fund began to falter. Eventually he cashed out his funds—at a loss to most of his investors—but still he himself came out in reasonably good shape, with perhaps $70 million, Palmer estimated.

But then Warren began to invest in things he knew very

little about, a couple of small start-up companies and other things. "The most bizarre item," Palmer said, "was mice."

"Mice?"

"Specially bred for the pharmaceutical industry that replicate some kind of desirable DNA drug companies are looking for and cost $30,000 apiece."

"Thirty thousand dollars for one mouse?" Arnie asked. "You've got to be kidding."

"I wish I were," said Palmer. "In any case, none of this really panned out, and a few months ago Warren was in a bad way: he still had a few million, but for him that was pennies on the dollar."

While talking, we had ordered and eaten our lunch, and by this point, had finished. The waiter arrived, picked up our plates, and asked if we cared for dessert. I demurred, saying I would just have a decaf coffee, but Arnie spoke up: "They have a great rum raisin ice cream—homemade." I'm a sucker for ice cream and reluctantly agreed to try it. Arnie ordered a bowl of fruit and Palmer a slice of cheesecake, and the waiter left.

"On the subject of Warren," I asked Arnie, "do you know anything about this new enterprise with a young man from St. Louis?"

"I've heard something about it. It seems that the boy's father remembers Warren from the old days when he made money with him, but knows very little about his recent history. He has staked Warren and his son to a new venture. A couple of the young associates in our law firm tell me they know the boy. They've seen him at parties and at a local watering hole."

The waiter brought our desserts, and I dug in. Meanwhile,

around a mouthful of cheesecake, Palmer said, "From what I hear, Warren is not in good shape these days: distracted, having mood swings. Anyway, given all that, to my mind he couldn't possibly be the one who did this to Dorothy: put this whole scheme together, even if he decided to take such drastic measures."

"I'm sure you're right, Palmer, and I'm glad you said something."

"He appears to have become flakier and flakier," Arnie said. "Ebullient and over the top one moment, eerily silent the next. Reggie Butler, who has been in the same golf foursome with Warren for years, says that a couple of months ago Warren became so erratic, forgetting tee times, seeming distant and out of it, that they had to ask him to drop out of the group for a while."

"What's this about Warren living in a carriage house?"

"He'd already sold the house—into a down market, by the way—and had taken an apartment, but there was some problem there, so Aubrey Nichols threw him a lifeline: lent him his carriage house on Round Hill Road."

"Which Warren gratefully accepted."

"Exactly."

It was time to leave. Arnie and Palmer didn't need a check because you never do at these places; the waiters know whom to charge the lunch to. Downstairs, I thanked Palmer profusely for being so generous with his time and providing me with so much helpful information.

As Arnie and I were saying goodbye, I asked him, "About this young partner, Stuart Ross."

"As I said, quite outgoing, I understand."

"If you could ask the young men you know what Stuart

was doing last Monday night, I would really appreciate it."

"I'll do what I can. It's a long shot, but nothing ventured, nothing gained. Right?"

"Right."

• • •

After I arrived at Grand Central, I headed to the loft. The phone was blinking: a message from Monaghan. I called him.

"Where have you been?" he asked.

"Stamford, Connecticut, as I mentioned to you earlier."

"Learn anything?"

"Warren has been acting strangely. I'll tell you about it. Anything from you?"

"Ever hear of someone named Troy Hildebrand?"

"Let me think. He's in Minneapolis, right?"

"*Was* in Minneapolis. Last Monday night he was at your theatre."

"You mean the night that Dorothy . . . ?"

"Exactly."

"Wait a minute, Monaghan, I'm putting this on the speakerphone. I have to change my clothes. I'm due at the theatre for an early rehearsal."

Troy Hildebrand was an offbeat but talented director. When he directed a play in a straightforward way, as often as not it would be brilliant. But he was a great experimenter who could let his imagination run wild. He might, for instance, move *The Three Sisters* from Russia to a small town in the Midwest, with the sisters desperate to get to Chicago, or present *Hamlet* entirely from within a series of nets like the safety nets put under trapeze artists in the circus—the hero as a man caught in a net or spider web. When this sort of thing worked, it could be a revelation, but more often than not, it missed the mark entirely or appeared self-indulgent.

The Centre Theatre Group, the company producing our play, was originally Troy's brainchild, but what made the theatre successful was his teaming up with Ardith. Gradually, however, Ardith edged him out. One of her great talents was ingratiating herself with the members of her Board of Directors. Quietly but persistently, she convinced most of the directors that Troy was too erratic and unreliable to be an artistic director. Finally, one of his productions went way over budget, and the Board ousted him, making her the sole artistic director.

I turned on the speakerphone. "The last I heard of Troy, he was head of a well-regarded theatre in Minneapolis."

"Apparently he lost his job. It seems he and the woman who headed the board out there had a falling–out. When we went back to the cast and crew of your production to ask about third parties that may have wandered in Monday night, the sound man, Ollie Simpson, says this Troy fellow was there, in the light booth with Samantha whatever her name is."

"Samantha Orenstein," I said.

It was clear that Monaghan was pleased that his hunch that someone besides cast and crew might have been around Monday night. "I gather," he continued, "that Troy and Samantha are buddies. Anyway, the Simpson guy seems to be the nosy type, interested in everyone's business. He says the rumor is that the head of the board in Minnesota is a good friend of your Ardith: a college roommate, or something. So Troy believes that Ardith had something to do with his dismissal, and the sound-man says it had happened before. So the assumption is that Troy has it in for her."

"What does this have to do with Dorothy?"

"Maybe nothing, but it seems weird that he would show up on the night all this went down. We've checked with the light character."

"Samantha."

"At first she denied that Troy was with her, and, when we made it clear we knew otherwise, she reversed herself and said not only was he there, he was with her the whole time, never left the booth. But at this point her testimony is thoroughly suspect."

"I would say so. Look, Monaghan, you should definitely pursue this. In the meantime, I really have to get to the theatre."

• • •

On Thursday night, arriving home from rehearsal, I wanted to grab as much sleep as possible, so I had turned off my house and cell phones. I set the alarm for 9 a.m. Friday morning, at which point it went off—louder, I thought, than usual. I took my time making a pot of coffee. Finally I turned on the phone. It rang almost instantly.

"Where the hell have you been?" demanded an angry voice.

"Who is this?" I asked. "Otto? Is it you, Otto?"

"Of course it's me," said Otto, a scene designer who was also the town crier. "I've been calling since 7:30."

"I'm in a show. Remember?"

"Show be damned. Have you seen it?"

"Seen what?"

"Nasty's latest."

"Otto, I just this second woke up. I haven't even shaved or had breakfast."

"You do take the daily rag, don't you?"

"As a matter of fact, I don't. I find it goes better with a second cup of coffee down at Anton's."

"Put on your bathrobe and rush out now."

"What in the world are you talking about?"

"Nasty."

Nasty, I should explain, is Nat Pomeroy, who writes a theatre gossip column for what Otto referred to as the daily rag. Called "Nasty" by everyone, Nat specializes in dishing the dirt about the theatre community. No rumor is too remote, no innuendo too inconsequential, no accusation too outrageous, no snide suggestion too implausible for Nasty. He attempts to give himself cover by using such phrases as "reliable sources report . . ." or "it is alleged that . . ." or "it is widely believed that . . ."—caveats that supposedly protect him from libel suits. The truth is, however, that if you put Nasty's words through a sieve of accuracy, there would be only a few drops at the bottom; the bulk of his writing would be the sludgy dregs at the top.

"I don't need to go out in my bathrobe. I'll get it online."

"Call me the minute you've read it."

I looked at my cell phone. There were eleven calls since

early morning. I was certain they were all about the same thing, so, without actually checking, I headed for the computer to find the already infamous column.

### Feydeau in the Midst of Tragedy

This week the New York theatre community has been in shock, mourning the loss of producer Dorothy Tremayne. Her death was all the more poignant because it occurred in the confines of a theatre, and during a rehearsal. No one in Manhattan's theatre world was more respected or more admired than she, and it is generally agreed that this is the most heartrending loss the profession has suffered in many years. "Her taste, her integrity, her enthusiasm are irreplaceable," said Ardith Wainwright, head of CTG.

Ironically, it is against this backdrop of tragedy that another story has unfolded, a story that by contrast can best be described as a British sex farce or a bedroom comedy à la Feydeau. One of the persons interviewed by police in connection with the crime was Sybil Conway, a former partner of Ms. Tremayne's. Detective Kevin Monaghan, head of the investigation, pointed out that Conway is not a suspect or even "a person of interest," but that the police are speaking to everyone who knew the victim well.

When asked where she was on Monday night, Conway said she was at a performance of Mamma Maybe and when asked to provide a witness, she named Wilfred Covington, a Texas tycoon who has recently teamed with Ms. Conway in backing Broadway musicals. When Covington was asked, however, if he was at the theatre with Conway, he quickly said no, erasing her alibi.

It turns out that Covington's wife, Lorinda, is an avid bridge player; some have even described her as a fanatic. On frequent occasions she uses her husband's jet to carry bridge-playing friends and professionals to tournaments around the country. She is also a jealous wife. Aware of this, Covington, even with his wife out of town on one of her jaunts, last Monday did not want to be seen entering the theatre with Conway. Originally, she sat toward the back of the theatre, but when the lights were lowered, moved to the front to join Covington.

When a detective called Covington to ask if he was with Conway that evening, he immediately assumed that this was a private detective hired by his wife, and his emphatic response was "no." This, of course, blew Conway's alibi out of the water. When she was confronted by detectives, she put in a desperate call to Covington explaining that he had made her a prime suspect. At that point, realizing he had no choice, Covington did the honorable thing and contacted Detective Monaghan to tell him the truth, explaining that the two of them were, in fact, at the theatre together.

What effect this confession has had on the domestic situation at the Covington home, we have not been told. We can only assume that the drama is still unfolding. Stay tuned.

Sybil had her alibi, but at a considerable price in publicity.

# CHAPTER TEN

On Friday morning, a lengthy article by Gina and Drew on the Metropolitan Museum homicide appeared in the *New York Times*. The crime was still no closer to being solved, they wrote, but from talks with Met officials they were able to report that the perpetrators (at this point it was assumed by everyone that there was more than one) were extremely well informed on several fronts. They certainly knew the layout of the museum: backstairs, entrances and exits, corridors, in fact, all the out-of-sight intricacies of the building. They also knew the ins and outs of museum schedules, not only when the rooftop exhibition would close but internal workings as to which committees of the trustees would meet on what days, at what hours, and who would be attending. In short, it was obviously an extremely sophisticated, well-rehearsed operation.

Most of the article, however, focused on Mulholland in his pre-Chicago days, starting in Kansas City. Obviously, one of the *Times* writers, probably Drew, had gone out there. This was the place, it was noted, where Mulholland had made his fortune. After graduating from the University of Kansas in

Lawrence, he got a job with a bank in Kansas City. From the beginning he apparently was both devilishly clever and untiringly industrious. After only ten years with the bank, he, along with two others, formed KCVC Partners, the initials standing for Kansas City Venture Capital. A private equity firm in which Mulholland was the brains, KCVC was ahead of its time in the Midwest. Using borrowed money, they bought out ailing companies and, after a period of laying off workers and introducing new equipment, made them profitable.

In virtually every case, KCVC was able to unload these newly minted lean and mean companies in a few short years for a multiple of anywhere from 50 to 500 percent. This was not the mother lode, however. That came after Mulholland had left KCVC and gone out on his own. First, he put together an outfit called MAA, Medical Advisors Associates. A sharp physician friend came to him with an idea. Medicare was fairly new then, and doctors, his friend pointed out, were overwhelmed and baffled by the paperwork required. Why not form a company that would relieve doctors of all those details and file with Medicare on their behalf? The plan was a huge success; MAA signed up hundreds of physicians in nine states across the Midwest. Mulholland and his physician friend made millions. Strangely, just when it seemed to be reaching its peak, Mulholland got out—to everyone's surprise.

A year or two after that, it fell apart. Several watchdog groups had become suspicious and reported irregularities. It turned out that MAA, at the same time it was filing claims for their clients, was also adding a little extra to each fee. When it all unraveled, it proved to be the largest case of Medicare fraud uncovered to that time. Not only did MAA go under, Mulholland's physician friend and several of his fellow officers ended up in jail. They yelled and screamed that Mulholland was just as responsible as they were, but he maintained that he had no idea what was going on, and, if he had, he certainly would never have been a part of it. Amazingly, he had also seen to it that there was no paper trail, no emails, nothing to implicate him.

His next venture was Pharmegen, a pharmaceutical company in Des Moines, Iowa, that specialized in generic drugs—aspirin, ibuprofen, acetaminophen—but had moved into more sophisticated items: drugs for heart, liver, kidney, and blood disorders. The company knew to the day—almost to the hour—when the rights of a brand name would expire, and it began preparing well ahead of time to turn out the equivalent generic drug so that it could launch its product the moment it was legal. Before moving into the more complicated drugs, it announced it was setting up a lab in New Mexico, and indeed there was a small lab there. But the real reason for New Mexico was to provide a warehouse to store drugs made in Mexico that Pharmegen had begun distributing without saying they were prepared outside the United States.

The real problem came when Pharmegen got into the more complicated drugs such as those for epilepsy, diabetes, and arthritis. These drugs were considerably more expensive and difficult to manufacture than headache or cold remedies. In other words, they needed capital, which was where Mulholland came in. The expansion was a huge success.

Besides costs, there was another, much more troubling problem with these high-end drugs. A number of them, which seemed to work extremely well at first, eventually proved to have serious side effects, to the point that the manufacturers were forced by the FDA to recall them. Operating somewhat below the radar, Pharmegen continued to market a few of them, and, of course, had the market pretty much to itself. Besides, there was also a legal factor that played into the equation. There is a quirky drug law that says the generic manufacturers have less legal risk than the original name-brand company if their products allegedly cause harm. The law doesn't make much sense, but there it is, and it proved an irresistible temptation to Pharmegen to continue selling these extremely chancy products. For a while the money was pouring into Pharmegen, but then, seemingly all at once, the warned-against side effects from several of the drugs arrived with a vengeance, to the point of causing not only numerous life-threatening illnesses but more than a few deaths.

Once again, Mulholland had been the canary in the coal mine. Having made a fortune in the early days of the venture, he had cashed out well before the debacle. When Mulholland left, things were going so swimmingly that the CEO of Pharmegen was baffled. "We're just getting started," he told Mulholland. "I need the money elsewhere," Mulholland told him, "but I wish you all the luck in the world." When the axe fell, and the company, faced with multiple lawsuits, was forced out of business, the CEO, hearing that his erstwhile backer had pleaded complete innocence of what had gone on, was apoplectic. Mulholland proved, however, as he had before, to be a miracle worker, a quick-change artist of the highest order.

Having amassed close to $1 billion, which over the next

decade only increased, Mulholland undertook what was to be a series of reinventions of himself. His wife, Cornelia, had always been a person with a strong social conscience, supporting things like Meals on Wheels and shelters for the homeless. Moreover, Kansas City was a wholesome, homespun town—the home, after all, of Hallmark. Retiring from active participation in finance, Mulholland became a serious, dedicated philanthropist, not only joining his wife in her work, but also becoming a strong supporter of Kansas City's first-class art museum, the Nelson-Atkins.

When, four years later, Cornelia contracted pancreatic cancer and died, Mulholland's ties to the financial world had been all but forgotten. And he himself was ready to move on.

• • •

When I finished the article, I called Drew at the *Times* to congratulate him on his terrific research. When I couldn't reach him, I called Gina and asked her to pass along my congratulations to Drew.

"Quite a story, isn't it?" she remarked.

"I'll say. First-rate reporting."

"Did you see the piece next to ours on the inside page—a four-column box on a man named Izzy?" she asked.

"No."

"Read it."

Izzy Schwartzman has a small store, Tux DeLuxe, on West 37th street in the Garment District. Inherited from his father, it specializes in men's formal wear: tuxedoes, tails, cutaways, morning suits—rented or sold. Through the years the business has seen a slow but unmistakable decline. Informality—the advent of dress-down Fridays, the emergence of blue jeans and the T-shirt as acceptable for all occasions, Broadway theatre audiences without a single necktie in sight—has become the order of the day.

In such a world, formal wear has landed near the bottom of the food chain, which is why a few years ago Izzy found himself one hot October day—it was spring in Colombia—getting off a plane in Bogotá. Speaking what little Spanish he could manage (anyone in the clothing business in New York City has to speak some Spanish), he was about to ask someone for help when a sharp-looking dude appeared at his side and introduced himself. It was Manuel Escobar, who was as thin as Izzy was overweight, with hair as dark and shiny as Izzy's hair was thin and wispy, and a nose as thin as Izzy's was flat and wide.

Manny, as he was known, took Izzy in hand, whisked him into a Mercedes S550, and headed out of town. About three miles outside the crowded city, they turned into an industrial area. Most of the buildings were old, a bit rusted and weathered, and Izzy began to wonder what he had gotten himself into, when, just past an empty warehouse, they turned a corner and headed toward an impressive, new-looking shed of corrugated steel where they disembarked. One of Manny's assistants took Izzy's bag, another assistant opened the door, and Manny ushered him into the building. Inside was a long, rectangular building about the length of half a football field, most of which was occupied by a hundred or more women hunched over sewing machines, ignoring everything except the garments in front of them.

In one corner were enclosed offices, and next to those was a long table on which were laid out samples of Manny's products: formal wear, sportswear, business suits, overcoats, sweaters. Behind the table were mannequins dressed in the same garments. Manny was beginning to show Izzy his line when the latter's eye was caught by something in a far corner of the building. He saw a man standing, facing another man who was aiming a pistol at him. All of a sudden, the man with the pistol fired point blank at the other man. Izzy was dumbstruck, even more so when nothing happened. The bullet appeared to bounce off the man's chest onto the floor.

"Did you see that?" asked the startled Izzy.

"What?' asked Manny.

Izzy pointed to the far corner, "That man just shot another man in the chest."

"I'm sorry," Manny said. "I should have warned you. That's our test area."

"But, but . . . nothing happened."

"Of course. That's why you're here."

Manny had gotten into the bulletproof garment business at the height of the Colombian drug wars, outfitting various drug lords and their associates in impervious clothing. Along the way, he had spread out in two ways. He included more and more styles in his inventory: blazers, figured vests, leather jackets. He also perfected ever thinner, stronger, lighter fabrics out of which to make these garments. In addition, he had developed materials that would ward off knife blows as well as bullets.

The result of all this was that Manny had become one of the premier exporters of bulletproof gear. Izzy, hearing of Manny's enterprise, thought that maybe, just maybe, this might be a way to expand his own business and prevent the sinking ship of tuxedoes and morning suits from disappearing altogether, which was why he was now in the unlikely environs of Bogotá. The outcome of the visit was that Izzy began to carry Manny's merchandise in Manhattan, joining outlets that Manny had around the globe: Hong Kong, Singapore, Paris, Istanbul, Dubai—you name it.

After Izzy made his deal with Manny, he had his nephew, a computer nerd, develop a fancy web site and enlisted a female cousin in the design world to prepare a glossy brochure. In a relatively short time, he had established a reliable supplementary income in state-of-the-art protective gear with such customers as prominent political figures and mob bosses along with their lieutenants in New Jersey, Brooklyn, and Bridgeport.

Izzy did not read the New York Times. His news sources were the Post and the Daily News, along with local TV, of course. He was aware of the murder at the Met, but since there was a regular drumbeat of murders in the five boroughs and the tristate area, and since he had never been inside the Met, he did not pay too much attention. He was astonished, therefore, that on the Friday morning after the crime at the Met, he began to get phone calls from chauffeurs and security guards for prominent social and business figures. Day after day following that, limos were lining up on 37th Street, and a stream of men, and some women, thronged into his shop.

After the murder, one the first things trustees of the museum and, indeed, of all the large arts organizations did was check with their people to see how their security measures stacked up in this new world of trustee assassinations. They were concerned, not just for themselves, of course, but for their wives, children, and small grandchildren headed for private schools and soccer games. It was understood that in addition to beefing up the private security at the entrances to their apartment buildings, a number of trustees also engaged security personnel to ride shotgun next to their chauffeurs. Inquiring of their security advisors what else they might do, they discovered, almost simultaneously, Izzy's enterprise. Not only chauffeurs and security men arrived, but in some cases the principals themselves, who wanted to be sure that they got the right fit and style, as well as maximum protection, by trying these things on.

In between waiting on customers, Izzy phoned every relative or friend who had ever been near the shop and asked them to get there as quickly as possible. Watching his stock disappear, he put in an urgent call to Manny in Bogotá for as many items as Manny could spare, plus urgent orders for more. Izzy has sold more in a matter of days than he sometimes previously had in a year.

• • •

Dressing for Dorothy's funeral, I put on my one and only dark blue suit; my one white shirt, a subdued, patterned yellow tie; and black dress shoes and headed out. As I emerged from the subway at 50th Street and Sixth Avenue, my cell phone was ringing. It was Arnie, calling from Stamford.

"I've been trying to get you," he said.

"Had my cell turned off. I'm on my way to the funeral."

"I assumed as much. Half of southern Connecticut is headed down this morning."

"What's up?" I asked.

"The junior associate I mentioned, the one who knows the scene in the business community?"

"Yes?"

"He says this young man you asked about, Stuart Ross, doesn't hide his light under a bushel, especially at a local watering hole: McGonagle's Pub. Monday night is Happy Hour at McGonagle's, when all the young try to make the scene, and last Monday Ross, who goes by the name of Stu, was there. The reason my associate remembers is that Stu and another fellow, a left-leaning environmentalist, got into a heated political argument."

"What time?"

"Happy Hour is from 5:00 to 7:00. Somewhere in the middle of that."

"Arnie, I can't tell you how helpful this is." I looked at my watch. "Sorry, but I have to ring off. I'm almost there. Thank you, thank you, thank you."

• • •

Monaghan and I had agreed to meet near the church in Paley Park, a tiny, vest-pocket park on 53rd, just east of Fifth Avenue. He was there when I arrived, dressed in a quiet gray suit, blue shirt as usual, and a muted white-and-red striped tie—his churchgoing outfit, I assumed.

"Have you tracked down Troy?" I asked.

"Late last night. He's staying with an actor friend, someone named Halliday. Seems they're all friends, Samantha the lighting woman, Halliday, and Troy. Troy admits he was there. Said he'd heard about the playwright and the director but had never seen their work and wanted to take a look. He was supposed to leave town before the previews begin, so Samantha invited him to sit in the light booth. One of my people talked to him—Elena, a sharp Hispanic girl. He's angry all right, but he denies having anything to do with Tremayne's murder. He did leave the booth briefly to go downstairs to the john, but that was earlier, he says, and he came right back. Once the news of the murder was reported, he immediately skedaddled. As for wanting to kill Tremayne, he says no way: 'She's one of the only decent producers in the theatre: If I'd wanted to kill anyone, it would have been that bitch Ardith,' he's quoted as saying. We're checking to see who remembers seeing him. It still could have been one of those unintended things."

"Obviously, there's something off-kilter here, what with his being in the booth and Samantha denying it. Also, he's known to be a volatile individual." I then told Monaghan about my conversation with Arnie. "In other words, Warren's alibi, that he and that young man were in Stamford working late, seems not just problematic, but untrue." I changed the subject. "You've never seen Warren, have you?"

"No."

"He'll be at the funeral, and probably his sister from Tucson and her husband as well. We'll go to the church separately, but when we get there, stand at the back corner on the right-hand side. It's dark there, and I can point people out as they come in. The family has reserved a private dining room at the University Club—a block north of the church—for lunch after the service. I'm assuming Warren and his sister will go to that." We left separately, and headed for the church.

# CHAPTER ELEVEN

St. Thomas Episcopal Church, on the northwest corner of 53rd Street and Fifth, was built in the early twentieth century in the French High Gothic style. Not as enormous as the great cathedrals of Europe, it has its own grandeur, not only in the architecture but in the height and sweep of the interior, especially the magnificent white stone screen, rising nearly 100 feet, at the rear of the church.

I entered and signed one of the guest books. It was early, so only a sprinkling of people had arrived. I stepped into the sanctuary and turned right; there in the corner was Monaghan. He pointed across the way and down the side aisles to three of his men, dressed in black or dark blue suits, which meant they could easily be mistaken for part of the funeral team from Campbell's rather than cops.

The same groups who had been at Dorothy's apartment for the visitation attended the funeral: The Connecticut contingent, the New York Upper East Side friends, and the two theatre groups: actors, directors, designers, and the more mainstream producers and managers. The chief difference was that for the religious service everyone dressed in slightly more formal and conservative outfits.

I wondered if Wilfred Covington would come, especially after that stinging piece in the morning paper. But he did appear, with someone who could only be his wife, Lorinda. Coming in quietly, almost stealthily, they sneaked down a side aisle and attempted inconspicuously to drop into their seats as quickly as possible. As various people of interest arrived, I pointed them out to Monaghan: Alistair, the former companion; Lance; other socialites; important theatre people. Some he recognized, especially those connected with our production whom he had interviewed: Ardith, Rowan, a couple of actors, and Elliott, the playwright.

The family, of course, would come in last and move down front. That was when I would have to begin speaking rapidly to identify the key players among Dorothy's relatives. At about ten to 11:00, the family gathered in the vestibule, and the funeral officials lined them up. In the front row would be Annie, Curtis, their children, Danny, and Dorothy's older sister from St. Louis with her husband. In the second row I pointed out Warren, with a couple I did not recognize, but who I assumed were his sister, and brother-in-law with their three grown children. Behind the immediate family were two rows of people, no doubt various cousins, nephews, nieces, and the like. When everyone had moved down to take their seats, I left Monaghan standing in the back corner, slipped across the way, and sat toward the back next to an actor friend.

The service began. The organ boomed forth, the boys' and men's choir processed down the center aisle followed by various clergy, and finally the two ministers, one the head clergyman of

St. Thomas and the other the Reverend Claude Merrivale, Dorothy's longtime minister from her church in Connecticut, who delivered an appropriate and heartfelt homily. The transcendent aspect of any service at St. Thomas is the boys' choir, the most highly regarded musical group of its kind in the country. It's safe to say that they produce one of the truly glorious sounds on the planet. At Dorothy's service they led us in singing "O God, Our Help in Ages Past" and "Abide with Me." On the final chorus of each one, the choir sang a descant, which elevated these ancient numbers even further.

After the service, I slipped out early and disappeared around a corner. When others had scattered, the family came out, and I briefly moved over and spoke to the ones I wanted to see: Annie, Curtis, and Danny. I moved away and started walking to the Savile Club ten blocks away, where I was to meet Alistair for lunch.

Alistair Hargrave was a "walker," a creature virtually unique to Manhattan. Walkers could vary in age from the mid-thirties to the mid-sixties, and, if well preserved, a tad older. They were always male and almost never overtly gay. They could be somewhat androgynous, even a touch epicene, but they must also convey a certain sense of solidity, a trace of masculinity—in other words, not be too louche. They are escorts for a variety of women: divorced, separated, widows, of course, and women whose husbands are frequently out of town or who have openly taken on a mistress.

A good walker has to be not only presentable but distinguished-looking, preferably bordering on handsome. He has to be well-read and up on current affairs—the *Times* and the *Post* every day, select books on the arts, fashion, travel, and the like. His knowledge need not be exhaustive but broad enough to keep up his end of the conversation in any circle: cocktail parties, museum openings, benefits. Moreover, in terms of masculine libido, he must achieve that tricky balance of being neither a limp dishrag nor a raging Lothario. On almost every count Alistair was the quintessential walker, which is no doubt why Dorothy took up with him a year or so after her divorce from Warren.

Alistair escorted her for almost three years; then she seemed to abruptly drop him. Maybe it wasn't all that sudden, but most people looked at it that way, and Alistair gave the stiff upper lip performance of a lover spurned. I had my own theory about why she ended the arrangement. As companionable and ideal as Alistair was, the code of the walker phenomenon is that it almost always excludes ongoing sexual intimacy, and one of Alistair's strong points was his adherence to the code. In this case, though, I think it began to work against him.

One thing that led me to this conclusion were the times Dorothy and I saw each another at openings and play readings, when I came to sense there was definitely a *frisson* between us. We both knew it would never go anywhere. But it was there: one of those unspoken but unmistakable feelings. Later I came to suspect that there was not only a desire for a man with more to offer than Alistair, but also her growing sense of wanting to be her own person.

• • •

The Savile Club is a four-story Georgian brick building on Fifth Avenue in the low sixties. The Upper East Side of Manhattan is a world unto itself. Lots of ordinary people live there, and it has the usual mixture of small groceries, florists, banks, dress shops, bookstores, and the like. But within that world there is another world. It has its architectural artifacts: museums, art galleries, condominiums, co-ops, expensive restaurants—which are an indispensable part of this other world. Condominiums, by the way, exist all over the world, but the co-op is unique to a certain part of Manhattan. There are financial differences, of course, between a condo and a co-op, but the most important difference is control. The board of a co-op has considerably more options when it comes to rejecting prospective apartment buyers. Put another way, a co-op can be far more exclusive than a condo.

As with any foreign land, enclave, or world-within-a-world, the Upper East Side has its own language with its own vocabulary, not to mention its own set of symbols. This has to do with where you went to school, what restaurants you frequent, where you go in the summer, where you go in the winter (in Florida, it may be Hobe Sound on the east coast or Boca Grande on the west). If you are born into this world, you imbibe all this with your mother's milk (or, if your mother does not breast feed, with the formula administered by your nanny). You may marry into it, of course, and if you are nimble and quick on your feet, you can adapt to it reasonably well, but, if you are neither born to it nor marry into it, you must absorb the codes, the signals, the sign language until they are second nature. You might send out a signal like a semaphore, but if no one responds, you remain in outer darkness.

An integral part of this unspoken code are the clubs. Not only must you know which ones they are, a husband and wife must each belong to several. We are not speaking here of country clubs in Connecticut or Long Island, but clubs in town. For the women, the Colony and the Cos Club; for the men, the Union, the Brook, the Knickerbocker, the Savile. You start with those and go on from there.

• • •

When you enter the Savile, the uniformed man at the door politely asks if he can help you.

"Mr. Hargrave?" I say.

"He's expecting you, sir. Upstairs in the lounge on the right."

You ascend a steep series of steps, past oil portraits of ancient worthies, and end up on a marble floor at the top. To your right is a dining room, not overly large but with understated elegance, strictly of the masculine variety. Just to the left of the dining room is a lounge. As I moved in that direction, Alistair, who was clearly on the lookout for me, rose and greeted me. His handshake was solemn and serious, a clear sign that he was grieving.

Alistair was about five feet ten, clearly fighting to stay as trim as possible but losing the battle slightly around the middle. With pink cheeks, a dimple in his chin, and gray temples, he appeared a bit cherubic. Always impeccably dressed, usually in a dark blue blazer and gray slacks, but today, because of the funeral, he wore a dark business suit, a blue shirt with white collar and cuffs, gold cuff links with his initials, and a yellow tie patterned with miniscule figures that looked like small yachts or country houses, I couldn't tell which.

"You've been here before, of course," he said.

"Edgar Lawrence is an old friend and kind enough to invite me from time to time."

"Lovely man, Edgar. Shall we have a drink? Sherry, wine, a cocktail?"

"I will take a glass of white wine, thank you, but if you don't mind, could we have it with lunch?

"Of course."

He steered me toward the dining room, whereupon the headwaiter took us to our table, in a corner overlooking Central Park and the silent, passing traffic on Fifth Avenue. After we had ordered drinks, we discussed the funeral service and agreed it was both infinitely sad and, at the same time, extremely inspirational.

"Truthfully, Matt, I'm devastated," he said. "I've hardly slept a wink since I heard. Finally, the last two nights I did something I rarely do: I took sleeping pills both nights."

"I know how close to her you were."

"I loved her, Matt. It was that simple. I know, someone like me, an escort—you're not supposed to be the kind that falls in love, truly in love, and I never did before."

"You've been the companion of a number of elegant, interesting women."

"Not like Dorothy. There was no artifice there, no pretense. She was smart, of course, attractive, quick, and clearly she loved the arts. I've never known anyone quite like her: all that intellectual power combined with grace and good taste."

"First the blow of losing her, and now this one. I would think it's almost too much to bear."

"I'm so glad you understand."

"That first blow, when she ended the relationship: that must have been difficult to understand."

"Impossible."

The waiter appeared with our drinks and asked if we were ready to order. We had not looked at the menu, but both of us were familiar with it, so we looked somewhat hurriedly and ordered: lemon sole for Alistair, a Cobb salad for me. When the waiter had disappeared, Alistair continued. "From left field, Matt. I never saw it coming."

"Awful for you."

"I was stunned. I still can't wrap my mind, my emotions, around it."

"There were no warning signs?"

"None as far as I could see. I've gone over it time and time again, and, as far as I can tell, there was not the slightest hint."

"I have a theory, Alistair."

"Oh?"

I then proceeded to explain my idea of Dorothy's notion of a kind of personal Declaration of Independence. Alistair listened with great interest. "I hear what you're saying," he said, "but I still don't understand why—"

"I think she felt it had to be across the board. My own hunch is that, if there was any one attachment she would have wanted to hold on to and hated to give up, it was you."

"Do you really feel that?"

"It's my sense of things," I said. I wasn't at all certain this was true, but Alistair was so shaken I thought there was no harm in reassuring him. Besides, I didn't want to spend the entire lunch listening to his lament. I had never thought of Alistair as a serious suspect, but now I was certain he was not. His grief was too genuine; besides, looking at him, I could never imagine this immaculate figure involved in any kind of basement skulduggery.

At this point the waiter arrived with our lunch, and as we began eating I turned to the other question I wanted answered. I was reasonably certain that Dorothy and Alistair must have travelled in the same circles as Mulholland and his wife, and I was anxious to find out what he knew about those two. "This murder at the Met," I said.

"Horrible, grotesque, truly repulsive."

"Did you know him, or his wife, Roxanne?"

"Dorothy was invited to their place for dinner, of course, but she didn't accept the first couple of times. As you can imagine, she could have gone out every night of the week. But she was a working producer and didn't have time for constant rounds of social engagements. Besides, more often than not she was bored to death. But she had heard that the Mulholland parties were different from most: smaller, more intimate, more intellectual. So we went to one and after that to several more."

"And were they?"

"What?"

"Different."

At this point the waiter returned with the coffee and macaroons and silently disappeared.

Alistair continued: "The key was Roxanne—a remarkable hostess. The apartment was impeccable, the height of good taste—restrained, lovely colors, just the right accents. And the food: she had hired a sous-chef from one of the Boulud restaurants as her cook. The menus were simple: straightforward dishes prepared with great inventiveness, and small portions of everything—a trick most people never learn. The company was carefully chosen, and there was always a museum trustee, maybe two, though sometimes it was a curator. Over dinner, Roxanne and the curator would strike up a conversation about some acquisition or upcoming exhibition. It made you feel that you were in on the ground floor."

"What about Clifford, the husband?"

"I never figured him out. He was invariably polite, and Roxanne was careful to defer to him periodically. Though he was generally part of the conversations, I never could tell whether he was genuine or playing a role."

"Maybe some of both."

"Maybe."

We moved from the table to the top of the steps, and I was ready to leave.

"By the way," he said, remembering that I was rehearsing a play. "How are rehearsals going?"

"It hasn't been easy; a difficult week, to say the least."

"But I pray it will be a success—Dorothy would want that."

"It's taking us time to regain our stride, but I think it will come right in the end. It's a good play with a strong cast. Keep your fingers crossed."

"I will."

I was starting down the steps, but he remained at the top. "I'm staying a while," he said. "I need to recover from this morning."

"I understand," I said. "Thanks, Alistair, for a lovely lunch. I'm just sorry it had to be under these circumstances."

"That makes two of us." As I started down the steps, he added, "Break a leg."

● ● ●

When I got back to the loft after lunch with Alistair, the answering machine showed I had a couple of calls. The most important by far was from Seymour Pascall, my friend in the coroner's office. I had been anxiously waiting to find out what the autopsy of Dorothy had shown. When I reached him on the phone, he told me it had revealed that strangulation was definitely the main cause of death, but she had also suffered a severe blow to the head with some blunt instrument—a small pipe, a hammer, something like that. I raised the possibility that it might be a wine bottle, since it happened adjacent to the bar in the lounge. He said they had thought of that and had asked the pathologist to examine her head again with that in mind— either before or after the blow, probably after, the person proceeded to strangle her.

"Any fingerprints?"

"Yes," he said, "but they haven't been processed so far."

"Would you let me know when they find out?"

"Will do," Seymour said. I thanked him profusely, telling him this report might certainly help lead to Dorothy's killer.

• • •

After I rang off, I went over the information I had so far on the murder itself. Someone had arranged it so that Dorothy would arrive thirty minutes before she was to meet Danny, probably someone who had stolen or had access to Danny's cell phone. The killer or killers had positioned themselves in the darkened basement ahead of time, possibly entering through the front of the theatre, but most likely coming in through the alley that exited on 50th street. After the murder they left by the same route. As for the murder itself, I continued to think they would find upside-down fingerprints on the neck of the wine bottle. The murderer or murderers might have used gloves, but somehow I thought it had all the earmarks of an impromptu, unplanned event. There was intention to intimidate Dorothy—but to kill her? I was not so sure.

• • •

Friday night was our first dress rehearsal. It was supposed to have been earlier, but Dorothy's death pushed everything back. We would have a regular performance—costumes, lights, the works—with our first audience: about two dozen friends and relatives of the cast and crew. It went reasonably well, but as always, there were a few problems. The character of Mark,

121

the oldest of the three children, seemed a bit vapid and ill-defined. There was a slow spot midway in act two when the husband and wife were at each other's throats recalling past quarrels. On the technical side, two-thirds of the way through act one, the rain, thunder, and lightning were so loud that the actors could barely be heard. Then it was overcorrected and became more like a "gentle rain from heaven" than a storm. Obviously, a sound level between the two was the answer to this problem.

As for the other weaknesses, the director and playwright conferred and decided that the problem in act two—the scene where the forward thrust of the play seemed to stop in the argument between the spouses—could be largely cured with judicious cuts. Giving more definition to Mark's character would not be so easy, though Elliot, the playwright, thought he had an idea: an expanded scene toward the end of act one between Mark and my character, where he challenges me more and gets a number of things off his chest. Elliot planned to work on this over the weekend and get a new scene to us either Sunday afternoon or early Monday morning. We would work on the scene Monday afternoon and hope to put it in that night. For the most part, however, our small audience seemed impressed with both the play and the performances.

# CHAPTER TWELVE

The matinee performance Saturday afternoon went smoothly: The sound level for the storm had been corrected and other adjustments made, and as a result, the Saturday evening performance was our best so far. Afterwards, the cast wanted to go out for a drink; usually I went with them, but tonight I begged off, saying that with all that had gone on this week I was exhausted. In fact, I wasn't going home, but took the number 1 subway up to Columbia University area, hoping to track down Roger Morehead, the young druggie who had confronted Dorothy in her office. I knew the chances of finding him were slim, but I had to try. Monaghan had given me the address where Roger was supposed to be staying and without too much trouble I found the place: a six-story apartment house just west of Broadway, no doubt with reasonable rents that suited Columbia students as well as those attending nearby Union Theological Seminary.

I flashed a guard—half-asleep in the lobby—an NYPD detective's card, a fake one I had been given when I was on *Law & Order* and had kept for just such situations. A gunmetal gray elevator took me to the fifth floor, where I walked down a long corridor to an apartment at the end. From all the noise, it was clear there was a party in progress, and I felt I just might be in luck.

Not surprisingly, it took a series of knocks on the door to get someone to answer. "Yes?" the person inquired, seeing someone who obviously did not belong. When the door opened, even a crack, there was the raucous sound of rock music, complete with indistinguishable lyrics; a heavy drum and bass guitar beat; the sight of writhing bodies, not really moving together or even to the music, beer cans in virtually every hand; and the pungent smell of marijuana and God knows what else.

"Roger Morehead," I said. "Is he here?"

"Who wants to know?"

"Johanssen, is the name. Matt Johanssen."

"Is there a problem?"

"No problem. I have a message for him."

"From whom?"

"Someone he knows, an old friend."

"I'll see if I can find him." He didn't invite me in, but then, I didn't want to go in. I did, however, place a firm foot in the door so I would not be locked out. After quite a few minutes, Roger appeared. Rail-thin, he had greasy black hair pulled back in a ponytail, with stray hairs shooting out in places. Below a sharp nose, there was almost no chin, but he did have large ears. Also, there remained on his face traces of adolescent acne. My first thought was that, if I looked like Roger, I might very well have taken to dope myself.

"Do I know you?"

"A friend of Warren Tremayne."

"Is this about Dorothy?"

"Not really."

"The police already talked to me."

"It wasn't the police I wanted to ask about."

"What then? Look, this is an odd time for any kind of interrogation." He started to turn and leave.

I called him back. "Just a couple of questions and I'm gone." Before he could object further, I plowed on. "Warren has been reaching out to a number of people recently; I just wondered if he's been in touch with you."

He paused a moment. "As a matter of fact, he was. What of it?"

"Was he asking you to do something?"

"I thought he was going to; he acted like he was. Said he would pay me. But then changed his mind."

"Oh?"

"He didn't explain, but he did give me a couple of hundred bucks."

"That was nice of him."

"I always liked Warren."

"Better than Dorothy?"

"Never speak ill of the dead. Isn't that what they say?"

"Last question: When was this?"

"What?"

"When he spoke to you?"

"Two weeks ago, give or take a few days."

"Thanks. Sorry I interrupted the festivities. Go back to your party."

"I thought maybe you were fuzz."

"Not me." And I went on my way.

$$\bullet \quad \bullet \quad \bullet$$

It's strange, the quirky connections the mind can make. Riding home on the subway, a fairly longish ride from Columbia to the lower Village, my thoughts jumped from the raucous, youth-oriented party I had just observed to another party two decades earlier, a party standing in stark contrast to this one: a wedding reception for two young people, both from old money, on the roof of the St. Regis Hotel. I had stepped out onto a small terrace to get a breath of air when someone came up beside me, a girl a few years younger than I, which is to say, in her late twenties.

"This is it," she said, "The last hurrah."

"I thought it was just the beginning," I said.

"I don't mean the bride and groom. The whole affair. The final frolic of the WASP world. Surely you've noticed the crowd: a few Catholics, three blacks, and a couple of Asians, but essentially this is WASP country. Laughing, mingling, dancing to Gershwin and Cole Porter—as if there were no tomorrow. But of course there is, and they don't know it, or possibly they do know it and don't want to face it. Better to live in ignorant bliss than be aware and scared to death." After a slight pause she continued, "You're the actor, aren't you?"

"And you're the designer."

"Assistant designer, actually, second assistant designer."

Her name was Sophie van Deventer, and everyone knew who she was, at least everyone in the crowd at the reception.

From Minneapolis, she had a classic look, not that of the whole-some, pink-cheeked lass, but more continental than mid-American. Reasonably tall, just under six feet, she had dark chestnut hair, piercing blue eyes, high cheekbones, a beautifully proportioned nose and chin, and flawless skin. Clearly as beautiful as any model, she would never be mistaken for one because of her animation, not to say her intelligence. Her face seemed infinitely mobile, breaking out in a wide smile one moment, a serious mien the next, followed by a sly smile, and then arched eyebrows when skeptical. Men swarmed all over her—stockbrokers, lawyers, investment bankers, real estate deal makers—but so far she had resisted them all.

She stuck out her hand. "I'm Sophie."

"I know," I said. "I'm Matt."

"So here we are: the last of the Mohicans."

"I hope not."

"But, darling, we are. Of course, the clubs, the out-of-town watering holes, the Upper East Side, they will go on, but the clock is ticking."

"Did you come with someone?" I asked.

"Inky Lawrence."

"Don't know Inky."

"No reason you should. And you, are you alone?"

"No. Teeky Walters."

"Don't know Teeky."

"No reason you should." After a slight pause I continued, "Shouldn't we get together some time? Soon, from what you were saying. We could hold a wake or perform last rites for all those people in there." I indicated the dance floor.

She reached into a small purse. "Here's my card," she said. "Do you have a pen?"

I handed her one. She wrote on the back. "The number to call is this one."

• • •

That's where it began: my three-year affair with Sophie. I'd never met anyone like her, and I haven't since. She had come east and gone to Brown, and while in Providence attended classes at the Rhode Island School of Design. In New York, she quickly landed a job with a fabric house in the D & D building, then within two years joined Barbara Acorn. Called Babs by everyone, Acorn was known as the decorator for Old Money, though, as Sophie pointed out, there was a lot of new money in the mix as well. Babs specialized in understated elegance that included masterful recreations of faux English and faux French. Sophie's forte was color. With the naked eye, she could distinguish eight or nine shades of yellow, twelve or more of green, and no telling how many of red or blue. But she also became a whiz at fabrics, wallpaper, and furniture.

We were both tentative at first. As glamorous as she was, I was fearful that I might be in over my head. On her part, having fended off men for so long, she was not sure she could break the habit. I think my being an actor helped: I was not a cookie-cutter man with a briefcase. On the other hand, it was also a help that I wasn't some off-the-wall beatnik character. In any case, we became a regular item, so regular that within six months we had bought an apartment on Riverside Drive overlooking the

Hudson. It was large enough for each of us to have our own "space," as it was put in those days. Naturally, she decorated it.

Sophie was extraordinary: adventurous, impulsive, improvisational. We would take the ferry to Governor's Island one week, visit the Brooklyn Museum the next, travel to Long Island—not to Southampton or East Hampton, but all the way to the end, to Montauk. She seemed always to know the latest, small, unknown but soon to be discovered restaurant. As an actor, I alternated periods of intense activity with days when I was relatively free, and she seemed to have the knack of being free at the same time. I taught her about theatre, and she taught me about art. A trip to a museum with Sophie—the Metropolitan, the Guggenheim, MOMA, the Whitney—became a course in art history, not to say art appreciation.

As if all this were not enough, there was the sex. In many ways I found this the most miraculous part of all. I had been involved from time to time with young women—some of them actresses, some not—who were willing partners, and with a couple of them I felt the sex was about as good as it could get. But always, even with the most willing and experimental bedmate, the tension never went completely away. Invariably there was something in the air: a hesitancy, an uncertainty, a question mark whether my performance would be acceptable. Of course, when things worked out, the tension was dissipated, but there was no denying it had been there at the start.

With Sophie, it was never there at all. Whether foreplay or fulfillment, the experience was amazingly relaxed, at the same time that it was as intense and exciting as anything I had known. She was as adventurous in bed as she was in our other escapades.

Everything was up for grabs: time, place, positions, whatever. It could be at any moment: after a leisurely breakfast on a Saturday or Sunday, or following a walk on the beach in Montauk, one never knew.

We were together three years. Toward the end several things happened. She had passed the thirty-year mark, and those were the days when the term "biological clock" was very much in vogue. Women began to consider the possibility that time might be running out. I think one of the things that worked so well for Sophie and me is that neither one of us ever raised the notion of marriage. We were as close as any married couple could be; ironically, one thing that allowed that to happen was that we were so evenly balanced, each one wanting what we had and nothing more. Unconsciously, we probably realized that there was a time limit on such a relationship.

The split, about which there had already been a few hints, came when I went out of town on a lengthy tour, playing Sky Masterson in *Guys and Dolls*. She had decided that she wanted to go out on her own as a designer, and had begun moving in that direction. While I was on tour, I would come back over a Sunday night and a Monday, but we both sensed that we were turning a page and beginning a new chapter. During my absences she began seeing a doctor, an up-and-coming neurosurgeon, who loved her madly and wanted to get married. He turned out to be just what she needed at that point. And so our affair ended—amicably and with a vow to remain good friends, which we did, and continue to do to this day. They, by the way, had three children, each one by the looks of things headed toward becoming a notable success in his or her chosen field.

By the time my subway ride ended, my reverie was over, but it accomplished one thing. For the previous seventy-two hours, I had thought of only two things: the play, and finding Dorothy's killer. My reminiscence let me forget for a time what had been so uppermost in my mind, and I had the first good night's sleep I had had all week.

• • •

Sunday morning I slept in. I had turned off my phone and deliberately did not check my emails. Instead I fixed a leisurely breakfast, made my way slowly through the Sunday *Times*, and did a little laundry. At noon I checked my phone messages. Most could wait. But one, I thought, could not. Beginning at 9:00, and then every twenty minutes or so, I had had calls from Sonny Beaufort: he had to see me. So the one call I returned was to Sonny.

"You read Friday's paper?" he asked.

"Of course."

"I must talk to you."

"Why?"

"I'll explain."

"You can't tell me now?"

"Can I come down?"

I looked around the loft. "It's a mess here."

"This is not about interior design."

"Is 2:00, 2:30 all right?"

"Fine. See you then."

∙ ∙ ∙

Sonny Beaufort grew up in the family home near Chester, South Carolina. Chester was also the home of Summer Tree Mills, a textile business that had been in Sonny's family for four generations. His grandfather, Lucius, after whom he was named, had been running the mill during and just after World War II and had expanded the business exponentially, first by becoming one of the major suppliers of parachute cloth to the military during the war and later by being one of the first to get into no-iron fabric for sheets and shirts. When Sonny's father took over, he kept things going by turning out denim for blue jeans. Summer Tree was booming, and, not surprisingly, it was expected that Sonny would enter the family business, in fact, that he would *run* the family business.

Sonny was sent to Princeton, the favorite Ivy League school for the sons of Southern gentlemen. Two years behind me, he was an enthusiastic member of the Triangle Club—the group that since 1891 has been presenting musical theatre productions at the university, boasting such well-known alumni as F. Scott Fitzgerald, Booth Tarkington, Josh Logan, and Jimmy Stewart. The highlight, year after year, is a group of male students dressed in drag who form an outrageous kick line.

Sonny proved to be an indifferent singer and dancer but showed genuine talent as a costume and set designer. Early in my senior year, after we had finished the fall production, he sought me out as a sort of mentor, or at least as a sounding board. What he was chewing over was his future—namely, how to avoid returning to South Carolina to take over the family business, a thought that sent shivers through him every time it surfaced, which was all the time. The burden of history weighs heavily on the heir to a long-standing family enterprise, and in Sonny's case it was particularly distressing because he had discovered at Princeton, if not before, that a career in the arts was where his heart was.

I tried to offer what advice I could, but mostly I listened. The one thing I did counsel was that he try to postpone the inevitable as long as he could. Then, when the point of no return arrived, he would either have to knuckle under or, if he felt fervently enough, fly in the face of family history and go out on his own. He did, in fact, hold off as long as he could, first with a year abroad, and then two years of graduate work at the Pratt Institute of Design. Fortunately for him, just when it looked as if he could delay the decision no longer, fate intervened. Those who ran the textile business had not yet seen the sun setting in the west and rising in China. They had no idea that within fifteen or twenty years hardly a single piece of fabric or furniture would be manufactured in either South or North Carolina. In the boom just before the bust, Cannon Mills and Burlington got into a bidding war over Summer Tree, offering a price no one could sensibly refuse. A deal was struck, and the business passed to Burlington.

For Sonny it was a blessing in more ways than one. Not only was he off the hook, career-wise, but he was a rich young man. He finished up at Pratt, getting an MFA in design, but shortly after getting his degree he realized that his real talent was not for design itself, but in spotting and supporting talent in the visual arts. He started a private foundation, and used its largesse to support painters, sculptors, designers, and the institutions that trained them. Occasionally he would also offer support to struggling theatre and dance companies.

He did a good deal of freelance writing: articles in *The New Yorker*, *The New York Review of Books*, and elsewhere, but he became best known for the monthly magazine he founded, *AV*, or *Arts View*. In his magazine, the prime targets of Sonny's ire were the industrial or financial entrepreneurs who had amassed fortunes by questionable if not downright dishonest means, then made a 180-degree turn, attempting to create the image of a model citizen and erase all traces of their previous careers. This attempted act of redemption was often achieved by becoming prominent in philanthropy, particularly in the arts.

There was a long record of such transformations in American history, the best example, no doubt, being the robber barons of the late nineteenth century—Carnegie, Rockefeller, Vanderbilt, Frick—who seemingly would do anything to achieve a monopoly or corner the market in oil, steel, or railroads, often destroying other people's lives in the process. A classic example of such corporate malfeasance was the Homestead Strike of 1892. The Carnegie steel mill at Homestead, near Pittsburgh, was managed by Carnegie's partner, Henry Clay Frick. When the workers struck, Carnegie and Frick were determined to break their labor union. To do so, Frick shipped in several hundred Pinkerton guards from Boston to confront the workers. During the showdown, seven workers were killed and many more wounded. Today, however, Carnegie and Frick are not remembered for executing workers but for Carnegie Hall and the pristine Frick Museum on Fifth Avenue.

For Sonny, things have not changed. A hundred years later, history is repeating itself. The particulars are different. Entrepreneurs no longer shut down the steel mills and coal mines of their opposition, but clever financial manipulators outsmart their competition with dubious tactics that amount to the same thing. They corner the market on mercury or basalt with computers, puts, calls, derivatives, IPOs, you name it. They hire the most expensive Washington lobbyists that money can buy to make certain that no government restrictions impede their progress toward ever higher profits for their enterprises, while those same enterprises pay virtually no taxes. And, once they have made their fortunes, they leave all that behind and reinvent themselves as model citizens, often by making large contributions to some institution like the Metropolitan Opera or New York City Ballet, then joining the boards of the same so they can hobnob with old money at galas and opera openings. Sonny had exposed more than his share of such parvenus.

# CHAPTER THIRTEEN

Sonny appeared at my door that afternoon wearing an old pair of blue jeans, a dark blue turtleneck with a gray sweatshirt over it, and running shoes. Sonny is short by today's standards, probably five eight or so. He has blond hair, pale blue eyes, and fair skin with a few freckles. His straw-colored hair spilled over his ears and shirt, and he had two days' stubble of beard on his chin.

"Like a beer?" I asked.

"Do you have decaf coffee?"

"I can make some."

"Milk and no sugar."

He followed me into the kitchen area while I started to make the coffee.

"I'm sorry about your producer."

"Dorothy."

"Did you know her well?"

"As a matter of fact, I did."

"Was there . . . ?"

"Anything between us?"

"She was divorced, right?"

"Yes. I cared for her a great deal, and admired her enormously, but, romantically, no."

"Still, a real loss."

"No question. It's hit me harder than I would have imagined."

"What about the show?"

"It's been rough."

"I can imagine."

"We've postponed previews and the opening."

"Everyone will understand that."

By this time we had moved into the living area; I was seated on the sofa, and Sonny on the edge of a straight-backed chair.

"Everyone thinks it's me," he said.

"What do you mean 'everyone'? Who? When?"

"Don't be coy. After that piece in Friday's *Times*? Who has been railing against this sort of thing for years?"

"Well, you."

"Exactly. Arrivistes, social climbers who've made a bundle, then want to polish their image by getting on an arts board."

"I admit it's been one of your crusades, you might even say your pet bête noire. But to connect you with the Met affair is a bridge too far, I would say."

"Not to others."

"What others?"

"I've been getting phone calls, emails: 'Taking matters into your own hands, have you?' 'Congrats, you've finally taken action.' That sort of thing."

"Stop reading emails; turn off your phone."

"Easy for you to say."

"Where were you that Tuesday night?"

"In North Salem. Where else?"

"Anyone with you?"

"Arlene, of course."

"There you are."

"They'd say I planned it all. Hired people."

"Look, Sonny. This was an extremely sophisticated operation. It took weeks of planning, and the people who did it were experts. You don't even know people like that."

"There's more."

"Oh?"

"My computer's been hacked into."

"You're sure? How do you know? Anything gone missing?"

"There seem to be some new files. Things I never saw before. My young guru is coming tomorrow to check it out."

"That is disturbing."

"I think someone is trying to set me up—make me the fall guy, the suspect. I don't know what to do."

"First, you ought to find out from your guru exactly what has happened. Then I'll call the detective on Dorothy's case, Monaghan, and get the name of the detective heading the Met murder. When I do, I'll let you know, and you should let his office know what has been happening. Call this man."

"Thanks, Matt." He paused. "This whole thing is filled with ironies."

"In what way?"

"This focus on the bad apples on arts boards—it's true I feel strongly about that, but I care even more about the good guys: the people who use their private wealth to support the arts. Without them we'd have no museums, no performing arts, no higher education, for that matter. I've always been a champion of these people. Every issue we feature the 'Philanthropists of the Month,' two people, and we go all over the country to find them: Seattle, Minneapolis, Little Rock, Atlanta. Of course, the other supreme irony is this murder at the Met. I very much wanted this whole racket exposed, but I would never in my wildest dreams have come up with the idea of murder, especially one carried out with such bizarre theatrics."

We started toward the elevator. "I know," I said. "It's as if someone took you more seriously than you ever intended."

We arrived at the elevator and, since no one had come or gone, the gate opened immediately.

"Good luck with the show."

"Let me know how it goes with Monaghan."

• • •

After Sonny left, I looked at my emails; there were two I wanted to answer. One was from the stage manager. Regarding Austin's feeling that his character in the play was too bland and needed to be more proactive, the playwright, Elliot, had decided that, instead of sharpening a confrontation in the first act, he would give Austin's character a monologue in act two. So I would not be getting a new scene to rehearse Monday afternoon, but I would have to come in for a rehearsal at 2:00 in order to adjust to the changes surrounding the monologue.

The second message was from Monaghan asking if I had anything new. I called him rather than emailed because I wanted to explain what I learned when I saw Roger Morehead the night before. I left a message telling him that I wished to give him a full report, so would he please call back. I went out to buy supper at Whole Foods.

• • •

Returning from the store, I was looking forward to a quiet Sunday evening. The moment I stepped into the elevator, I knew that was out the window. Standing there with his spiky hair, cutoff T-shirt, and a wide, studded belt was Danny's friend, Mikey, holding a pistol aimed straight at me. "Get in," he said. For a moment I was speechless, trying to take in the situation— not quite believing it, but realizing it was all too real.

"Mikey," I finally replied. "What a surprise."

"Forgotten about me, had you?"

"Not a chance."

"Push the button. Fifth floor, right?"

I pushed five, but was tempted to punch three as well. I had done this once before, some dozen years previously, in similar circumstances, when I found myself staring at the barrel of a gun pointed at me by a dark figure who, if not Mafia, I was certain had been sent by them. Dark hair parted in the middle and slicked back, with a heavy beard that even three shaves a day would not erase, he had come "to get a few things straight," meaning that I should look at things from his point of view or else. The elevator in our building was a holdover from its manufacturing days. A large metal enclosure, open at the sides near the top, it moved slowly, and, when it stopped on the third floor, it did so with a decided lurch. With my Mafia friend, I had pushed three, and when the lurch came he was momentarily thrown off balance. I head-butted him in the middle of his face and followed that with a knee to his groin. The head-butt resulted in blood gushing from a broken nose like water from a fire hydrant. In the pain and confusion, I was able to get hold of the gun, and after a time turn my would-be assailant over to the law.

I realized, however, that this wouldn't work with Mikey. The elevator was cavernous, and he had backed himself against the opposite wall as if the distance between us would increase his control, which in this case it did. Observing him, I couldn't tell whether he was unsure of himself, even frightened, and his bravura was an act meant to cover his uncertainty, or if he was actually a real tough enjoying his power and control.

"What's the gun for?" I asked as we edged upward toward five.

"You'll find out."

"You going to shoot me?"

"That's up to you."

"So I'd be number two, right?"

"Whatcha mean?"

"Two murders."

"I ain't murdered no one. That's one reason I'm here: to make that clear."

By this time we had reached my floor. The elevator was not automatic; you had to open the grill door.

"Open it," he commanded, which I did.

"Now unlock your door," which I did as well. I stepped

inside my apartment and kept walking.

"Stop right there," he barked. "Stop!" he yelled again, even though I had already done so. "Sit down."

"Where?"

"There." He indicated a straight-backed chair near the coffee table. I sat down, and Mikey, still aiming the gun at me, moved over to the edge of the coffee table and brushed a few objects (magazines, a couple of knickknacks) onto the floor, probably to reinforce his tough–guy image. I knew I had to be careful. A nervous novice, which was what he was, even a novice killer, can be more dangerous than a professional. In his desperation to establish his "creds," he might fire his gun at the slightest provocation.

He sat down on the edge of the coffee table he had just cleared.

"So?" I asked.

"I didn't murder her."

"Who said you did?"

"The fuzz. Maybe you. All those questions, innuendos. But I have an alibi."

"You said that before. Twice, and neither one held up."

"This one's for real—ironclad."

"Why tell me? Tell Monaghan."

"I plan to, but first I want to be sure you're off the case."

"I was never on it."

"Don't play games. You jumped into the middle of this thing with both feet."

"Look, Mikey. Dorothy was a friend of mine. You may not have liked her; I can understand that. But to me she was a colleague, someone I admired. If the fuzz, as you call them, ask me to help them get to the bottom of this, I don't think I can say no."

"They didn't ask you, and you know it. You've been sniffing around from the start, meeting with the cops every day, going to Connecticut. You might as well be wearing a badge."

"You seem to know all about me."

"Everyone knows."

"I don't think so. Someone's been talking to you. Who is it? Warren? Sounds like Warren. Why is he in such close touch with you? Did he kill Dorothy?"

"No," he said, much too emphatically.

"Does he know who did?"

"He's not mixed up in this; neither am I."

"Maybe he hired someone."

"Did you hear what I just said? Now I'm going to tell you what happened. That's why I'm here, and you're going to listen. And, when I finish, you're going to tell me you understand, and that you'll not only cut out all this interfering shit, this snooping around, but that you'll support us in our story."

"Us?" I asked.

"No more questions. I do the talking, not you. When I finish, if you don't agree, then—" For emphasis he gripped his gun tighter and pointed it toward my leg. "It would be too bad," he said, "for your career if you had an accident right now: a wounded leg, say, so shattering you couldn't be in your precious play. It opens when?"

"This coming week."

"So a serious mishap right now would mean you couldn't

143

be in it, and maybe the play after that." He paused. "Now," he continued. "Will you listen and not interrupt, or do I have to get careless with this thing?"

"Fire away," I said. "Oops, bad choice of words." After a moment I said, as seriously as I could, "I'm listening."

"I didn't kill that woman, and neither did Warren. We each have a solid, foolproof, ironclad alibi."

"Both of you claimed to have one, but neither alibi held up."

"This is different." After a pause, he continued: "I'm really an entrepreneur."

"So I've heard."

"Quiet!"

I became quiet.

"I have ideas, plans, projects, but I need money. The best idea I've had is for a club—a bar, restaurant, dancing—catering to gays and lesbians but also to straights. A lot of straights get their kicks from watching gays and lesbians. Some men especially get a thrill from watching two women together. Anyway, I've had this idea for some time, but I needed a place. Well, I found one: ideal location, right square footage, perfect setup."

"Where is this perfect place?"

"The Meatpacking District."

"Ah."

The Meatpacking District, in the West Village, runs along the Hudson River just below 14th Street. In the early twentieth century, it actually was a meatpacking district, known then as the Gansevoort Market, when it housed some 250 slaughterhouses and packing plants. Over the years the meatpacking industry moved elsewhere, and by the 1980s the site had become notorious as a hotbed of drug dealing as well as gay and transsexual prostitution. A number of sex clubs opened up—the Anvil, the Manhole, the Hellfire, the Mine Shaft—many of them Mafia-controlled. In the mid-'90s, however, another transformation occurred, and the place was cleaned up. Over the next ten years, it became a mecca of trendy restaurants and boutiques.

"Like I said," Mikey continued, "I found this great spot, a former bar and café on Little West 12th Street, just waiting to be handled properly. Two women ran it: didn't know their ass from home plate. Went bust three months ago. I can get the lease next week, but I need money. This is where Warren comes in. I've been telling him about my ideas for some time now, ever since Danny and I got together. Warren's smart—sees things I don't see. Most of my ideas he shot down, but not this one. This one he liked."

"When did you first tell him about it?"

"About three weeks ago. Why?"

"Just asking."

"You gonna make something out of the timing?"

"No, no. Not at all. Go on."

"He gave me money to get started on the lease. I took him to see the place last week. Then last Monday night I took him again. I wanted him to see it at night, get an idea of the street traffic, the other restaurants, the nightclubs, shops, all the rest—wide open, even on a Monday night. And it was."

"What?"

"Crowded. Some places, the sidewalk was so packed you had to get out in the street just to move along."

"And that's where you were last Monday night?"

"From 8:30 to 9:30."

"Both you and Warren, right at the time of the murder. Anyone see you?"

"There you go: sounding like a cop. Yes, people saw us, but I'll wait and tell my story to the NYPD."

"So what do you want me to do?"

"Number one: don't go trying to knock down my story, asking around, trying to poke holes in what I say. Let the cops do that. It's their job, not yours. Number two: Don't tell anyone I was up here. I'll know if you do, and, if you start snooping, then I won't just aim this at your leg; it will be another part of your anatomy. And don't think you can get away; you have to be at that theatre every night."

It was at this point that my cell phone rang.

# CHAPTER FOURTEEN

The ring on my phone is the opening bars of Cole Porter's *Anything Goes*. When Mikey heard the sound, he tensed, his gun at the ready.

"Don't answer," he barked.

"I have to. Connie, the stage manager, said she would call, and tell us about new dialogue we're putting in tonight."

"Make it short."

I answered: "Matt here."

On the other end: "Monaghan here."

"Hello, Connie."

"You're not alone?" Monaghan deduced.

"No."

"Friends?"

"No."

"People in the show?"

"No."

"Danny?"

"No."

"Mikey?"

"Yes."

"Keep him there."

"Right, Connie. See you tomorrow."

I hung up. "Who was that?"

"You heard: the stage manager, Connie. Just as I thought."

"When are you supposed to be there?"

"Early afternoon."

"You may not be there at all. You know that, don't you?"
What I knew at the moment was that I had to get the gun away
from Mikey before Monaghan arrived. I thought fast.

"Look, Mikey, like I said, this idea of yours sounds promising."

"Promising? It's dynamite."

"Right. And I'm curious to know more about it: the total
cost, the projected revenues and profits."

"Warren has all that. Don't forget, he's an ace businessman."

"Right," I said, "but first I'd like to get a clearer idea of just
where it is. I have a map on the wall here of the Chelsea area
and the West Village." I indicated the spot on the wall where I
had my posters and paintings. The map was one of those lam-
inated squares, shellacked on the front, with little illustrations:
a café here, a firehouse there, a farmers' market elsewhere. "I've
never known the difference between West Twelfth Street and
Little West Twelfth." I stood up and started walking to the wall.

"Stay where you are," he commanded.

"It's right there. You can show me in a second, and keep
the gun on me all the time."

Curious despite himself, he looked toward the map. I

could almost see the wheels turning in his head. Perhaps, he was thinking, if he pointed to a spot on the map, it would make his story more convincing. After a moment, holding his gun tighter than ever, he growled, "Get up." We walked toward the map. "Find the meatpacking district."

I moved closer to the map. "In here?" I asked, pointing toward the general area south of Fourteenth Street near the river.

"Yeah. See? West Twelfth is down below, just south of Jane Street. But look up at West Thirteenth Street. Then, just below that you'll see Little West Twelfth."

"Looks to be only two blocks long," I said.

"Right, but it's in the heart of things."

"Which one of the two blocks is your place in?"

He began to gaze intently at the map, straining a bit to see exactly where his proposed spot might be. This was the moment I was waiting for. A detective I had seen use the move called it the "double dip." I moved as quickly as I could. I brought the heel of my shoe as hard as I could down on the toe of his left shoe, and at the same time clasped my hands together and brought them down with all my strength on top of the forearm of his hand holding the pistol.

He screamed, and didn't know whether to reach for his arm or his foot. More to the point, he dropped the gun. Unfortunately, it slid to his right, away from me, with Mikey in between. There was no carpet on this part of the floor, so it slid a good eight feet. I ran after it, reached down for it, but before I could have it fully in my grasp, he had recovered enough to come at me. He was on me from behind: the double blow had not been enough to put him out of action for very long. He covered me and grabbed my hand holding the gun, attempting to wrestle it away from me.

It was a struggle not only for the gun, but for survival. And he had an advantage. He was not only much younger than I, but also seemingly in good shape, with particularly well-developed pecs and abs, as you might imagine. We twisted and turned; he tried desperately to wrest the gun from me, while I held on for dear life. Meanwhile, our bodies were struggling for supremacy: he trying to smother me as I attempted to writhe out from under him.

Somewhere in the midst of this, we heard a knock on the door and a voice yelling, "Matt!" After a few times, I realized it was Monaghan. I renewed my efforts to get a firm grip on the pistol, but Mikey, hearing the voice, fought more desperately than ever. In the midst of this, I remembered that there was a small table along the wall near us, with a lamp on top. I kicked as hard as I could with one leg in that direction and hit a table leg. The lamp came off, falling on Mikey. He was temporarily stunned, but soon regained his equilibrium, got up, grabbed the lamp, and was ready to hit me over the head with it, but I had the gun. I rolled over on my back and pointed it at him. "Freeze!"

At just that moment Monaghan burst through the door, with two of his men behind him. I should have remembered that the NYPD has ways of opening doors the rest of us do not. Monaghan and his men entered, guns drawn. He pointed his gun at Mikey: "Put the lamp down." After hesitating a moment, Mikey did. To me, Monaghan said, "Get up. Whose gun is it anyway?"

"His," I said.

"You bastard," Mikey spat at me. "You goddam son of a bitch."

"Shut up," Monaghan told him. "Sit down." He pointed to the chair near the coffee table on which I had been sitting. "Clarkson, cuff him to the chair behind his back."

After a bit of resistance on Mikey's part, Clarkson proceeded to do just that. Monaghan then told Clarkson and the other man to wait outside. "Put the gun on the table," he instructed me, which I did. "Is that yours?" he asked Mikey.

"No."

"But you were carrying it. It has your prints on it. Right?"

"I want my lawyer," Mikey said.

"You'll get one," Monaghan said. "Plenty of time for that." Turning to me he asked, "What happened?"

"He was waiting for me downstairs when I came back from the grocery. Ordered me up here."

"What was the idea?"

"He and Warren have a project. They were working on it the night of the murder, he says. Each one can provide an alibi for the other."

"Neat," Monaghan said. I then proceeded to give a capsule version of what Mikey had told me about a nightclub in the meatpacking district. When I had finished, he said to Mikey, "Is that the story?"

"Absolutely. He left out a few details, but basically it's correct."

"Why pull a gun on Johanssen?"

"We wanted him to back us up."

"Why not come directly to us?"

"We were afraid you wouldn't believe us."

"Why not? If it checked out, it would have been much simpler."

"Glad to hear it. Maybe that's what I should have done."

"There's only one problem, Mikey."

"What's that?"

"With or without Johanssen, it wouldn't have worked."

"What do you mean?"

"Some tests just came back from the lab. The morning after the murder, my men found a few wine bottles in one of the trash cans at the end of that small alley behind the theatre."

"I don't know no alley."

"It turns out your prints are on one of those bottles."

"My prints? You don't have my prints."

"Yes we do. Remember when you came in for questioning, you had a cold drink: a Diet Pepsi, I think? We picked up the prints from that."

"That's illegal. I demand a lawyer."

"Like I said, there'll be plenty of time for that." As if to say, "This may take a little time," Monaghan went over to the dining room table, picked up a chair, and brought it over, facing Mikey. He placed a small digital recorder on the coffee table and spoke into the mike: "I'm placing a device on the table to record a conversation with Mikey Wyskovski." Monaghan sat down and began: "You've got a few choices to make, Mikey. Coming after Johanssen with a gun, bringing him into his apartment with the piece pointed at him—that alone would send you up for a few years."

"It wasn't my idea."

"Maybe not, but you did it. Anyway, that's not the point."

"Which is?"

"Dorothy's murder. The way I figure it, you can go one of two ways: tough it out and be charged with her murder—"

"I didn't kill her. I swear."

"Or you can tell us who did." He let that sink in. "If you didn't kill her and someone else did, and you know who that someone is, you could tell us, help us get the person, and I can assure you things will go easier for you."

"What do you mean?"

"The main thing in a murder case is to get the killer, or the planner—usually the same person."

"Suppose it was an accident?"

"The key question is who did it, accident or no accident. That's the person we want. Let's say that someone else did this— Mr. Tremayne, for instance—and you saw what happened and know what happened. You may have helped the person before or after, which means you cannot go scot-free—you'll do time—but it will be less, much less, if you can help us. Maybe you were tricked into this thing, or persuaded against your will.

"Look at it from another angle," he went on. "Let's suppose there were two people involved—you and someone else—and the other person was an older businessman. You are both accused. What do you think this other person, this well-to-do person, will do? Take the fall if both of you are charged? Will he say 'I did this? The young man here, with the tattoos, he just unlocked the door?' I don't think so. I think he will hire the most expensive lawyer he can find and lay the whole thing on

153

you. Make you take the fall. Remember, he's from the privileged class, the upper crust. People like that have no scruples. He'll throw you overboard so quickly you'll hear the splash before you hit the water."

Monaghan said nothing more: just let it all sink in. Mikey sat stock-still for a long time. Finally, he spoke. "And if I do help you—"

"Yes?"

"You can promise me less time?"

"I'm not a judge, or a jury, so I won't have the final say, but I can tell you one thing: my office will have a lot to do with preparing the indictments, and it's a far different thing to be charged with being an unwitting partner, an accidental accessory who had no idea it would go down this way, rather than a murderer. I can't promise you leniency, but I can certainly recommend it." Monaghan paused, then continued, "On the other hand, if someone throws his lot in with the killer, decides to go down with the ship, as they say, that person is on his own."

Monaghan paused, then turned to me. "Can I have a drink of water?" This, of course, was to give Mikey time to consider his next step. I started to offer Mikey a drink as well, and then realized that his hands were cuffed behind his back. I went to the kitchen and noisily got two glasses of water. I came back, gave one to Monaghan, and said to Mikey, "Like a sip?"

"Yes." I held the glass for him while he took several swallows. Then Monaghan spoke: "So what will it be?"

"It wasn't supposed to happen this way. Everything I said about the club is true. I've had this idea for some time, and I found the perfect spot. If you saw it, you'd agree. But I needed money. Danny's mother turned us down flat. One day, about two weeks ago, I had a call from Warren. From time to time I'd told him my ideas for various projects, but he seemed tied up with this new business he was starting. This time, after I described it, he told me it sounded interesting. He suggested we meet, but he told me to keep quiet, not even tell Danny.

"He met me on the corner of Little West Twelfth and Washington. We walked by the place, then had coffee in a Starbucks nearby. He gave me $1,000: up-front money, he said. He wanted to know how much I needed. I said about $50,000 to start, and another fifty soon after. He said he needed money too, that we should go after it together. I asked where. He said Dorothy; she had more than enough to spare, and most of it was his money anyway."

"That's absolutely not true," I interjected, but Monaghan quickly motioned to me to be quiet. I got the point: I was not to interrupt, no matter what he said. Monaghan nodded to Mikey.

"He said he'd tried to meet her at her office and her apartment," Mikey continued. "But she'd refused to see him. He said she should at least listen to him. Also, she should help me as a friend of Danny's, someone who had been so good to him. He asked me about this theatre where her play was rehearsing. He understood that she had met Danny there a few times. Maybe we could see her there. That's when it started. He asked me to scout out a place in the theatre. I told him I knew Danny and his mother had met a couple of times in the downstairs lounge. He said that sounded fine.

"I got there early one time when I was supposed to meet

Danny and cased the place. I found a door at the back of the basement, off a storeroom, that went out on a small alley. I put a block of wood in the door, followed the alley and saw steps with an iron gate with a lock. I went up the steps and saw that the passageway joined another small alley that went through to the next street. Later I got a pair of cutters from a biker friend of mine, a heavy-duty thing they use to cut the chains on Harleys, and cut the lock, but left it looking like it was still closed.

"Danny was meeting his mother last Monday night. I had stolen his cell phone earlier, and that afternoon sent Dorothy a text message saying to meet him at 9:00 p.m., a half hour before they were supposed to meet. I met Warren on the corner of Eighth Avenue and went down the alley through the iron gate and the door, into the lounge about a quarter to 9:00. We hid behind the bar, and just at 9:00 we heard Dorothy coming down the steps. She called, 'Danny?' a couple of times. When she was all the way down, Warren stepped out. She saw him and gave a little shout: 'Warren, what are you doing here?' He said he had to talk to her, and she said she was leaving. By that time I had stepped out, too. We blocked her way up the steps, and she started to yell. He told her not to scream, and moved toward her, asked her to hear him out. 'Give me ten minutes, and then I'm gone.' She was frozen to the spot. She kept asking, 'What's gotten into you? Are you threatening me?' He said, 'Just this once, and I promise it will never happen again.'

"She kept yelling for Danny, and Warren moved toward her and raised his hand, ready to put it over her mouth. 'Don't do that,' he said. 'I don't want to lay a hand on you, but if I have to, I will. Ten minutes.'

"He had a crazed look in his eye, and I knew she could tell he was dangerous. She said she'd listen. He told her about my idea and that I needed cash, and she said she'd already said no. He said, 'Not an investment, a loan, and he needs $250,000.'

'Two hundred and fifty thousand? Are you kidding?' she asked.

'For the two of us, $300,000.'

'Warren, are you out of your mind?'

'You don't understand.' He said, 'If I don't get a quarter of a million in the next few days, I'll have to declare personal bankruptcy.'

'It's that bad, is it?'

'Seven percent interest. Eight percent. Nine,' he yelled.

'Warren, this is insane.'

'If I weren't at the end of my rope, I wouldn't be here.'

"That was the first I had heard of any kind of bankruptcy. I thought this was a really rich man—megabucks.

"Then she said, 'It's ironic isn't it: just at the point where my life is more together than ever before, yours has fallen apart.'

'You can moralize all you want, but I need the money. Now. So what's the answer?'

'The same as it's always been. No.'

"That's when it happened. He snapped—went berserk— lost it completely. He grabbed her by the shoulders, pushed toward the bar, all the time saying in this singsong voice: 'Lend me the money, lend me the money, lend me the money.' She started to scream but he put one hand over her mouth. She broke free and was about to scream, again when he picked up an empty wine bottle from the bar and hit her over the head. She went down. It all happened so fast I couldn't believe what I'd seen. The next thing I knew, he was on top of her, choking her. He was a madman. I grabbed his shoulders, pulled him off of her. 'What have you done?' I yelled. 'Are you crazy?' Looking down at her, I saw a slight twitch, then she went still.

'We've got to get out of here,' I said. 'Fast.' I pushed him toward the back, into the storeroom. He was in a fog. I slapped him across the face, hard. He was stumbling, lurching. We were halfway to the back exit when I remembered the wine bottle. I went back and grabbed it. I pushed him out the back door into the alley, picked up the block of wood, and shoved him down the alley and up the stairs. I knew we had to get out of there. I opened the cut lock, got him out the iron gate, fixed the lock, and led him down the alley that ran to the street behind. I dropped the wine bottle and wood block in a trash can, hailed a cab, and headed to Grand Central so he could get a train to Connecticut."

He stopped. "Can I have another sip of that water?" he asked. I went over, tilted the glass, and let him drink.

"So it's your idea that when she wouldn't give him the money, he went off the rails, lost it completely, and that's when he killed her?"

"You should have seen him: wild, out of control. I've never seen anything like it, and believe me, I've seen a lot of crazy stuff in my time."

"And you're willing to stand by this?"

"I wish I'd never met that family. Danny is a good kid, but weak—a washrag in the shape of whoever wrung him out last.

Dorothy—well, I won't say what I think of her. And Warren's a psycho-weirdo, over the edge."

Monaghan went over to the coffee table and picked up the recorder. "I have it all here if you need to refresh your memory."

"I can remember it."

"And swear to it in court."

"I'll keep my end of the bargain if you keep yours."

Dead serious, Monaghan said to him, "You have my word." He called out to the two men who had been waiting outside and told them to come in. He ordered them to uncuff Mikey from the chair, take him in, and keep him under guard. He was to talk to no one until Monaghan got back to the precinct. Also, he told Mikey that he could get in touch with his lawyer now. The three of them left. I began to straighten up.

"Well," Monaghan said, "he tells a good story."

"Do you believe him?"

"Yes. Do you?"

"Makes sense to me; I always thought Warren had to be involved."

"Okay. I'll get my men on rounding him up."

"I'd also get that young man who works with him."

"Right." Monaghan exited, and I collapsed on the sofa.

# CHAPTER FIFTEEN

I had to get out, get some fresh air. I grabbed a parka, headed downstairs, turned north toward Washington Square Park. Walking, I deliberately didn't dwell on what had happened. At the park, I found an empty space on a bench and sat down.

What had just happened? The answer came in bits and pieces—a stream-of-consciousness mélange. You cross the street, a bicycle comes from nowhere—there's a collision. You survive, injured but okay. Dorothy goes downstairs to meet her son and gets killed by a crazed husband. The loss, the tragic irony. How to deal with what I had just seen and heard? So many "ifs." If Monaghan hadn't called me. If Dorothy had only known how far gone Warren was. If someone had interrupted them. Sometimes people survive; other times they don't. There's no rhyme or reason, no logic, no fairness, no justice. How fragile, on the knife edge, it all is. I'm here; the people in this park are here. Dorothy's gone.

I shook my head, knowing there would be no answers tonight. In a day or two, when they track down Warren, maybe for some people it will be what today they call "closure." But for far too many that's a mirage. An innocent coed killed by a dope-addled stalker, a soldier shot down in battle, a tornado, a tsunami—there is no quick fix, maybe no fix at all, ever.

Then my mind shut down. The whole thing was too much. I slowly made my way home, ambling, not minding anyone around me. At a corner stand, I bought a hot dog, lots of mustard. I continued walking. Back at the apartment, I poured a glass of wine, took a few sips, put the glass down. Went to the bathroom, took a Diazepam, didn't brush my teeth, took off everything but shorts and a T-shirt. Got into bed.

• • •

The main purpose of the rehearsal Monday afternoon was to put in the new scene for the oldest son, Mark, played by Austin Estabrook, and if it worked well, it would go in that night. Originally, Elliot had thought he could tweak lines in the first act, but on second thought he came up with a monologue for the character in the second act and emailed it to Austin over the weekend. Austin and Rowan worked on the scene on Monday morning.

As rehearsal of the scene that afternoon got underway, it was clear that the character came alive once he launched into his monologue. He chastised the other family members for their whining and complaining: "Uncle Roy was terrific to everyone here, loaning money to you, Mom and Dad, to buy this house—at no interest—giving both of you (indicating his younger siblings) funds for private schools and summer trips. Now he sets up this system to arrive at some kind of equitable distribution of our inheritance—but, more important, for us to examine what is really best for this family—and all you've done is whine, bicker, and argue. I've had enough." He turned to my character: "Mr. Stanhope, I don't know how you can possibly give any of us money. I certainly want no part of it—but the rest of this family (he made a broad sweep of the others) are so self-centered, so egotistical they can't think of anything else. Once and for all, count me out." And with that he exited.

The cast tried it. For the character of Mark, it changed everything, and for the other characters, nothing was quite the same either. Of course, as far as the script was concerned, there was work to do after Mark exited. For example, exactly how should each of the others react? How does the play get back on course? Elliot said he wanted to work on that, too. He suggested that we take a break and come back in about forty-five minutes, when he would have new lines. Everyone agreed it was worth spending as much time as possible that afternoon to put the new material in that night. Since I was not in the scene that followed, I was able to leave.

• • •

I was on the way to the subway when my cell phone rang. It was Monaghan. "Where have you been?"

"Rehearsing a play, remember?"

"How could I forget?"

"What's so urgent?"

"He's gone."

"Who?"

162

"Tremayne. Disappeared."

"How? When?"

"You tell me."

"No trace of him?"

"The carriage house is empty. Apparently he hasn't been seen since early yesterday."

"What about Stuart Ross, his junior partner?"

"Gone too."

"Is Warren's car gone?"

"Still there."

"Ross's car?"

"Gone."

"God. I don't know what to say."

"At least this confirms he's our man."

"I don't think he can be impossible to catch. He's become unhinged, and Ross doesn't seem too bright."

"I've put checks on everything: airports, trains, border crossings."

"At this point the man is not going to be too alert. At the same time, he's a desperate individual. All I can say is, good luck."

"If you have any ideas, let me know."

"One other thing," I said.

"Yes?"

"I want to talk to Annie, the daughter, and to Danny. Annie has been calling me every day to ask where things stand. I didn't want to tell her about last night, but I think I need to let her know that Mikey is in custody and Warren has disappeared."

"I wish you would wait till we have Warren."

"I really think I owe her this—and Danny."

"Say as little as you can, and ask them not to breathe a word."

"Absolutely."

• • •

I called Annie, and got her machine. I asked her to call back, which she did half an hour later. "Any news?"

"Yes, though it's not too good."

"I was afraid of that."

"Mikey is in custody."

"Did he do it?"

"He says not."

"Do they believe him?"

"I hate to say this."

"Go ahead."

"He claims he was with your father the night it happened—in the theatre."

"Go on."

"He says they had no intention of hurting Dorothy; they were trying to get money, both of them, and things got out of hand."

"And what about Dad in all this?"

"Mikey claims your father lost it—went off the rails—and went too far threatening her."

"Oh, God. It's worse than I thought."

"Nothing is definite. Nothing proven."

"Where is Dad?"

"He seems to have disappeared, along with that young man he started the new company with. They're looking for both of them now. The fact that he can't be found makes things worse."

"Sounds just awful."

"I agree. For what it's worth, these last few days I've been talking to old friends of Warren's, and they all say he's changed. He's sort of lost it."

"I've had a suspicion, a fear, really, that something like this might happen. But, of course, I hoped against hope it wouldn't. Have you told Danny?"

"I called you first. I plan to call him now."

"I invited him to come up here and visit us for a few days."

"That's a terrific idea. I'll urge him to do it."

"I just can't believe how this is turning out. It couldn't be worse."

"I agree. One thing: it's not any real comfort, but you should know the show is going beautifully. We're all doing it for Dorothy, and I've never been in a production where the cast was so dedicated."

"You're right; nothing is any comfort right now, but I'm glad for everyone else—and for her memory, of course."

We rang off, and I faced the unpleasant task of having to go through the same exchange with Danny. As might be imagined, he was far more hysterical than Annie, having not only lost his mother but been betrayed by Mikey and his father. We got through it, however, and I told him I understood that Annie had invited him to come to Boston. I told him I thought the best thing he could do right now was get away from all this and stay with Annie for a few days. He told me he would think about it, that he had a great deal to absorb. There was no doubt about that.

• • •

The preview that Monday night went better than we had any right to expect. There were a couple of hiccups, but essentially the new scene worked beautifully and improved the entire last part of the play. I went home greatly relieved, especially when I compared this night to the one before. The chief worry now, of course, was the disappearance of Warren. I tried to come up with some idea about what had happened, but nothing had come to mind by the time I went to sleep.

When I was making coffee the next morning, it hit me. Maybe it was Monaghan's mention of border crossings, or it may have been my coffee mug. I knew it was a wild idea, perhaps an insane idea, but I thought it was worth a try. The picture that had popped into my head was a shelf in a kitchen. On the shelf were twenty or more colorful, picturesque coffee mugs. The kitchen was in Dorothy and Warren's house in Connecticut, where I had first met them some years earlier. When Dorothy asked what I would like to drink, I said a beer. She told me I could find one in the fridge, and a glass in the cabinet beside it. I got the beer, opened the cabinet door, saw a tall glass and took it, but I also saw, on the shelf above, two dozen or more mugs with names on them, which I soon figured out belonged to various inns or bed-and-breakfast establishments:

The Old Drover's, Highfield House, Stone Creek, Willow Bend, Copper Kettle, Wild Strawberry, Mount Pleasant, Maple Grove, Blue Heron, White Swan.

Back in the living room, I asked about the collection, and Warren explained. When he and Dorothy were first married, they began visiting small inns and B and Bs in northwest Connecticut, western Massachusetts, and Vermont: Washington, Cornwall, Stockbridge, Middlebury. In some cases encouraged by the owners, in other cases surreptitiously, they brought home mugs. After Annie and Danny were born, the trips became less frequent, but they never forgot the getaways taken during those early days, and the mugs reminded them of that.

As soon as I had shaved and dressed, I searched through my maps and called Monaghan. "This may be crazy, but I have an idea," I said. "Warren and Dorothy used to visit a lot of inns in Connecticut, Massachusetts, and Vermont. Also, Warren has a cousin in Montreal who idolizes him. The cousin made a lot of money with Warren and thinks he can do no wrong. Warren is not thinking too clearly right now, and his young partner is not the brightest bulb on the tree. Warren might have thought of the first thing that came to mind: head for one of those inns and then go on to Montreal. They'll stay away from interstates and toll roads and probably try to cross into Canada somewhere between East Franklin and North Troy. My suggestion is that you contact the police in all those small towns along Route 7 going north and, further on, between Interstates 89 and 91. See if the two of them have stayed in an inn or B and B. Also, the kid's car will have a Missouri license plate."

"If you ask me, that's reaching for it."

"I agree. Don't bother with it yourself, but, if some kid in the office is free, put him on it."

"I'll see what I can do. By the way, do you think the young man is part of this?"

"Probably not. Warren may well have told him that he is innocent and being pursued by old enemies in the financial world, people trying to frame him. Stuart Ross is just naïve enough to believe him."

"I hope you realize, Matt, that I'll be pursuing this scavenger hunt just for you."

• • •

Just after noon on Tuesday, I had an email from someone named Phyllida Fairchild. She said she wrote for *Vanity Fair* and was hoping to do a piece about Dorothy for the next issue. Would I please phone her? I called, and after four rings she answered.

"Thanks for calling back, Mr. Johanssen."

"Please, call me Matt. You're thinking about writing about Dorothy?"

"I'm hoping to. We haven't quite decided what to do, whether to combine something on her with the murder at the Met Museum or to do a short piece just on her."

"I can't help you with that."

"I know. But I would still like to learn more about her; I understand you not only knew her, but you knew the husband as well."

"Yes," I answered tentatively.

"Could we possibly get together—at your convenience, of course. I know you're in a show that's about to open, so maybe this is not a great time."

"True."

"Still, if you could squeeze something in."

I looked at the calendar on my phone. "We have two previews tomorrow, a matinee and an evening show. In between I'm going to have a bite to eat with Elliot, the playwright, at a small French place nearby. We'll be having a quick supper. He has to leave early to meet the director. Maybe you could come for a cup of coffee or a glass of wine at 6:30."

"That'll be fine."

"It's called Mon Plaisir, on 49th near Ninth."

"Mon Plaisir it is."

# CHAPTER SIXTEEN

The preview on Tuesday night had gone well, and the audience was the best one yet. I got a good night's sleep. Early Wednesday, Monaghan called.

"There's good news and bad news."

"I'll have the good first."

"Your hunch was right. They're headed north. Two men answering to the descriptions of Warren and the boy spent last night at the White Birch Inn north of Rutland, Vermont."

"The bad news is—they got away."

"Right. They left in the middle of the night, maybe as early as 2:00 or 3:00 a.m. We had all the crossings from Vermont into Canada covered, but so far no sign of them."

"I didn't think of it before: they may have turned west into upper New York and gone over that way."

"We were wondering the same thing."

"This seems almost certain to mean that he's headed for the cousin in Montreal. I looked him up on the Internet. His name is Josh Tremayne and he lives in an upscale district called Westmount."

"We'll check it out."

"Good luck."

• • •

After I hung up with Monaghan, I called Annie in Boston and told her what the police had discovered. I explained my hunch that her father might be headed for Montreal, where he had that young cousin. "Josh," Annie said.

"It may not be as bad as it sounds."

"But it doesn't sound good."

"No. If they do catch him, they'll bring him and Stuart Ross, who is apparently with him, back to the city and charge them, along with Mikey. Stuart and Mikey might try to turn state's evidence against Warren. All in all, it looks bleak."

A subdued Annie listened and then thanked me. I told her once again how desperately sorry I was, and how much the family had always meant to me—Warren in the past, Dorothy in the last few years, and Annie and her brother ever since I had known them. I said I would try to reach Danny. She said there was no need; he was on his way to Boston. I told her that was exactly where he should be just now. I repeated that if there was anything I could do, to please let me know.

"You've been a great deal of help already."

"Not nearly enough," I said.

• • •

Knowing that he got to his office early, I put in a call to Lance Middlecoff and told him that he should get in touch with his friend in St. Louis.

"Arthur Ross?"

"If he's the one whose son is working with Warren, you should let him know that the young man may be in need of legal help."

"How so?"

"It seems that he and Warren are on the lam. The detective thinks they may be headed to Warren's cousin's house in Montreal. If they are, the boy will need a lawyer, and I thought it only fair to let the father know what is happening."

"Sounds wild."

"I agree, and there may be nothing to it, but I wanted to tell you so you can warn the father."

"I'll give him a call; the rest is up to him."

"If I hear anything more definite, I'll let you know."

I couldn't reveal any more than I had, and I knew Lance thought I sounded half-crazy, but I thought I owed it to him and the Ross fellow.

• • •

The audience for the preview on Wednesday afternoon was not as enthusiastic as the one the night before, but that frequently happens at matinees. Still, the show seemed to be on a solid footing. After I had changed, my playwright, Elliot, and I headed for Mon Plaisir. It's off the beaten track and a bit seedy, but I have always liked it. Besides, the food is authentically French, rare for a small bistro, and there is more room between tables than usual. Another advantage: I'm well known there, so they always save me a table near the window, the quietest spot in the restaurant. Gerard, the waiter, asked what we wanted. Since he had very little time, Elliott ordered a bowl of mushroom soup, a small endive salad, and a beer. I ordered scallops and a glass of white wine. Then we talked about my scene near the end where I announce my decision about the division of the inheritances. I wasn't quite sure how to approach it, which was the point of our meeting.

At 6:30, Elliott left, but so far Phyllida Fairchild had not appeared. In the true French style, Mon Plaisir prefers to offer the salad after the entrée, so Gerard brought me a small plate of arugula. I had almost finished it when the door of the restaurant opened and a woman entered who could only be the one I was expecting. I don't know what I thought she would look like, but it certainly wasn't the person I saw coming toward me. Tall, about my height if not taller, with slim legs and arms, she had a more than ample bosom. Her eyes were green, she had high cheekbones, and her lipstick was pink, accenting her surprisingly pale face, which was surrounded by an aurora of soft auburn hair. Her mouth seemed always in a half smile, though I learned later that, with a barely noticeable shift, it could register many things, from the sardonic to an expression of genuine pleasure. She was not glamorous, with the vacant stare of a model, but her appearance, both intriguing and appealing, drew attention whenever she entered a room. I assumed this had to be Phyllida. She walked toward me smoothly, easily—one could say, almost regally. I rose and extended my hand.

"Sorry to be late," she said. "I was stuck in traffic. I finally got out of the taxi and walked."

"A New York moment."

She shook hands. "Phyllida Fairchild," she said.

"Matt Johanssen."

Gerard helped her to her chair. "A drink, madame? A glass of wine?"

"Black tea," she said. "Milk, no lemon or sugar."

As Gerard departed, I said, "Phyllida? Sounds English."

"My mother was English," she said, and continued, "Thank you for doing this; I know it's an imposition."

"Anything to help Dorothy get the recognition she deserves."

"That's one of the things I want to be up front about. I'm an associate editor of the magazine, but none of us, from the editor-in-chief on down, knows quite what to do with all this. I'm pushing as hard as I can for some kind of piece on Dorothy, but I don't know how it will turn out. One reason I want to do this is that I met her a couple of times."

"Oh?"

"I used to go to the theatre off and on."

"I don't remember seeing you, and if I had, I'm sure I would have remembered."

"I was dating Ashley Sullivan at the time."

"Oh."

"Yes, 'oh.'"

Ashley Sullivan was the wealthy scion of a family that had made its money in pastry-related products: crackers, frozen pizza, cheesecake. He dabbled—almost bought a small chain of four theatres, invested hither and yon, brought shows over from London. But it turned out he was a manic depressive, and in one of his down periods he became so despondent that he swallowed more pills than even Lenox Hill's finest could save him from.

"It was always at a social gathering: backers' auditions, fund-raisers in plush apartments, opening night parties. But Dorothy stood out—genuine, serene, quietly intelligent. The idea that someone took her from us offends me to the core."

"True. The theatre needs every single person of her caliber it can find."

Gerard had brought her tea, and she continued: "I've seen you in half a dozen shows over the years. You're good. Alive, authentic, versatile, always believable. What I think of as the backbone of the live theatre."

"Thank you, if you mean even part of what you say."

"I don't flatter people, and I don't throw compliments around."

"We've just met, remember, but I take you at your word. Now, about you."

"I suppose the simplest thing is to say is I'm a writer, though I've been through half a dozen careers: translating at the UN, teaching at Barnard, editing for a small press. But for ten years now—which is a record for me—I've been a freelance writer. Mostly in the glossy magazines—*Vogue, Vanity Fair, Architectural Digest.* Four years ago I was made an associate editor as well as writer at *Vanity Fair*, which pays better than I deserve."

"A bit of an independent income, perhaps?"

"How did you guess?"

"You must be good, though."

"I write well enough, but mostly I seem to be able to get stories no one else can land."

"Like thinking about Dorothy."

"Exactly."

Gerard, who had already given me the check, appeared with my credit card. I signed it and said, "I'm sorry to be so abrupt, but I really have to get back to the theatre. Would you like to walk back with me?"

We exited the restaurant and headed east. "It's hard to know where to start about Dorothy."

"Start anywhere."

"She was sound, of course, really well grounded, as a person but also as a theatre producer. She truly loved the theatre and was a fast learner who was just coming into her own."

"There's a lot to cover in each one of those."

"I want to come back to something you mentioned earlier," I said.

"Which is?"

"The uncertainty of your fellow editors."

"It's a problem, more for me than for you. But as a writer, I try to stay ahead of other writers. I pursue stories on all sides, and, if one out of every three works out, I'm ahead of the game. It's because of this that I have this contract. But I must confess that, while I have a genuine interest in Dorothy, I have an ulterior motive."

"Which is?"

"You."

"Oh?"

"I've always wanted to get to know an actor. I've been close to a few, but they were always special cases: too obviously gay, a character actor who plays the same part over and over, someone much, much younger than I. So I'm intrigued."

"Not by me. You don't even know me."

"You don't think the whole town doesn't know about your behind-the-scenes detective work."

"Oh, that."

"Yes, that."

"There's one thing I want to get straight," I said. "I'm willing to talk about Dorothy, and I'm willing to talk about the theatre, but my avocation, my occasional sideline, is strictly off-limits."

"Understood and agreed to. As you say, this whole thing calls for more talk. I know how tied up you are with these previews and the opening next week. When can we talk again? Friday? Saturday? Sunday?"

By this time, we were only a few steps from the stage door. I hesitated. I have to confess I was conflicted. I was busy, what with my involvement with the murder case and the forthcoming opening night. At the same time, Phyllida intrigued me. She was obviously bright as hell, accomplished, a bit offbeat, and perhaps great fun. It had been some time since I had had any real contact with a woman my age—with any woman. In short, a long time between drinks.

"Right through this stretch, it changes from day to day, even hour to hour." I looked at my calendar on my cell phone. "Whew," I said. "It's a rough weekend. Can we talk tomorrow?"

"Absolutely."

I headed toward the stage door. "I'm sorry—I have to run."

"Thanks for working me in."

"Give me a call tomorrow. We'll try to set a time to talk about Dorothy."

• • •

The Wednesday night preview went better than the matinee and gave us the same feeling we had had the night before: that we were getting there. Also, the talk I had had with Elliot helped me enormously in my scene near the end. My intentions were clearer, and I felt much more confident. The big news that night, however, was not our preview but events occurring just north of us on the Upper West Side, at the American Museum of Natural History.

Later, when I read the papers and talked to people, some of whom had been there, I was able to piece together how the evening unfolded. The museum was holding its annual gala, their most important event of the year, socially and financially. All of its top-tier trustees, donors, and supporters were invited, along with important political figures, especially those from the city who were in a position to assist with financial aid to the institution. It was black tie, of course, and the more fashionably conscious women would not dare appear in anything but a recognizable designer dress. Events at the Museum of Natural History were not as pretentious or self-important as those at the two Mets—the opera and the museum—but they were nevertheless grand affairs.

The Museum of Natural History is on a four-block stretch on the Upper West Side of Manhattan, running from 77th

Street to 81st. For the gala, the U-shaped driveway to the south, ordinarily closed to vehicular traffic, was opened so that limousines could drive in from 77th Street under a high-ceilinged porte cochère where guests could alight and enter the Grand Gallery, the most notable feature of which was an amazing sixty-three-foot wooden canoe suspended from the ceiling. Originally created in the Northwest, it was thought to be the largest surviving carved canoe in the world.

After being marked off a list, guests were greeted by the museum's director and the chairman of the trustees, who directed them to a fleet of electric trolleys waiting to whisk them to the site of the dinner at the Milstein Hall of Ocean Life. An immense space of nearly 30,000 feet, it was a spectacular setting for the gala. The centerpiece of the hall was a model of a ninety-four-foot blue whale suspended from the ceiling in a graceful curve, as if it were floating rather than making its way through the ocean deep. With its tall ceiling, large ground floor, and spacious upper gallery running around the entire circumference, it could accommodate an event like this and still not seem crowded.

On both levels of the hall, there was a bar set up, and an area for socializing before the dinner. Off to one side on the lower level, a society orchestra was playing old favorites: Rodgers and Hart, Gershwin, Jerome Kern. The tables were beautifully decorated with flowers, each with a centerpiece featuring a small ocean creature of some sort—a starfish, a snail, or the like—cast in silver. The lights were brighter than usual, and the atmosphere overall was not only appropriate but notably festive.

Certain locations in the hall were considered the most

desirable—tables for ten, for example, that cost $50,000. Prices went down from there, but even the least expensive were not cheap. A $250 ticket allowed you to have drinks, but you had to leave before dinner. There was also the opportunity to make larger gifts, which would be announced with some fanfare at the end of the evening.

Following the murder at the Met Museum, there had been discussions between senior staff at Natural History and the executive committee of the board that perhaps they should cancel or at least tone down the celebration. In addition to the fact that this was a high-profile event, there would be a large number of additional personnel entering and leaving the premises. In the end, it was decided that the Met incident, hopefully, was a one-off event and that they should proceed. The museum did, however, beef up security considerably by bringing in an outside firm, which doubled the number of guards and surveillance teams.

The highlight of the evening was to take place after the main course had been served and just before dessert. The cocktail hour was to last forty-five minutes to an hour, after which guests who were staying for dinner would take their seats. A first-class caterer had been engaged, one who did not proffer the usual limp salad and bland chicken. No, there would be a salad with a "divine" dressing, with choices for a gourmet main course.

The new addition to be unveiled was a graceful, fourteen-foot baby whale suspended from the ceiling, to be moved later toward the center as a sort of accent or punctuation mark to accompany the large whale. On the west side of the gallery level, opposite the entrance, the balcony widened in the center; it was here that the small whale was concealed under a white covering. At the critical moment, a man on each side would pull a rope raising the cloth to reveal the replica of the small whale. It would be what the Elizabethan theatre referred to as a "discovery."

The guests were finishing their dinners. The evening so far had been a huge success; as the wife of the chairman said to the director, everything was going "swimmingly." The orchestra sounded a fanfare; the Chairman moved to the microphone; the room grew quiet. The Chairman exclaimed what a special night this was for the museum. He thanked all those present for coming and for their support; he also mentioned by name the people who had made larger gifts; he thanked the staff. "And now," he said, "the moment we have all been waiting for. An addition to our glorious Hall of Ocean Life, which will only add to its excitement and its appeal." He pointed to the covered object on the balcony. The orchestra played a chord, and he nodded to the two men holding ropes on the balcony.

It was the signal for them to raise the cover, which they began slowly and ceremoniously to do. First visible was the bottom of the baby whale in a curved position, like its larger counterpart in the center of the room. As they raised the cover higher, it became apparent that there was something else coming into view. The men hesitated, but then continued. When they had pulled the cover free, there, astride the small whale, was a man dressed in tux and black tie. He had a shock of red hair and a round face with protruding ears. There was an audible, almost universal gasp. It was one of those moments that passes in an instant and yet is indelibly imprinted on the visual memory of everyone who saw it.

There were choked attempts at speech. "Is he—?"

"Oh no—"

"It's not—"

"I can't believe—"

Finally one man, sitting in the gallery near the scene, exclaimed in horror and disbelief, "My God, it's Wally!"

Seeing the stiff figure in his tuxedo atop the whale, people didn't know what to do. Everyone was in shock. There were shouts from all sides: "Call the police"; "Get security." Some put their dessert forks down, picked up their things, and made a hasty exit. Others looked at the frozen tableau, transfixed by the sight. Still others gazed and then looked away, shaking their heads. Gradually, everyone left except those directly concerned: the staff, several trustees, guards who had been summoned, all of whom had slowly made their way to the scene. On close inspection, it was confirmed that the man was dead. Somehow, he had been strapped securely to the baby whale, which his corpse appeared to be riding like a cowboy. Also, there were straps under his arms. As the two men pulled the ropes that raised the cover, the man had been drawn erect as well. Later it would be pointed out that, at the gala exactly one year before, the victim had been on that same balcony being honored as the "trustee of the year."

# CHAPTER SEVENTEEN

As I was leaving the theatre after the performance Wednesday night, I overheard disjointed references from the assistant stage manager, who was glued to her cell phone, about a disturbance at the Museum of Natural History, but her information was vague. When I turned on the 11:00 news, however, there it was. TV crews had rushed to Central Park West to the main entrance of the museum, which features a large statue of Teddy Roosevelt on horseback in front. Commentators breathlessly told us about the grotesque, bizarre events that had occurred inside during this elegant, black-tie gala. It was impossible not to relate this to what had happened at the Met Museum only two weeks before. The label "patron murders," plural, was now all too true.

Unlike the Metropolitan murder, this time there were plenty of photographs. First, there were the shots taken by the museum's official photographer who was on hand, and then there were dozens of images taken on cell phones and other handheld devices. TV wasted no time in getting their hands on these. Reporters tossed out terms like grotesque, horrific, bizarre, freakish, monstrous, and perverted to describe the scene.

The victim, Wallace Weatherby, turned out to be a Texan who had moved to New York with his wife, Sheryl, twelve years before. Wallace had been invited to join the Board of Trustees six years previously. A spokesperson for the museum appeared on camera for an impromptu press conference explaining what an exemplary and hard-working trustee he had been and what a dastardly, cowardly, and demeaning act this had been, the work surely of a sick, deranged mind. As for the perpetrator, like the earlier murder at the Met it appeared to be the work of more than one person, in addition to which there were very few clues: no obvious signs of a break-in, though, of course, the investigation—which would leave no stone unturned—was just beginning.

My reaction to all this was that there had to be some kind of backstory. There was clearly a thread running through both museum murders—a strong statement echoing some of the feelings that Sonny Beaufort had long expressed—but at the same time there was something diabolical and over-the-top about it.

The next morning Gina and Drew had a lengthy, front-page piece in the *Times*—they must have been up all night. Wallace Weatherby grew up in Abilene, Texas, and went to Texas A&M, where he studied engineering. He had been enormously successful in the energy business: oil, coal, natural gas. He had met his wife, also from West Texas, at A&M. Unlike most billionaires, who seem to shed wives like old overcoats, he had kept Sheryl by his side. In fact, she had been with him every step of the way, transforming herself from an Aggie with a Texas twang into a quite respectable Southern lady. It was said, for example, that she had successfully apprenticed herself to the social doyennes of Dallas and Fort Worth, leaving behind not only her twang but all vestiges and mannerisms of a down-home cowgirl.

The husband, Wally, by all accounts was outgoing, affable, very well liked, and apparently a masterly storyteller, not just tall tales from Texas but more sophisticated narratives that never failed to amuse. He was also regarded as a shrewd businessman who could break down a balance sheet with remarkable speed and acuity. The combination of his bonhomie and his sharp mind appeared in the eyes of many to make him an ideal trustee of a not-for-profit board. That, plus his amazing generosity— stepping in to make large gifts to causes and institutions just when they seemed to be most in need of support.

His wife, distraught and badly shaken, revealed that her husband had received a call at 4:00 p.m., purportedly from the director's office, asking him to come to the museum early to meet with a potential donor who was attending the gala and was considering making a sizeable donation for the refurbishment of an entire wing. The donor wanted to meet with the director and two or three trustees before the cocktail hour to discuss the gift. In order to keep the meeting secret, Weatherby and his wife were to direct their driver to come to an entrance at the north end of the museum near the adjacent planetarium. Accordingly, Weatherby asked his driver to bring the car earlier than planned. The couple arrived at the designated entrance and were greeted by a well-dressed man with a mustache, wearing dark glasses, who escorted them in. Once inside, the husband was grabbed and whisked away, and Mrs. Weatherby was taken by two men in masks to a bathroom in a subbasement, where she was locked in along with a woman employee of the museum, a maid of some kind. Later, after the horrific events of the evening, a call came in to the museum explaining where she could be found.

Despite their many similarities, the murders at the Met and the Natural History differed in important respects. First, there were obviously more people involved in this operation. Second, while the murder at the Met was a very quiet, private sort of thing, this latest murder could not have been announced in a more public way, with the results being dramatically displayed to several hundred attendees at the gala. As before, there was no obvious evidence: no broken windows, surveillance tape, or fingerprints. But, unlike the Met operation, there were a few solid clues: three guards were found bound and gagged, though when questioned they had no idea what their captors looked like, as they had all worn masks. Two uniforms and passes from the catering staff were missing; these were from the kitchen staff, not the waitstaff, and so they were never exposed to general view. Also, the surveillance tape had been rigged so that the reel that appeared in the control room in the period from 5:00 to 8:00 p.m. was actually a repeat of the tape from 2:00 to 5:00. Perhaps most revealing of all, a fire alarm went off in the Milstein Hall at about 5:30. The room was emptied briefly until an all-clear sounded fifteen minutes later.

In other words, not only was this operation far more elaborate, but there appeared to be much more to go on than there had been in the previous murder. Still, there was no clue whatsoever as to when or how the perpetrators entered the museum or when or how they left. The man who met the Weatherbys at the side entrance was probably disguised. For the record, the police precinct in charge of the museum area was the 20th, whose headquarters were on West 82nd Street.

In terms of his personality and marital history, Wallace Weatherby quite obviously stood in contrast to the Met Museum victim. The important question was whether the two were alike in their financial history—in the manner in which they accumulated their fortunes and the ethics, or lack of them, with which they conducted their business affairs. To find out, it was my guess that Drew had taken the earliest possible plane out of LaGuardia headed to Dallas.

• • •

As might be expected, the story was all over the early morning news and talk shows. Headlines screamed phrases like "Heinous Assault on City's Cultural Elite" and "Madman Murder at Museum." Expert consultants were interviewed to voice their weighty opinions. One, for example, spoke of how "porous" the Museum of Natural History was. The entire acreage on which it was placed was surrounded only by a low fence. The large windows around the sides and back of the building itself were guarded by a wrought iron fence that could easily be surmounted. As for the sensors on the windows, which would send an alarm if one was opened even a crack, the controls at a central station could easily be disabled so that no report registered or siren went off. There was a driveway and entrance at 78th Street that came from Columbus Avenue straight to a loading dock for deliveries. It was heavily guarded, but this was no guarantee against an entry or escape there. The entire setup would be child's play to real professionals, which was obviously what they were dealing with. There was also the question of motive, and it was open season on that.

• • •

Just as I finished reading about the latest museum murder, the phone rang. It was Monaghan.

"Congratulations."

"You got Warren?"

"In Montreal, just as you thought. Yesterday afternoon."

"Congratulations to you."

"I can't talk now. I'll be tied up all day today and tomorrow. The two of them are being brought down this morning. We'll be interviewing and processing at least till tomorrow night. Could you make lunch here on Saturday?"

"It would have to be early; I have a matinee."

"How about noon? We'll order a sandwich. You won't believe the story when I tell you. It was like one of your comic dramas."

"A farce?"

"That's it."

"I can't wait to hear."

• • •

After talking to Monaghan, I hit the pause button. Too much was happening too fast. Three weeks ago I was rehearsing a new play about to open on Broadway, definitely a better-than-average play, which was rare. Even better, it was being produced by someone I admired as much as anyone I had ever worked with in the theatre. No question: it was one of those rare moments, among the most fulfilling events of my career. Then, out of the blue, the world turned upside down.

In quick succession, an unprecedented, totally bizarre murder occurred at the Metropolitan Museum, and shortly after that Dorothy was killed in a senseless, obscene fashion. I could not get my head around the contrast between the two deaths. The first, the Met murder, reeking of sensationalism, was carefully planned, required weeks of preparation, and was intended to be as shocking as possible. Dorothy's murder, on the other hand, was an unplanned, miserable affair that took place in an obscure basement. Now, on top of everything else, there was this latest horrendous slaying.

I needed a break. I headed for Anton's, my favorite coffee shop on the corner of my block, run by a young couple, Mica and Anton Fielding who were always there, always friendly, and kept the place spotless. I ordered a latte and settled at my favorite table. Just as the coffee arrived, my cell phone rang. It was Phyllida. "Can you believe this? What a horrific spectacle." She was referring, of course, to the Natural History murder.

"No doubt about that."

"It's macabre, Grand Guignol gone mad."

"I agree."

"Where will it end?"

"No one knows."

"I have to talk to you."

"I can't today, or tomorrow. Maybe a quick bite tomorrow night before the show."

"Great."

I thought quickly. "There's a pub, the Rose and Crown, right around the corner from the theatre on Eighth Avenue. Serves things like shepherd's pie. I could be there at around 6:15."

"I'll be there. My God, it gets worse and worse. The magazine doesn't know where to turn."

"I can imagine."

• • •

After I finished talking to Phyllida, I turned off my cell. I needed time to think. I had no idea who had masterminded these two museum murders, or why. One thing I did decide was that this second victim probably had a personal history very much like the first—that is, someone with a very shady business background who wanted to put it behind him and burnish his image by becoming a philanthropist and arts patron. I would be very surprised if Drew didn't turn up just such a biography after his research in Dallas.

I realized, however, that it would be next to impossible to guess at the motive. Perhaps it was an obsessive reformer who wanted to make certain the lesson about questionable board members was driven home. Or someone who had known these two men years ago and felt wronged by them and wanted to get even. Or even a fanatical New York patron who resented the invasion of outsiders. I knew no one could guess the answer without a multitude of additional facts. I decided the answer lay not with the "why" but with the "how."

Several things were clear. Whoever masterminded this had excellent information about the arts scene in New York, about the makeup and selection of trustees, about exhibits and schedules, about the inner workings of museums and concert halls. The person also had access to an incredible team of computer experts who could hack into almost anything and program anything. Probably most important, the person had at his disposal a first-class team of experts at clandestine search-and-seizure, including assassinations. It was time to get in touch with Hunter Waldrop. Hunter was a young guru who had helped me solve my computer problems for more than ten years and had been a key player in solving a case I had worked on some years before. At the time, I was acting in a courtroom drama, *The Defense Objects*, playing a cameo role as a young doctor giving expert testimony. In real life—not in the stage drama—the murder victim was the show's lighting designer, Oliver Zelsky.

Oz, as everyone called him, was a brilliant designer: skillful, innovative, and imaginative. He was also an egotistical bastard who alienated everyone in sight. Everyone, that is, except a series of young, unsuspecting females whom he seemed to have an incredible knack for seducing. On the night after the second preview of *The Defense Objects*, Oz was found dead, hanged by the neck and dangling, like some Elizabethan criminal, from a metal catwalk high above the stage.

Given how many people detested Oz, there was a long list of suspects, and the police went about interviewing them. During their interrogations, it was discovered that a mystery man had been seen in the theatre during the final days before previews. Cleverly, when asked, he told the lighting people he was on the stage crew, the stage crew that he was a costume assistant, and the costume group that he was a lighting gopher. Once Oz was found dead and people began comparing notes, he became an obvious suspect. He claimed his name was Parker Burlingame, but that was obviously an alias. There were no photographs of him. Someone had taken a photo of the sound crew on an iPhone, but when the person checked, she found that her photos had been erased. Theatre people, however, are unusually observant, and when they pooled their impressions they came up with an unusually accurate sketch of his face. The only thing was, he was long gone.

That's when Hunter came to the rescue. I got in touch with him, showed him the sketch, and explained the problem. I also told him that the suspect might be someone with a bent toward eighteenth- or nineteenth-century methods of execution: hangings, guillotines, etc. I admitted this was a needle-in-a-haystack situation, but he seemed to relish the challenge.

This was in the early days of Myspace and Facebook, and Hunter eventually identified him. His name was Roger Watkins, and he had decamped to Spokane, Washington, where he lived in a sort of time warp. Rather than a theatre person, he was into heraldry, honor, and retribution. His motive for killing Oz was that his first and only love was an innocent young lady named Rosalind, whom the dastardly Oz had induced to take drugs so he could seduce her. She had a violent reaction to whatever Oz gave her and lost not only her purity but her life. From that moment on, Roger had vowed to avenge her death, plotting, planning, in fact, devoting his whole life to it. Once I learned the circumstances, I felt great remorse that I had been the one who helped track him down.

It was near lunchtime. At Anton's I ordered one of their jambon beurre sandwiches: thin-sliced French ham with marvelous butter and cheese on a freshly baked baguette. Sandwich in hand I returned to the loft, emailed Hunter, and told him that I needed to talk to him—urgently. I left a similar message on his cell phone.

• • •

I then put in a call to Annie in Boston. She was away temporarily, but Danny was there and answered the phone.

"I hear Dad's been arrested in Montreal," he said.

"That's what I understand."

"They'll bring him back to New York?"

"I think so, yes."

"Do you think he did it—killed Mother?"

"The police seem to believe so."

"Is Mikey involved?"

"Again, the police think so."

"Oh, God. This couldn't be worse. How could Dad do this? I know he was mad at her, but to—I just can't believe it."

"I'm sure if he was involved it was probably accidental."

"But to go this far . . ."

"We can't do anything but wait at the moment, none of us. One thing I have learned, talking to his old friends in

Connecticut: he hasn't been himself lately. He's become more and more erratic."

"I've noticed that too, and I was worried, but something like this . . ."

"One thing you can count on, Danny. He'll have the best lawyer anyone could find, someone who will be on his side all the way."

"I should come down there and see him."

"I'd wait if I were you. They'll have him tied up for the next few days and won't allow any visitors, even family." I didn't know if this were true, but I knew Danny should stay where he was. Also, I wanted to change the subject, so I began talking about the show and our schedule until opening night. This week was previews, I said, and next week—Monday, Tuesday, and the Wednesday matinee—would be the press previews. The opening would be next Wednesday night. I told him what a marvelous production it was, especially of a straight play without a lot of bells and whistles. I asked him to please pass this along to Annie, and said that either one of them should call me anytime they felt like it. I also told him that the moment I had any more news about Warren, I would call straightaway.

• • •

Hunter got back to me shortly after I finished talking to Danny and said he could meet me sometime around 4:30. He would be in the Wall Street area—an emergency. Could I meet him at the Starbucks at Broad and Beaver? I said I'd be there.

He was only ten minutes late. I told him it had to do with

the patron murders and therefore had to be absolutely confidential. I then explained what I wanted.

When I finished, he said, "You don't need me, you need Buzz Pegram."

"Who the hell is Buzz Pegram?"

"To put it one way: my people charge $150 an hour. Buzz charges anywhere from $1,200 to $2,000 an hour."

"He's worth that?"

"The best computer software man outside the Defense Department—maybe better than anyone *in* the Defense Department."

"How can we get hold of him?"

"I'll try to reach him. I don't ask him for things very often; if I explain how important it is . . . Well, we'll see."

"You have my cell number. I'll meet him anytime, anywhere. The only caveat is that I'm at the theatre from 7:00 to 10:30 tonight."

"Noted." And he was off.

# CHAPTER EIGHTEEN

Friday morning Gina had a piece in the *Times*, the main thrust of which was the way in which the city's social and arts elite were reacting to the Met murder. In view of the second horrible and very public crime of the previous evening, the information she had gleaned was more timely and relevant than ever. In reviewing the future of New York's large cultural institutions, she relied largely on off-the-record conversations with well-placed sources—people in the hierarchy who kept abreast of behind-the-scenes developments.

On one front, it appeared that conversations were underway among the Old Guard, quietly and informally, indicating that established institutions should rethink the way they take on new trustees, especially those from out of town who, after making a fortune elsewhere, move to New York and make a convincing show of being worthy of joining the elite among the city's cultural leaders. Perhaps they were sometimes paying too high a price for taking on a generous donor whose cash was badly needed but who himself might not be what he appeared to be in terms of background and integrity. In addition, the Old Guard had extended their concerns to another phenomenon:

naming concert halls, museum wings, and the like after wealthy donors who contributed enormous amounts of money in exchange for having a sort of ownership of the space. Perhaps there should be a reevaluation of this all-too-common practice as well.

It was understood that several high-profile donors now serving on boards, who had migrated to the city in recent years, had become especially concerned that they too might become targets. Accordingly, several had left town temporarily, deciding to visit one of their many homes elsewhere, taking family and servants with them. For those who remained, there was a conspicuous increase in security. Chauffeurs were given additional background checks, extra doormen were hired for lobbies in high-profile buildings; additional guards were signed on to escort young children to their private schools, and security people were engaged to remain outside those schools the entire time the children were there.

After the second murder, the question on everyone's mind was what the next target would be. A strong consensus had emerged that the obvious choice was Lincoln Center. Halfway through a ballet or an opera, instead of a piece of scenery descending from above, a trustee dressed in a tuxedo would fall into view, a noose around his neck.

· · ·

Our performance on Friday night was the best one yet. When the cast invited me to join them for a beer afterwards, I was happy to do so, not only to join in the camaraderie but also because it happened to fit in perfectly with my plans for later. Just before leaving for the theatre, I had an email from Hunter's contact, Buzz Pegram, giving me explicit instructions on where and when to meet him later that night: an address on Lexington Avenue, between 52nd and 53rd Streets at exactly 11:50 p.m. I had just enough time to join the cast for a beer, though I stuck to the nonalcoholic kind so I could be as sharp as possible when I encountered the computer prodigy.

I arrived at the designated building on Lex at 11:45 and found a number of black town cars and limousines lined up outside. This had become a ritual in Wall Street and midtown office buildings. In high-pressure law offices and financial institutions, associates and junior partners worked well into the evening, night after night. To make this more palatable, firms signed up fleets of limos to drive the late-night workers home in luxury, no matter what the hour.

The lobby of the office building was an antiseptic cube of glass, white marble, and stainless steel. I arrived at the security desk at 11:48, and two minutes later, on the dot, an elevator door opened. Four young lawyers emerged and went through the turnstiles headed for their limos. A fifth person emerged and walked to the security desk. If I had not known otherwise, I would have said that Harry Potter in the person of Daniel Radcliffe had stepped off the screen and started walking toward me. No more than five feet six or seven, he was a thin young man with a sharp nose and chin and large, round, black-rimmed glasses that seemed to cover his entire upper face. He was wearing black sneakers, black jeans, and a wrinkled blue Apple T-shirt, and his black hair covered his collar and the top of his ears. "Mr. Johanssen?"

I nodded yes.

He spoke to the security guard, who looked at my ID and printed out a security badge. I went through the turnstile and followed Pegram, who was already on his way to the elevator. We rode to the twelfth floor, where he indicated we should get out. Except for my name, he still had not spoken a word. Taking a cue from him, I had not spoken either. We turned left and went to the end of the corridor, where we turned right and headed down another corridor. Halfway down, he stopped at a door that had a number on it but no name. He punched in a series of numbers on a key pad, reached for the door, and opened it.

"The code changes every six hours," he said.

"How do you keep up?"

"Every week I memorize the ones coming up for the next seven days."

We entered a relatively small reception room with a guard sitting at a desk where I assumed a receptionist usually sat. Pegram went to another door off to the side, punched in another code, opened the door, and indicated that I should enter ahead of him. We passed down a short corridor with three or four carrels on each side and came to a small, bare office with a metal desk on which papers were scattered, three metal chairs, and a series of computers lined up on a long, low table. He indicated a chair, and I sat down; he sat in another.

"Thank you for seeing me," I said.

"Hunter and I have been friends for a long time."

"He tells me you are a master of the supercomputer."

Pegram pointed behind him at a large glass window,

behind which I could see an array of machines that I assumed to be the so-called supercomputer.

"It's a Japanese K, the most advanced computer in the world. Each one is custom made for individual clients: governments that can afford them, the Defense Department, large multinational corporations. These days it's the K plus the Cloud. This organization does work for companies not large enough to have one of their own. I don't know exactly what they charge. I think it's around $150,000 an hour."

"I don't have . . ." I started to say.

He cut me off. "Don't worry. I do software programming for them. One of the trade-offs is that I can use it after hours if there is not another urgent project in the works. You're lucky: this weekend there's a bit of free time."

"I'll get to the point," I said. "You've heard, I assume, about these recent murders at the two museums, the Metropolitan and the Natural History."

"Yes."

"The police are totally baffled, but I have a thought. I wouldn't even call it a theory, more like a strong hunch."

"Which is?"

"I think there must be a connection somewhere. There are two victims, but it seems to me there may be a third coordinate, and maybe even a fourth. If we could sift through all these and see if any names come up, names that might be connected to all the coordinates, it might tell us something. These computers, I gather, make thousands of connections a minute—"

"A second," he said.

"They could be given three or four points of reference, and

we might discover a name or two that registered with all of them."

"I couldn't promise anything, but it's worth a try. I've been buried in a project on molecular biology and just before that, quantum physics. This would be a welcome change of pace."

"That's good to hear. Here are the names of the two victims, and a little bit about them. And here are coordinates three, four, and five, with explanations about them." I took four pieces of paper out of my jacket pocket and handed them to him.

"I'll see what I can do." He pointed behind him at the stack of computers and started out of the office. I followed along behind him.

"If you could crack this, the whole city will be indebted to you, not just the museums and the police, but everyone."

"If I get something, you mustn't tell anyone where it came from."

"Absolutely. Of course, I'll have to give the police the results."

We reached the elevator. He pushed the button. I thanked him again; the elevator arrived, and I was on my way.

• • •

On Saturday morning, Drew's piece from Dallas appeared in the *Times*. There would be more to learn about Wallace Weatherby, but already a few facts were clear. Wally, as he was known, definitely had a different personality from the other victim, Mulholland. Whereas the latter was quiet and somewhat reserved, Wally, his old friends insisted, was "outgoing as all outdoors." Hearty, effervescent, but not overly effusive, he was liked by almost everyone—at the Downtown Club in Dallas, the Cattle Club in Fort Worth, the country clubs in both cities. In the same way, his wife Sheryl was extremely popular in the Dallas Garden Club and everywhere else. Their friends in Dallas were horrified and deeply shocked by the murder at the Museum of Natural History, and could not believe that it was anything but a cruel mistake.

Even when moving to New York, the Weatherbys had kept a large apartment in Dallas and maintained their ranch in Abilene. They went back for two or three weeks every spring and fall—seeing friends, shooting birds, riding on the ranch—and also at Christmas to give their holiday party, which remained one of the highlights of the year in Dallas.

As with Mulholland, however, there turned out to be another side to the story. At Texas A&M, Weatherby had majored in chemical engineering and proved to be an ambitious young man. An early sign of his ingenuity was a project for the coal mining industry. A friend of his from college had joined with others to buy a series of family-owned mines in West Virginia and eastern Kentucky. The friend let Wally know that they were concerned about the cost of "seals" in their newly acquired mines. Seals close off mined-out areas and isolate shafts susceptible to explosions or spontaneous combustion. One of the chief methods of building seals is called "cast-in-place foamed cement."

Weatherby developed a much less expensive way to construct the cement seal. His mine owner friends were thrilled and paid him handsomely in money and stock. His mine seals, however, turned out to be time bombs. Effective for a while, they were found to be less durable than older, tried-and-true methods, particularly if they were not properly monitored. As a result there were catastrophes at several mines, most notably at the Lower Silver Springs and Solonica mines in West Virginia, where the loss of life was twenty-seven in the first case and eleven in the second. Weatherby, however, had long since sold his cement seal process to a third party and had cleverly removed virtually any trace of his original involvement.

A much more important initiative was Weatherby's contribution to "fracking" to extract natural gas trapped in shale deep underground. These deposits, found three or four miles underground, had been known about for some time. The trick was to get at them. It was discovered that, if you go down to the desired depth, near the deposits, and then drill horizontally, you could break up the shale and extract the gas.

The key is the fracking: pumping a solution of water, sand, and chemicals into the shale, under extremely high pressure. Even though they make up only 2 percent, the chemicals from such a toxic mixture can be lethal. In their television ads, energy companies are fond of pointing out that they cannot be harmful because the process takes place at least a mile underground. What they don't say is that the liquid compound can work its way up to ground level. Even worse, when the expended solution is brought back to the surface, the company doing the fracking often buries the toxic waste in a porous, shallow pool, or sends it to a supposed reprocessing plant that may be nothing of the kind. The results had been innumerable cases of serious contamination and not a few deaths.

Weatherby was an important player in the early days of

fracking, developing a chemical compound of benzene, methanol, ethylene glycol, and boric acid that frackers found very effective. He patented the compound but very early in the game sold the patent for a huge sum and had long since vanished when the trouble started. Asked about it later, he claimed the people he sold it to had changed the formula. A pattern was developing: Weatherby, like Mulholland, had been on the scene early, taken out the money, lots of money, and, when the roof fell in, pled total ignorance. As I had suspected, though Weatherby and Mulholland were involved in different schemes, their early careers were remarkably similar.

· · ·

Saturday at noon I appeared at Monaghan's office to find him sitting at his desk and an aide standing near the door.

"What kind of sandwich do you want?" he asked.

"What choices do I have?"

"These people can do anything."

"Ham and brie on pumpernickel."

"Mustard or mayonnaise?" the aide asked.

"Both," I said.

"And to drink?" asked Monaghan.

"Nonalcoholic beer."

The aide departed and I sat down and began: "Before we get to Warren, what do you make of this other business, the museum murders?"

"What do you make of them?'

"Weird."

"To say the least. I'm glad neither one is my case. I don't envy Markham or Steinmetz."

"Steinmetz?"

"The detective handling the case for the 20th—on the Upper West Side."

"Is there any precedent for this kind of thing?" I asked.

"None that I know of, and I imagine the same goes for them."

"There's something outside the box here, something truly grotesque. But tell me about Warren and this farce."

"The crime unit in Montreal had been watching the Josh Tremayne house, pretty sure Warren and the boy were there—in fact, spotting them through the window with long-range glasses. Also, they located the boy's car in a garage nearby. Wednesday afternoon they decided to move in. Two plainclothes men went to the door, showed their badges, and, after some little time, were shown in. Once inside they discovered that a lawyer Josh had hired for Warren had just arrived and was with him in the dining room. Only minutes later another lawyer appeared, hired by the boy's father to represent him. So you had two detectives and two lawyers appearing at the same time, just like one of your stage plays.

"The boy and his lawyer went into the kitchen, and when he and Warren reappeared it was clear that their lawyers had told them to remain silent, which didn't mean anything. Both were charged and taken to the local jail. Meanwhile, I had three men on the way up there, and, after all the extradition business was taken care of, they brought them back the next afternoon. They're here now, each with a new lawyer, and we have been interviewing them while preparing the indictments."

"So what have you learned?" I asked.

"As we assumed, the young man, Stuart Ross, claimed that he had known nothing about Warren's involvement with the murder. Warren told him that a man to whom he owed money had hired white-collar mob figures to come after him. It was all a mistake, he told Ross; his former accountant had screwed up, and Warren didn't realize it until too late. To avoid his pursuers, he asked the young man to give him an alibi on Monday night and then help him escape. In the meantime, Stuart, on the advice of the topflight lawyer hired by his father, has been cooperating to the hilt."

Switching gears, I asked about Mikey.

A few days ago, Monaghan explained, Mikey had acquired a lawyer, and a good one, too: an older man, silver-haired, impeccably dressed, gay, and smooth as silk. Warren, of course, had a team of top-drawer lawyers who were all over the case, but they had an uphill fight. New evidence was coming in almost every day. The wine bottle, for instance, that had Mikey's prints, had Warren's as well, but what was particularly damning was that Warren's were upside down. In other words, he had grasped the bottle to use as a weapon, not to pour wine. When things got tighter, no doubt Warren's lawyers would move to an insanity defense, but Monaghan didn't think they could make that stick.

"What I can't understand," he added, "is how it came to this. I know money problems among the wealthy can be rough, but at their worst they're not like what people face when they're destitute."

"It was the kudzu."

206

"Kudzu?"

"A green, broad-leaf plant with an insatiable appetite to smother everything in sight. Originally brought here from Japan in the late 1930s, it was planted throughout the South to control soil erosion, but, if ever a cure proved more deadly than the disease, it was kudzu. Early in my career I played Brick in a bus-and-truck tour of *Cat on a Hot Tin Roof.* We traveled through a good part of the South, and I will never forget riding down highways in Georgia, Alabama, and South Carolina and seeing mile after mile of this green blanket covering the countryside. Wherever you had once seen a young elm, oak, maple, or magnolia tree, a rhododendron or azalea bush, you now saw only this smothering green carpet.

"Beginning in the late nineties, the financial world went crazy. First, geeks from MIT found they could program computer models to make a zillion trades in a matter of seconds. If these phantom trades worked out, they made billions. If not, it was the customer's loss, not theirs. Then came derivatives—the bundling, slicing, and dicing of everything in sight. No one knew what was in these so-called 'instruments,' and no one cared. When they went bust, millions of people lost their homes, their life savings, and more. The perpetrators went scot-free. The oaks and the elms of probity, fairness, and decency, were smothered under a blanket of fraud, greed, and deception. Kudzu."

"And is Warren part of this?"

"Not really. In his own way, he's a victim too. Before this reached fever pitch, Warren had already begun to lose his way. But when he started to fight back, he found he too was buried under the kudzu. He didn't know where he was; he saw all these other people making tons of money, but the new world was foreign to him. Desperate to catch up, he lurched from one thing to another, getting in deeper and deeper."

Monaghan changed the subject. "You've got an opening next week, right?"

"Wednesday night."

"My wife wants to see the show."

"What about you? Are you interested in seeing the show?"

After a pause, he stammered, "Yes, of course, but I'm not quite sure when we can come. Once we know, could you get us tickets?"

"Of course. Any time. Just tell me what night."

"Can you make that three tickets? We've got a niece who wants to be an actress."

"No problem, but at some point you have to give me a date."

"Right. I understand."

"Now it's time I was off. Saturday is matinee day."

"That much I know."

# CHAPTER NINETEEN

The performance that Saturday evening was perhaps our best one yet. Afterwards I checked my cell phone for messages, only to find that there was one from Buzz Pegram: "Call whenever you can, no matter what time." I took him at his word.

"I'm closing in on this," he said.

"You're kidding."

"Another two or three hours should do it. Do you want me to call you then, or first thing tomorrow?"

"How early would 'first thing' be?"

"7:30, 8:00."

"Do you ever sleep?"

"Yes, but probably not when you do."

"8:00 will be fine. Do you really think you—?"

"We'll see."

• • •

As tired as I was, I didn't sleep very well, waking up several times to wonder what Buzz had come up with. At 7:30 Sunday morning, when the alarm went off, I got up, put on a robe, started the coffee, and put a bagel in the toaster oven. At 8:00, while I was eating, my cell phone rang.

"Are you up?"

"Yes."

"I'll join you."

"You're coming down here?"

"I'm already here."

"Where?"

"Downstairs. Buzz me in."

"Okay. By the way, the elevator's tricky."

"I'll manage."

I quickly put on a pair of trousers, a T-shirt, and a sweater and went to open the door, just as Buzz arrived in the clanking elevator. He had his computer case in one hand and a small paper bag in the other.

"I was just finishing breakfast. Want some?"

He held up his bag. "I brought my own," he said, whereupon he took out a cup of hot green tea and a prune Danish.

"So you think you've found him?"

"Who says it's a him?"

"I assumed . . ."

"Just kidding." He looked around the loft. "Is there a place here I could crash?"

I pointed to the guest room. "But aren't you going to tell me who it is?"

He opened his computer case and took out a sheaf of papers. "It's all in here," he said, and handed me the papers as he started toward the bedroom.

"One minute."

He paused.

"Let me tell you what I'm planning to do. First, I will read this thing. Then, if it's what I think it is, I'm going to call my contact, Monaghan, and ask him to contact the two detectives in the 19th and 20th precincts for a meeting as early as possible this afternoon.'"

"Do what you like; at this point, I'm out of it."

"But I need . . ." I was talking to empty air. He had gone into the spare room and closed the door.

I made a new pot of coffee, threw away my unfinished bagel and put a new one in the toaster, and went to the sofa to begin reading.

Marshall Bigelow III was born and raised in Wichita, Kansas. The largest bank in the city, CBT, the Commerce Bank and Trust Company, was founded by his great-grandfather. When his grandfather, Marshall Bigelow Sr., was president, the bank lent money to three aviation pioneers: Bill Lear, Walter Beech, and Clyde Cessna, all of whom, in the 1920s and '30s, started aircraft companies in Wichita. In addition to the bank lending them money, Bigelow's grandfather invested very profitably in all three companies. Marshall the Third took over in the early 1980s, and under his leadership the bank reached new heights in deposits, income, and trust accounts. It also moved into the late twentieth century in its adoption of the latest in digital and computer technology. Bigelow himself invested wisely in individual opportunities throughout the Midwest. In 1998 CBT was acquired by a conglomerate, and Bigelow retired with a sum estimated at just below $1 billion.

Bigelow and his wife, Constance, were considered model citizens of Wichita and were among the most generous members of the community, both in financial support and participation on boards of charities and nonprofit organizations. Mrs. Bigelow's particular interests were the local symphony and the garden club. An active member of the Garden Club of America, she eventually served as president of the organization. The Bigelows had three residences: a large home in Wichita, an apartment on the Upper East Side of Manhattan, and a compound in Marrakech, Morocco. The last had been their winter retreat for a number of years.

Bigelow had known both Mulholland and Weatherby for many years, his bank having lent large sums of money to them individually and for their various capital ventures. As their banker he was well aware of the accusations aimed at them from time to time. He himself was never implicated in wrongdoing of any kind.

A defining moment for Bigelow was his participation in the Vietnam War as a Navy Seal. Through the years Bigelow kept in close touch with his former comrades, attending annual reunions and the like. Along the way he had helped innumerable ex-Seals and others who had been injured or fallen on hard times, not just from that war but from subsequent engagements. As part of this, he set up a rather large charitable foundation dedicated to assisting ex–covert operatives, helping them find jobs and providing financial and psychological assistance.

Thomas Sterling Catlett, known as Tomcat, was a Denver entrepreneur and money manager who headed three major funds: Mile High I, a conservative fund with $48 billion under management; Mile High II, a mixture of high-value and slightly more speculative investments in a portfolio valued at $33 billion; and Mile High III, a higher-risk fund, which managed $29 billion. In business, Catlett ran MAAC, the Mid-America Agricultural Corporation, an agricultural conglomerate, which, along with Archer, Daniels, Midland, was the largest in the country. In creating MAAC, Catlett secured agreements and licenses from thousands of farmers over a fourteen-state area. Catlett himself was said to be worth something between $11 and $12 billion.

Catlett attended the University of Colorado at Boulder, where he was a star athlete in football and track. When he graduated in the mid-1960s, a few years before Bigelow, he also served in Vietnam, eventually joining a unit of the Army's 5th Special Forces Group. For Catlett, too, this experience had left an indelible mark on his character, and he too continued to stay in close contact with former colleagues, and later supported, financially and personally, ex–special forces troops fighting in Iraq and Afghanistan. Increasingly, his friends said, Catlett had become disenchanted with what was happening in the United States in its policies with regard to war. The Iraq War, for example, was particularly galling to him: a trumped-up war, he felt, not of necessity but of political chicanery, and the most wasteful, costly, ill-advised foreign policy blunder in our nation's history.

During his career Catlett crossed paths with both

Clifford Mulholland and Wallace Weatherby. In the case of Mulholland, the wife of one of Catlett's vice presidents had a serious liver condition for which she took a flawed generic drug manufactured by Pharmegen. When she died, Catlett took care of all her expenses, including suing Pharmegen, but, before the suit came to trial, the company declared bankruptcy. When Catlett discovered that Mulholland was a principal investor in Pharmegen, he confronted him with his participation in that company's unscrupulous and fatal practices. Mulholland's response was that he was merely an investor, and therefore "not responsible." This went against all Catlett's principles of ethical stewardship. He had also learned that Mulholland was an investor in the Mile High II fund, whereupon Catlett sent Mulholland a notice that his $17-million investment in Mile High II was being returned forthwith and that any further attempt by Mulholland to invest in any of the funds would not be accepted.

In the case of Weatherby, it had to do with land leases. Catlett was known far and wide as a preeminently "fair" businessman. In putting together his agricultural behemoth, he made certain that every single farmer who signed on was treated equitably and participated in all profits. A crucial part of this was the lease on the farmer's property. In reviewing each of their own leases, Catlett's staff came across other leases on the same properties attempting to secure drilling rights for oil and gas. Many of these, with obscure and opaque fine print, were demonstrably unfair to the farmers and might end up destroying their crops.

Catlett's conglomerate began actively to review all the leases on land where they were entitled to the agricultural products and discovered innumerable leases that also involved drilling and sometimes fracking. Advising their farming partners of the unfairness of these leases and the need to correct them, they ran afoul of the oil and gas interests. The latter banded together and asked Weatherby, widely admired and considered a true heavyweight, to take the matter up with Catlett. Weatherby flew to Denver and met with him, strongly suggesting that Catlett stick to farming and let energy companies take care of exploration. Weatherby was met with a withering lecture on exploitation. When Catlett discovered shortly after the meeting that the practice had been reduced but not eliminated, he wrote a blistering letter to Weatherby and doubled his efforts to protect his farmers' leases.

Some twenty years ago Catlett had built a large home just outside Aspen, Colorado, and fifteen years ago he and his wife had moved there. In the meantime, he had turned the day-to-day operation of his various businesses over to one of his sons, a son-in-law, and various lieutenants. Catlett's wife, Alicia, died one year ago. They had always been extremely close. For many years she had been deeply involved in the Aspen Institute, and was an active board member as well as chairperson of the Aspen Arts Festival. It should be noted as well that she was a subscriber to the magazine *Arts View*, published by Lucius Beaufort.

Victor Arundel, a private equity, venture capital entrepreneur known for his aggressiveness and, some would say, ruthlessness, was born in Des Moines, had gone to the University of Iowa and then to the Wharton Business School in Philadelphia, but had dropped out of business school to begin his financial career. Having made and lost several fortunes, he was now in the $4- to $5-billion range. His main office was in Des Moines, but he also had offices in New York, San Francisco, and Charlotte, North Carolina. He bought run-down companies cheaply, using mostly borrowed money, and either closed the companies down and took a huge tax write-off, or cut them drastically before reviving them to the point where he could dispose of them at an impressive profit. Admired by some for his ingenuity and persistence, he had been accused by others of stopping at nothing to get what he wanted, including reneging on agreements whenever it suited him. He had had several brushes with regulatory authorities, in some cases paying substantial fines, and in others escaping punishment, but was never actually forced to admit guilt.

Arundel knew both Clifford Mulholland and Wallace Weatherby. Some years ago he and Mulholland were the major investors in a surgical supply company in Omaha, Nebraska. They turned the moribund operation into the largest medical supply operation in the Midwest before selling it for an impressive profit. In the case of Weatherby, the two of them formed a joint venture in Oklahoma that successfully developed a more sophisticated version of the "Christmas Tree," a vital piece of equipment necessary for oil drilling.

Arundel had several homes: a Colonial-style mansion in Des Moines, apartments in both San Francisco and

New York, and an eighty-acre spread on the Virginia–West Virginia border, where, among other activities, he raised horses. Arundel himself was never in the armed services, but he had a close associate, a man named Henry (Hank) Herkimer, who was in a Special Operations unit that he left under cloudy circumstances. Herkimer was known to have a number of friends on the fringes of Special Forces: men who flunked out, served but were discharged, or turned rogue after serving. Apparently, Herkimer had been involved with Arundel for many years, not in operations dealing with finance, acquisitions, or individual corporations, but as an "enabler," a trusted associate who assisted Arundel in corporate espionage, in enforcing contracts and the like.

Arundel divorced his first wife some years ago but in recent years had been close to a woman named Anita Gomez who originally resided in Santa Fe. It was not known whether they were actually married or had simply been living together.

Buzz had done his job well enough, but what was one to make of this news? Moreover, two of the men appeared to be upstanding, exemplary citizens, as far from criminals as one could imagine. Could it be true that either one of them had arranged not one but two ingenious assassinations that had rocked the New York arts and cultural establishments? The third man, however, an extremely ambitious and acquisitive entrepreneur, was someone who might have been capable of an elaborate, perhaps deadly, undertaking. In spite of this third possibility, I had misgivings about showing the report to the two detectives in charge of the operation. Thinking it over, I finally decided that, since I had gone this far, I should probably see it through. It was 9:15; I called Monaghan on his home phone. It rang for seven, eight, nine times: maybe he didn't answer on Sundays. Just as I was ready to hang up, a woman answered.

"Yes?"

I hesitated a moment.

"Is someone there?"

"Mrs. Monaghan?"

"Who's calling? If this is one of those charities . . ."

"No. No. It's Matt Johanssen."

"Who?"

"Matt Johanssen."

"Never heard of you."

"A friend of Detective Monaghan."

"No one I know."

"A recent friend."

"Do you know what day it is, what time it is? My husband . . . Forget it. Call back."

I spoke quickly, "Please, Mrs. Monaghan. I know it's Sunday and it's early, but this is very, very important."

"It better be."

Then I heard hoarse voice. "Florence, who is it?"

"You find out." Presumably she was handing the phone to Monaghan.

"Monaghan here."

"Kevin, it's Matt Johanssen."

"What in God's name—?"

"I know, I know. But hear me out."

"We've already solved this thing; the man's in jail."

"This is the other one."

"What other one?"

"The museum murders."

"That's not my case."

"I know, but I had a hunch about it."

"What kind of hunch?"

"The person who did it."

"If this is some kind of joke . . ."

"Kevin, I promise. I got someone, a computer genius, to run a program, and he came up with a weird answer."

"If it's weird, why do you think it's correct?"

"It's so off the wall it could just be the key."

"Matt, the best minds in law enforcement have been on this for two, almost three weeks now."

"This is outside the box."

"So?"

"It just might be the answer."

"Even if it was, why call me?"

"What I would like is for you to get in touch with the detectives at the 19th and 20th precincts. Tell them I have new, crucial information that I think might solve the case."

"Then what?"

"Arrange a meeting with the two of them and you and me."

"For when?"

"This afternoon."

"You're kidding me."

"These guys have been knocking themselves out with no progress, nothing, zilch, day after day. Besides, the more time that goes by, the better chance this person has to cover his tracks."

"Where would this meeting take place?"

"Anywhere they say—67th Street, 82nd Street."

"Let me think about this."

"Kevin, believe me. If we can do this, I'll never ask another favor as long as I live."

"We? What's this 'we'? I'm not part of this."

"You have to be."

"Why?"

"To vouch for me, to tell them I'm not a kook. Besides, I don't want to face those two alone."

"You're asking a lot."

"Don't I know it? And if this doesn't work out, I'll be the sap of all times."

There was a pause, a long pause. Then he spoke: "All right, I'll call them, but if they say no, that's it. What time were you thinking about?"

"Whenever they say. Tomorrow if we have to."

"I'll call you back, but it may take time."

"I'm right here."

• • •

At 11:40 Monaghan called. "You've got two very upset chief detectives."

"I can imagine."

"Let's only hope this will prove worth it. We'll meet at 2:30 at the 20th precinct, on 82nd between Columbus and Amsterdam."

"I'll be there. I know you've gone out on a limb—way out—and I can't thank you enough . . ."

"Don't say it."

"I won't."

He had already hung up.

I went to my copier and began running off five copies of the report Buzz had given me. At 1:30, just as I was about to wake Buzz, I heard the shower running. Ten minutes later, he emerged.

"Get some sleep?" I asked.

"Great bed," he said. "Great shower. Hope you don't mind."

"Not at all. They've called a meeting—three detectives and me. At the 20th precinct."

"You won't dare—?"

"What?"

"Bring me into this.

"No way."

"You swear."

"Absolutely. But suppose they ask a question I can't answer?"

"You can call, but under no circumstances let them know who I am or how to reach me."

"You have my word. One thing we haven't mentioned is a price, what all this cost."

He thought a moment. "As I told you, if it was the firm, it would be $150,000 an hour."

I raised an eyebrow. "Is that what it's going to cost the NYPD?"

"This was me, not the firm. Let's say $15,000 plus $5,000 for the report."

"That's either way."

"What do you mean, 'either way'?"

"Whether or not this is our man."

"Look . . ." he began to protest.

"I'm kidding." I said, "Of course, either way." I held up a copy of the report. "Dare I ask how you did it?"

"It would take as long as it took me to do it, and, with all due respect, you wouldn't have the slightest idea what I was talking about."

"I'm sure you're right." I said. I was suddenly aware of the time. "I have to be going."

"So do I." We both headed to the door.

# CHAPTER TWENTY

I took the subway to 79th Street, walked up three blocks, and went east on 82nd almost to Columbus. Between Amsterdam and Columbus, the 20th precinct, the only non-residential building in a block filled with brownstones and small apartment houses, is on the south side: a three-story building, brick on the first floor and rough concrete on the upper two. You enter a small, brick-lined lobby lined with photographs of honored and fallen members of the NYPD. Up two steps is the small lobby of the precinct itself, with doors on two sides and walls of vertical ceramic tile in a brown, red, and black pattern, a drab attempt at color and design.

I went to the glass window and announced myself. The woman at the desk spoke into a phone; I moved to the side and waited. Shortly, a woman in uniform, with the name Tracy Gammage above her badge, entered. She had close-cropped black hair framing a square face with a long, thin nose, and she exuded a no-nonsense, don't-get-in-my-way attitude. She led me up a flight of stairs to the second floor and down a hall to a small conference room at the back. The side of the room toward the hall was all glass on the upper half. In the middle was a rectangular metal table with a dark blue Masonite top. Nondescript chairs were scattered around the table and lined against three walls.

The officer opened the door, and I entered. Inside, Kevin was sitting at a table with two other men, one in a tweed jacket, the other in a worn blue blazer. Kevin barely acknowledged me.

"Matt," he said, raising his eyes slightly.

"Kevin," I said, nodding thanks. Then he introduced me to the other two, who remained sitting at the table. One was a large, burly man—the one in the tweed coat—whose belly spilled over his belt, which was worn well below his waistline; washed-out blond hair protruded from his ears. This was Vince Markham, the detective from the 19th precinct in charge of the Met Museum investigation. The other was a small, trim, wiry man with dark hair and a pencil mustache. In charge of the Natural History investigation, his name was Barton Steinmetz. Though much smaller than Markham, it was clear that he was the authoritative, take-charge guy in the investigation. Also on hand were three people in uniform who sat around the edges. I did not dare offer to shake hands with any of these people because I was fast sensing in the room what is meant by the term "a hostile environment."

Once we were seated, Steinmetz nodded to Monaghan, and he began, explaining that I was actually a career actor, appearing, in fact, in new play that was soon opening, information that drew absolutely no reaction from Markham and Steinmetz. Monaghan went on to explain that, though an actor, I had through the years quietly but successfully assisted the NYPD in solving half a dozen important cases. The latest example was the Tremayne murder, where I had played a key role in identifying as well as locating the suspect.

Monaghan explained that he had no idea I had any thoughts about the two museum cases until I had called early that morning. Taken by surprise, on his first day off in several weeks, he had no inclination to take me seriously, but I seemed so sure of my information and so persistent that he agreed to do what he could, which is how we all happened to be together now. When he ended, Steinmetz turned to me: "So, Mr. Johanssen, share with us this scoop, this great revelation."

I ignored the sarcasm. Speaking to Steinmetz and Markham, I said that there were two points I wanted to clear up before I began. First, that the name of the person who prepared the report—should it ever be discovered by them—must never be revealed; nor should my name. When asked why I should remain anonymous, I said that I had always been known as an actor and wanted it to remain that way.

I then turned to the question of cost. I explained that the research had been done on what's known as a supercomputer, in this case, a piece of equipment so advanced in capacity and technology that there were no more than half a dozen in the United States, including in the military. The firm that owned this one and leased it out to corporations and government agencies charged $150,000 per hour. There was a visible reaction: raised eyebrows, low whistles, head shakes. I went on to say that my contact, who did freelance programming for the firm, had the use of the computer in off hours, and was prepared to provide the information to the NYPD for $15,000 for the research and $5,000 for the report—a total of $20,000.

"Whether it shows results or not?" Steinmetz asked.

I answered that, if it didn't work out, I would absorb the cost. After getting their assurance both on anonymity and cost, I turned to the information itself. From the beginning, I told them, I felt there was something peculiar about these murders, unpredictable and off the charts. The execution of the crimes was so smooth, so seamless, so sophisticated that none of the usual rules seemed to apply.

"We have a few clues," Markham said.

"I'm sure you do," I said. But I went on to point out that in both cases it looked like a crime not committed by a criminal. Like everyone else, I continued, I began to ask myself who could have done this, and why. I put aside the *why*, focused on the *who*, and came to the conclusion that, because there was such exceptional planning and execution, someone very smart and very rich was involved. Also, the goal, I thought, was not primarily to end the lives of two people, but to make a statement. I didn't know what the statement was, but there was no question that these were two extreme acts: dramatic tableaus guaranteed to gain maximum attention.

More and more I came to wonder: how could these two murders have been carried out so successfully? The answer I came up with was that it had to have been an operation undertaken by some team like Special Forces units in the military who carry out covert missions, except in this case it would have been for evil, not for good. When I made contact with this genius with a supercomputer, I gave him five coordinates to process. Two, of course, were the victims. The third was someone super-rich who could afford to pay big bucks for computer expertise, surveillance, and so forth. The fourth was a person who might have had a past relationship with Seals or Green Berets and might know disaffected ex-members of those units. I also threw in a fifth coordinate: anyone who had a connection to Lucius Beaufort's magazine *Arts View*.

I stopped speaking and handed out copies of Buzz's report to the three detectives.

"This is it?" asked Markham.

"That's it." I asked where the men's room was.

"Down the hall, last door on the right," said Steinmetz. I excused myself and left the room.

• • •

I took my time returning to the conference room—had a cup of coffee, made a couple of calls on my cell phone. When I came in, the room was divided into two camps: those who thought this was utter nonsense, and those who, though highly skeptical, thought that the staff should at least make a few preliminary inquiries. At this point the ever-efficient lady cop, Tracy, entered the conference room. Reading from a paper on a clipboard, she announced, "Here's the info you asked for on the Bigelow properties. The house in Wichita has already been given to the two daughters for tax purposes, and, as often happens, the Bigelow parents paid the daughters rent to live there. The apartment in New York has not been occupied for the last four months, though Mr. Bigelow may have spent one or two nights there during that time. Currently, Mr. and Mrs. Bigelow are at their compound in Marrakech. As for Arundel, he is out of the country in the Far

East. It is not known exactly when he will return."

The policewoman had just finished when we were interrupted by a voice from a speakerphone that had been set up in the center of the conference table. A female voice said, "Detective Steinmetz?"

"Yes?"

"The Aspen Chief of Police is on the phone. His name's Jasper Rawlinson."

"Put him on."

"Hello. Hello," Steinmetz said. "Chief Rawlinson?"

"Rolly, everyone calls me Rolly."

"Okay. Rolly?"

"Yes?"

"This is Detective Steinmetz of the 20th precinct of the NYPD in Manhattan. I'm on a speakerphone with Detective Markham of the 19th Precinct."

"What is it? What's this about?"

"Sorry to bother you on a Sunday afternoon."

"It's not the best time. I'm in a ski lodge at Snowmass. My grandson's about to begin the downhill. It's his first race."

"I'll try not to keep you, but this is important."

"Go ahead."

"We're trying to locate a man named Thomas Catlett. Do you know him?"

"Are you serious?"

"Very."

"Everybody knows Tomcat."

"Detective Markham and I wish to contact him."

"You can't."

"Why?"

"He's not here."

"Is he away? On business? A vacation?"

"He's disappeared."

"What do you mean 'disappeared'?"

"Just what I said. Vanished. Evaporated. No one has seen him since Wednesday."

Everyone in the conference room was on high alert. "But you know where he is," Steinmetz continued.

"No. That's what I'm telling you. He's gone. Poof. Tomcat has his own landing strip between Basalt and El Jebel—the longest strip in the area. He has two planes and two helicopters. The largest plane is a Boeing BBJ 3, which can fly halfway around the world. Thursday morning we got a report that there was a lot of coming and going in the early morning hours at the airstrip. I sent someone out there, and they discovered that only one helicopter remained.—everything else was gone."

Rawlinson was interrupted at his end. "What? What? No, I can't. Go ahead without me; wish Teddy good luck." He spoke to us again, "Sorry, the race is about to start."

"Would you like us to call back?"

"No, no. This sounds important."

"It is."

"Is Tomcat implicated in something?"

"He may be."

"I can't believe that."

"There's nothing certain."

"Where was I?"

"His planes had disappeared."

"Right. Later that morning we got a call saying that something was going on at his house. We went over there, and when we arrived not a soul was in sight. We walked around the outside and saw that Tom's office has been stripped bare, and all the books were gone from his library. My men wanted to break in, but I didn't want to do that. I got in touch with Emily Ballentine, a real estate friend who checks out the house when he's away. She told me that six weeks ago he had transferred ownership to his daughter and son-in-law. I asked where the daughter, Shirley, was—she's in the Caribbean with her husband. We got in touch with the sons, and they said they had no idea where their father was."

"Do you believe them?"

"Not sure. Anyway, we went back to the house with the key. All the furniture was there and the carpets, but every single piece of electronic equipment was gone: phones, faxes, computers, satellite dishes."

"Do his friends know anything?"

"They say they're as baffled as we are. Frankly, I'm worried. Tomcat is not only our number one citizen; he's our number one, two, and three citizen. We lost his wife last year; I would hate to lose him."

"I understand. Look, Rolly. I think one or both of us might come out there. I hope that's all right."

"If you can shed any light on this, by all means."

If there had been any doubt as to whether the two detectives would pursue Bigelow, Catlett, and Arundel further, it was dissipated with this report of Catlett's strange disappearance from Aspen.

• • •

I thought Catlett was probably not the guilty one. Nevertheless, the first thing I did when I got home was go online to look up the countries around the world that did not have an extradition treaty with the United States—that is, countries not required to return to this country those requested by legal or other authorities. The place Bigelow had gone, Morocco, was one of them. As for Catlett, if he had left in such a hurry and so completely, he might be headed to such a place for reasons other than being guilty. Once online, I was surprised to find more than fifty countries with no U.S. extradition agreements. Aside from places like Russia, they seemed to come in clusters: the Persian Gulf, the Far East, and several island countries such as Samoa and Cape Verde.

Very early Monday, I called the office of Trent Broadhurst, and was put through to his secretary, who told me that he had taken the red-eye back from San Francisco the night before and wouldn't be in till about 10:30. I asked her to have him call me. Trent and his wife, Libby, were from San Francisco. She had been a younger, aspiring actress training at the ACT when I was studying there. When she married Trent, she gave up acting but not her love of theatre. After finishing Stanford undergraduate and business school, Trent went into his father's travel business, which he eventually took over and expanded exponentially. His firm's specialty was the high-end trade: safaris in Africa, skiing in South America during their winter. Sometime later he moved the company's headquarters to New York, and we renewed our friendship.

Around 11:00, Trent called. "How's the show going?"

"As well as could be expected, given what happened."

"God. How awful. Did you know her well?"

"Very well."

"I know the show is supposed to go on, but traditions don't make things any easier."

"No."

"I understand the opening is day after tomorrow. Libby and I wanted to be there, but she's in San Francisco putting an aunt into assisted living. We plan to come next week."

"Let me know what night. I'll have tickets set aside for you, and we'll have a drink afterwards."

"Sounds good. What's up?"

"Just some information I was interested in. I have some good friends in Aspen, and a close friend of theirs, a man named Thomas Catlett, has suddenly disappeared, vanished without a trace, and they are desperate to find out where he is."

"What is it you want me to do?"

"They seem to believe he may have decamped for one of those exotic places, you know, that have no extradition treaties with the United States."

"Matt, with all due respect, this sounds like needle-in-the-haystack time."

"I realize that. The truth is, this person is apparently a true eccentric, and he's been talking about moving someplace outside the reach of the government."

"So, again, what am I supposed to do?"

"All those nice, warm places. Could you possibly check

with your many contacts, see if some American seems to have moved there permanently?"

"It's crazy, Matt, and if it were anyone else, I would say absolutely not. But for you I will make one quick pass at it. Okay?"

"That's all I ask."

# CHAPTER TWENTY-ONE

Monday afternoon I called Annie and Danny in Boston. This time I reached Annie. She said that Danny had passed on the message about the schedule and asked how the show was doing. I thought she was about to cry again, but she got hold of herself, and I was able to tell her how beautifully the performances were going and how proud I thought Dorothy would have been. I explained that the press would be at the show Monday and Tuesday evenings and at the Wednesday matinee; as she knew, Wednesday night would be the opening.

I explained the plans for the opening. Ever since the date was set, I had been thinking it could be an occasion to honor Dorothy in some small way. I didn't have in mind any public recognition, more of a private one. I alerted the management about my idea, asking them to set aside eight or ten pairs of good seats. I then called a number of Dorothy's old friends whom I thought might be interested in coming: the Moreheads, Charlie Winthrop, Lance Middlecoff, Alistair Hargrave, and half a dozen other couples. Two said yes right away; others called soon after. I also asked them to let me know of others who might like to come—friends I wasn't aware of.

I asked Annie how Danny was doing. "Holding up," she said. He had begun to help her with babysitting chores with her young children. "He's doing a remarkably good job," she said.

"That's terrific," I said. "He needs something to take his mind off this whole affair. I think he was looking for somewhere to turn, somewhere completely different. I would imagine taking care of small children fits the bill as well as anything I can think of."

• • •

Wednesday morning Gina and Drew had a short piece buried inside the front section of the *Times* saying that rumor had it there were perhaps two "persons of interest" in the museum murders. One was a man named Bigelow, originally from Wichita, who had an apartment in New York but also a home in Marrakech, where he seemed to be at present. The other was a man from Aspen, Thomas Catlett, who strangely had disappeared the very night the murder occurred at the Museum of Natural History. A reporter in Denver had confirmed that Catlett had vanished completely, apparently abandoning his home and other possessions. Moreover, the same reporter stated that two detectives from New York City had been in touch with the chief of police in Aspen. Another strange fact: both Bigelow and Catlett seemed to have crossed paths with the two museum victims many years ago.

• • •

As I was finishing the article, Trent called.

"I've got news," he said.

"That was quick."

"I have a computer whiz on the staff who keeps wanting to impress me with what a genius he is; I put him on it."

"And?"

"The Gulf States are no good, neither is Samoa, but something is happening in Cape Verde. Do you know anything about the place?"

"Not much."

"A group of ten islands in the Atlantic Ocean about 300 miles off the west coast of Africa, on the longitude of Puerto Rico, divided into the Windward and Leeward Islands. The largest city and capital is on one island, a deepwater port on another, and an international airfield on a third. About two months ago, a man named Sinclair showed up there. Ever heard of him?"

"No."

"He said he was representing a third party, someone who was interested in bringing his family and friends there but was also interested in investing in wind power and a desalinization plant. A Portuguese businessman with a large villa with lots of land around it got into serious money trouble and had to sell. Sinclair scooped it up. Last Thursday night, a plane of the type you described landed at the main airport. Later, a smaller jet, a top-of-the-line Gulfstream, arrived."

"Is there any confirmation that this is Catlett?"

"I spoke to a man named Felipe Jacinto, the manager of the Atlantic Grand in Cape Verde, and he says the word is that an electrician who had been at the house recently had seen a man fitting the description of Catlett. It also became clear, he said, that there was a firm understanding between Catlett and Cape Verde officials that he was not to be bothered or approached by anyone."

· · ·

After the call from Trent, I put in a call to Steinmetz. The operator put me through to Tracy Gammage, Steinmetz's aide. "He's on his way to see Markham," she said. "If you call Markham, you might be able to talk to him." I did as she suggested, and after a few moments Markham was on the phone. I told him that there seemed strong evidence that Catlett had taken up residence in Cape Verde. He said that was one of three places they had narrowed it down to, and he was glad to have one of them confirmed. I then turned to another subject. "What's happening?" I asked. "There was this piece in the *Times* this morning pointing to Catlett and Bigelow but not a word about Arundel."

"Can we completely trust you?" he asked.

"With all due respect, I'm part of this—at least unofficially. You have these three names, and I gave them to you. As far as I know, you don't have a single other suspect."

"Point taken." After a pause, Markham continued, "From the beginning we've been in close touch with the FBI; early Monday morning we called them in and told them about the information you gave us. Together we began to plot a strategy. Everyone agreed that, despite Catlett's sudden departure and the amazing coincidence of the timing, Arundel was the most likely suspect. When it was discovered that both Bigelow and Catlett were in countries without extradition treaties, our strategy began to emerge. The point is we want Arundel to think that these other two are our only suspects, especially the way Catlett left so suddenly and both men have headed for safe havens. Also, the fact that Catlett and Bigelow had known both victims, and knew the whole story about their shady behavior in the past.

"We hope Arundel will be thrown completely off the scent. Which means we have to keep their names alive with as many stories on TV and in the press as possible. We heard that both Bigelow's lawyer and Catlett's were about to call press conferences and offer proof that their clients are innocent. The FBI got in touch with both men and asked them to hold off, to let everyone think not only that they are still suspects, but that perhaps one of them is guilty. In the case of Bigelow, someone said he was ready to return to the United States, and the Bureau asked his lawyer to explain to him that we would greatly prefer it if he remained right where he is. Also, there is one place you might be able to help us. The Bureau is learning a great deal about Arundel, but they don't know the full story here in New York, particularly about the ins and outs of this patron business. If you could find out anything more about that, it would be a great help."

"It's a chancy strategy, but it might be your best hope," I said. "As for finding out about Arundel, I'll do what I can."

"Anything will help."

I had an idea of whom I should call, but it would have to

wait. I had a matinee coming up, and after that, opening night.

• • •

When I first began in the theatre, opening night was just that, a single night when everyone was present: producers, friends, celebrities, and critics. Performances on opening night began early, at 6:30 or 7, so that critics could rush away and file their reviews before their 11:30 deadline. Gradually, it all changed. Twenty years later it was entirely different. Instead of a single opening night, critics were invited to any one of the last two or three previews, and naturally they took advantage of this—it gave them more time to write their critiques. Today's opening nights, which begin at the same hour as regular performances, are largely for investors and have lost much of their luster. We had had our three press performances on Monday and Tuesday evenings and at the Wednesday matinee. Fortunately, they had gone as well as could be expected.

Despite the fact that opening nights these days are mostly ceremonial occasions for producers, backers, and friends, I hoped that our opening could be framed as a tribute to Dorothy. *The Unwitting Executor* would be her last production, her *envoi*, as it were, and on the title page of our *Playbill* were the words: "This production is dedicated to Dorothy Tremayne." That night I was happy that the people I had invited, a good two dozen, were on hand. They were going to be a good audience, no matter how they honestly felt about the play. But in the end, there was no need for a claque—the performance went beautifully. I think everyone felt that we were doing this for—well, for the playwright, of course, but most of all for Dorothy. Of course this didn't matter to the critics—they had already been there—but it did create a wonderful ambiance for all who were there, a feeling that carried through to the reception after the performance that was held for friends, CTG personnel, cast, and crew in the elegant small ballroom of a hotel half a block away.

As for the reviews, most cast members, if they did not linger at the reception, rushed home to go online to see what the morning papers were going to say. I let it be known that I preferred to wait to read the papers the next morning. I did allow one person, the stage manager, to call around 11:30 and tell me basically if the reviews were good or bad, and the word I received was encouraging. The papers and online reviews the next morning confirmed that. There were a couple of exceptions, reviewers who felt it was a bit retrograde, but fortunately those articles were in minor publications or websites. By and large, the reception was better than for any new play in the recent past. The positive piece in the *Times* mentioned the play's strong central action, the witty dialogue, and the first-rate acting. The review also pointed out that the play should have a wide appeal to the general audience, along the lines of such plays as *Proof, Doubt*, and *August: Osage County*. In today's theatre, it continued, plays with a broader reach were the exception rather than the rule, and this play should take its place alongside those.

Most of the reviewers recognized that, like so many other contemporary offerings, *The Unwitting Executor* was concerned with a dysfunctional family, but there was a difference in that ours pointed to a solution, not with some Pollyanna approach, but with a clear-eyed look at the situation. One of the devices in the play was a two-part challenge my character issued to the five family members. Each one was to write out for me, first, how they themselves would spend a $1 million inheritance should they receive it, and second, how they would allocate $1 million among the other three members of their family, excluding themselves. Would they divide it four ways, give most to one person, or what?

My character had said early on that, by the end of the play, he would render his judgment, but part of the strength of the play was that by the time that moment came, the answers were already fairly clear, not just to the audience, but to the family members themselves. If not arriving at a full understanding of themselves and others, several of them had become painfully aware of their pettiness and downright selfishness. One could assume that out of this understanding would come better individuals and family members in the future. As one reviewer put it: "In the end, the absent uncle saves the family not because of the money he leaves its members, but because he forces them to come to terms with each other, and more important, with themselves." If not the best review of a play I had been in, it was up there near the top, and that was good enough for me. I had a feeling it would have been good enough for Dorothy as well.

• • •

Mid-morning on Thursday I called Peter Chalmers. I had met Peter and his wife, Alice, at parties in Dorothy's apartment, but I really got to know them a number of years before, completely by accident. I had double-dated with an actor, Tony Dupres, and the Chalmers's daughter Cornelia. My date was an old friend, Elsa Travis, who had taken Cornelia under her wing and brought me along as protection. A smooth-as-silk operator, Dupres had a dark side; when drinking too much, which happened all too often, he could become a nasty piece of work. Cornelia was smitten with him, and he was smitten with her father's money. Sure enough, the night the four of us were together, he got drunk, became belligerent, and lashed out at Cornelia, calling her a bitch and almost striking her. I intervened, and Elsa and I took Cornelia home. That ended the relationship, and Cornelia's parents, Peter and Alice, had always given me credit that I didn't deserve.

My reason for calling Peter was that to my mind he knew more about the world of arts patrons and trustees than anyone in the city: the best route for an outsider to become an insider, how to navigate the mine fields—in short, how to play the game. Tall and trim, with a full head of gray hair that had touches of white on top and at the temples, he had a strong chin and sharp features but wore a perpetual smile that widened into a grin when he met you. I always thought of him as the handsome patrician personified.

He returned my call about thirty minutes later, congratulated me on the success of the show, and then turned immediately to Dorothy and began talking about what a loss her death had been. We chatted about the show and how sadly ironic it was that she was not around for its success. He was shocked beyond words that Warren would do such a thing, and I replied that I was certain Warren had not been himself recently. It was my understanding, I explained, that he had gone off the rails. Peter acknowledged that it had to be something like that because nothing else made sense.

"You know," he continued, "I had the funniest feeling when I heard. I thought immediately of young people just starting their careers—a soldier sent into battle, a boy or girl killed in an automobile accident or a fraternity brawl—and how an entire life was suddenly cut short. I saw Dorothy as that young person, just beginning her career in producing and having this extraordinary future spread before her."

"An exceptional image," I said. "Apt and, of course, devastating."

"But you didn't call me to talk only about Dorothy."

"No. It was really about this whole business of people who have made fortunes in finance or the commercial world who want to break into the inner circle of trustees on arts boards."

"Well, that's certainly on everyone's mind these days. These grotesque murders have brought home to all of us the ideas Sonny Beaufort has been writing about for years."

"I also wanted to ask about one or two people in particular."

"Not the ones who were killed?"

"No, others, but also the whole realm of trustees and patrons. Is there any way I could see you, have lunch maybe, and ask a few questions?"

"Are you involved in this? Plying your amateur investigator's trade? The word is you were a key player in solving Dorothy's slaying."

"Not a key player—a friend of the court."

"What about the museum affairs?"

"I'm very much on the fringes, but the detectives in charge have asked me about one thing in particular."

I could sense he had been looking at his appointment book. "It just so happens that I was supposed to play squash at noon tomorrow, but my opponent has twisted his ankle. Could you make lunch?"

"Just tell me where."

"How about the Eustace Club?"

"Excellent. What time?"

"One o'clock?"

"I'll be there."

・ ・ ・

At 6:15 on Thursday, Phyllida and I met at the Rose and Crown. She thanked me for meeting and congratulated me on the reviews.

"It's doubly bad that your friend is not here to enjoy the moment."

"Death always seems to carry a lot of collateral damage."

"When can I see it?"

"Late next week would be best. This weekend I have friends coming in town, and I'll have to be with them; early next week Dorothy's son, Danny, will be coming back from his sister's house in Boston. Then there's the detective, Monaghan, who's coming and bringing his niece who wants to be an actress."

"A busy schedule."

"I want you to come when the two of us can be together, go out to dinner afterwards, if that's all right with you."

"Sounds good to me."

"Maybe next Thursday."

"That's a long time away."

"I've been thinking."

"What?"

"Sundays I usually try to unwind, stay close to home. If you wouldn't mind a low-key date?"

"Low-key, high-key, you name it."

"If you could come down to the loft, we could have a drink and then go for lunch in the neighborhood."

"I've been wondering when I could see this place of yours."

"In the meantime, what's happening at the magazine?"

"To be truthful, they're going crazy. They don't know how to handle it, what angle to take."

"Do you know Sonny Beaufort's magazine, *Arts View*?"

"I've read articles from it, and one of our editors has been saying that this is exactly what he's been talking about for years. Maybe we should do a piece on him."

"He wouldn't like that. But his magazine and his ideas would be a good place to start. You could do something on old-line trustees: the people whose families have been around for years and whose record of support for the arts is unimpeachable. Call it something like 'The Impeccable Past.'"

"Have you ever thought of being an editor?"

"Never." I realized the time. "I have to go; they'll be calling half-hour before you know it."

I had already paid the bill, and we made our exit. On the sidewalk she said, "Good luck tonight."

"Thanks," I said.

"I'll be thinking of you," she said, and kissed me on the cheek.

# CHAPTER TWENTY-TWO

The previous Wednesday, Gina and Drew had a short piece inside the *Times* saying that the second person being sought for questioning was thought to be Marshall Bigelow. Since that time, the papers and TV had pretty much assumed that this was the case. On Friday morning Gina and Drew had a longer piece about Bigelow and Catlett that included one fascinating bit of information about Bigelow that had not been reported previously—namely, that despite his reputation for caution and formality, he was an avid instigator of practical jokes, known in Wichita for the intricacies and expense of such escapades. He would think nothing, for example, of planning a golf match in which he and his opponent could choose any partner of his liking, and then, at a propitious moment, Bigelow would produce Phil Mickelson as his partner. At various times he had engaged such people as George Clooney or Julia Roberts. The victim of Bigelow's most elaborate hoax was Reginald Shawcross. The latter had attended Oxford for one semester and never gotten over it, becoming the ultimate Anglophile, with a pseudo-English accent and a vintage Rolls–Royce. His suits came from Savile Row, his shirts from

Turnbull & Asser, and his shoes from John Lobb. In Wichita the town was divided between those who were highly amused and those who thought the man was insufferable.

One day Shawcross received an engraved card announcing that he had been awarded a Knight–Errant medal by the Crown for his many contributions to the English tradition. A cover letter stated that it was hoped a ceremony could be arranged in Wichita at which a representative of the Crown could bestow a medallion upon him. Reginald wasted no time in setting up the ceremony, renting a small ballroom in the grandest hotel in the city, sending out invitations to the crème de la crème of Wichita, and brushing off the outfit he had once worn at Ascot. When the day came, an impressive gentleman with an impeccable English accent arrived and conducted a formal ceremony that ended with Shawcross kneeling before him while an impressive medallion on an embroidered strap was placed around his neck. A reception followed.

While Reginald was still basking in the glow of the event, it was discovered that his medallion was not the lion and unicorn of the United Kingdom, but the coat of arms of a pub called the Crown, located in Hammersmith. The man who had presented it was a hired actor, and the award had nothing whatever to do with the queen or Buckingham Palace. Chagrined beyond belief, Shawcross quickly departed Wichita, not for London, but for an extended visit to Australia. Though he denied it to the end, those close to Bigelow knew full well that the entire escapade was planned and paid for by him.

Fortunately, the plan of law enforcement and the FBI was given a further boost when other media types picked up on this last bit about practical jokes and hinted that the kind of person who could plan something like this might, perhaps, plan even more elaborate events. Who knew? Maybe even something like the museum episodes.

• • •

Just before 1:00 on Friday, I showed up at the Eustace Club to meet Peter Chalmers. The Eustace, in the low 60s near Madison, is a small, discreet club, like the Brook or the Links, that is also ultraexclusive. It's a double brownstone with no sign on the door: you tap a large brass doorknocker and are admitted by a man in uniform who takes you to your host. In this case I was led down a hallway to the small, tasteful dining room in the rear, where Peter was already seated at a corner table. After we exchanged greetings and ordered our meal, Peter began.

"Many financial arrivistes and parvenus view membership on an arts board as a trophy, like playing golf at Augusta or St. Andrews. They see no reason why, if enough people speak up for them and they contribute enough money, they shouldn't be invited to join any board they choose. Of course, the smarter ones realize that there is a right way to go about this and a wrong way. The clever ones are subtle and employ a good deal of finesse, hoping to convey the impression that joining a board is the last thing on their minds and that their sole motive is to serve. It doesn't hurt either, to have the right kind of wife."

"Like Mulholland's Roxanne?"

"Exactly. At least, I've heard that she fit the bill quite well. But for every person who knows exactly how to play the game, there must be dozens who don't. The worst of these appear to be totally tone deaf. They feel that if enough pressure is applied and they throw sufficient money around, they can hardly be denied. When they don't make the grade, they usually react in one of two ways: either they sulk and eventually slink off, or they cause a ruckus and even make threats, not realizing that they are digging themselves into an even deeper hole.

"What is more disturbing about this—and I think those of us in the arts governance have come to focus on it even more after these very public and horrific murders—is that in all the maneuvering and machinations, values and substance have been totally lost. It should not be enough for a would-be patron to contribute a huge sum of money; he or she should know something about the art form and should care deeply about it. As you know, I've been on the Philharmonic board for some time now, but my interest didn't suddenly appear out of the blue. My mother took me to the Friday morning rehearsals of the Philharmonic when I was still in short pants. My parents took me every year to Carnegie Hall to hear the Boston and Philadelphia orchestras; WQXR was playing in our house all day long.

"To my mind, this is where these two sets of murders, Dorothy's and these obscene trustee deaths, intersect. Of course, it's wretched that they ever occurred, let alone at the same time, but in an odd way the juxtaposition points up how much her world was the polar opposite from that of the two men. It underlines the contrast: pure versus impure, true versus false, with Dorothy being the pure and true."

There was a long pause. I realized I had long since stopped eating my lunch, and Peter pretty much had done the same. We each took a few bites. I looked up and said, "Peter, I hope you won't think I'm being some sort of flatterer, but I've never heard a more eloquent expression of what is at stake."

"It's something one takes for granted."

"I do have to ask, however, about a specific situation."

"Are you putting on your sleuth's hat?"

"You might say that."

"So?"

"One person I know, whose name has come up." I paused. "Peter, it goes without saying that what I am about to ask is totally confidential."

"I never thought it would be otherwise."

"Victor Arundel. I've been told he tried to break into the inner circle two or three years ago."

"Arundel?"

"Fairly aggressive, from what I hear."

He thought for a moment. "Oh, yes. I never really knew him. I may have been introduced at a gala or a season opening affair, but our paths didn't cross as far as I can recall. What I do remember is that Binky Butterfield took an instant dislike to him."

"Binky—?"

"A man who takes both his lineage and himself very seriously. Now that I think about it, I do recall the situation. Extremely pugnacious by all accounts. Ah, yes. Now it comes back. That's what it was. He's the one, I believe, who started with the City Opera but decided that was not good enough, so he set his sights on the Metropolitan Opera. He read somewhere that they needed $35 million, something about the chandeliers or the Grand Tier restaurant, so he got in touch with them and, without even being asked, gave them $35 mil outright. When, a few months later, nothing materialized in the way of an invitation to join the board, he went on the offensive. Alarmed, several of the old-line trustees got together and pooled resources to return his money. Meantime, they learned that Oswald Janovic at Goodman Sanders was his chief banker and got in touch with him."

"Goodman Sanders?"

"A firm almost the same size as Goldman Sachs but one that does things much more quietly. Anyway, Oswald cautioned Arundel that he had better back off or there would be hell to pay, and the whole thing ended."

"Did everyone know about this? I never heard a word."

"You should know by now, Matt, that the Old Guard never leaves a trace: no footprints in the snow, no marks in the sand. I do remember one thing, though. When the crisis was at its height, Binky said to anyone who would listen, 'I told you so, I told you so.'"

"Do you think I might meet this fellow, Binky?"

"You have to prepare yourself for a trip back in time."

"Might be interesting."

"He can certainly give you all the particulars on Arundel."

"Could I call him?"

"It won't hurt. Tell him I suggested it."

"Can you give me his phone number, or his email?"

"I'm afraid Binky hasn't quite caught up with email, but here is his number."

Peter took out one of his cards, wrote a number on the

back, and handed it to me. The waiter came to take our plates. We both declined dessert, and, after profuse thanks on my part, I departed.

• • •

Friday was the day that indictments were handed down in the Tremayne case. Warren was charged with first-degree murder, Mikey with being an accessory to murder, and Stuart with aiding in the escape of someone charged with murder. The next day, Saturday, I talked with Annie in Boston, telling her once again how sorry I was. When I asked to speak to Danny, she said he was out with the children. She also told me that he would be returning to New York on Monday morning. She would miss him, she said, because he had proved to be a wonderful babysitter for her children, who had become tremendously fond of him. More than that, she said the two of them had spent more time together than at any time since they were much younger. "Look out for him, will you?" she asked me.

"I will. I want him to see the show; also, I want him to meet a couple of people who I think could be helpful to him."

"Thanks, Matt. Keep me posted."

• • •

On Sunday Phyllida paid her first visit to the loft. I went downstairs to meet her because I didn't want her to have to navigate my clanging elevator on her own. She arrived shortly after I did, wearing tan slacks, a gray pullover, and a checked jacket of brown and blue. It was casual but on her looked pretty smashing. We went up, and I opened the rattling gate. She hadn't known what to expect, but, as people usually were, she was surprised by the wide open space. She'd seen a number of lofts before, she said, but coming from her vertical brownstone, she had forgotten how expansive they are.

I asked what she wanted to drink. I told her we were heading for an Italian place, Como Lario; she said in that case, she would have a glass of Pinot Grigio. I poured the same for myself, and we sat down in the living area.

"Anything new?" she asked.

"On what front?"

"Any front."

"The play's going well; we had a great night last night."

"I can't wait to see it."

"I can't wait to have you see it."

"Meantime, what about Dorothy's husband?"

"You may have heard, he was indicted on Friday for first-degree murder."

"Why do I have this feeling you had something to do with solving that?"

"I was able to help; after all, I knew Warren before I knew Dorothy."

"But you won't tell me how much you helped. And what about this other business: these bizarre museum affairs? Is it possible that you are also working on those?"

"I'm leaving that to the NYPD."

"I'll bet."

"Obviously, I read the papers and talk to a few people."

"People like the police."

"Not directly."

"Don't be coy. Admit it: you've been involved."

"Only around the edges."

"Some edges. More like in the middle of things, I would guess."

"Can we do this again next week?"

"Do what?"

"Be together, have lunch."

"Are you asking me?"

"Yes."

"I should make a show of looking at my iPhone, but—yes, the answer is yes."

"Maybe then I can tell you more."

"God, I hope so."

I indicated it was time to go. When we got to the elevator, I reached to open the gate.

"Aren't you forgetting something?"

I turned; there was no doubt what she was talking about. I took her in my arms and kissed her, not a casual kiss, a prolonged one. I touched her breast. She crushed my hand against her as she embraced me. We kissed again.

We both knew what was happening. We were at one of those moments when you have a clear choice: one direction or another. I'm certain the strongest impulse for both of us was to head straight to the bedroom. But we also knew that we wanted this thing between us to be right. We looked at each other and kissed again.

She spoke: "You think we should go to lunch."

"If I were on automatic pilot, the answer would be an emphatic no, but . . ."

"You think we have time."

"Don't you?"

"Not much time."

"Agreed. But a little."

"Very little."

• • •

At lunch, I learned more about her. We had been so much in the here and now—the murders, my opening, her magazine piece—that we had talked very little about the past. Her mother, I learned, had been a student at Oxford and met her father when he came over as a Rhodes Scholar. Back in the United States, her father became a well-known English literature scholar and teacher, specializing in the nineteenth-century novelists: Dickens, Trollope, Thackeray. Teaching first at Williams and then at Dartmouth, he got a double appointment at Radcliffe and Harvard, where he remained until his retirement two years ago.

Her mother, meanwhile, developed a very successful career as the author of children's books. She had created a ten-year-old heroine, Little Lotti, who survived a series of exciting but daunting childhood adventures through twenty-three volumes. Along the way Disney had made three animated films built around Little Lotti's derring-do.

Phyllida, who I discovered was fluent in French and Italian, also spoke passable German, Russian, and Mandarin Chinese.

She had travelled all over the place, writing travel and food pieces. But her strong suit was interviewing and profiling. Someone who knew her explained that she seemed to have a unique ability to get people to talk about themselves. A collection of her articles about interesting and unusual people had come out three years previously under the title *Who's Inside?* I admitted to her that, though I knew it had been on the best-seller list for eight weeks, I had not read it.

"Too busy solving mysteries, I imagine."

"Too busy reading scripts and memorizing lines."

I asked what was happening on their coverage of the patron murders and Dorothy. She said it had been decided that the museum material would be a long piece on its own, but she had persuaded them to have a one-page remembrance of Dorothy, based on something she had written contrasting Dorothy as an active participant with those so-called patrons whose contribution was almost exclusively monetary. The article would take up the whole page, have a nice border around it, and include a good photo of Dorothy, as well as a small photo with two cast members, one of whom would be me.

"Does this mean I will have my picture in *Vanity Fair*?"

"Your face will be the size of a dime."

# CHAPTER TWENTY-THREE

In the Monday morning *Times* was just the kind of article Markham and Steinmetz hoped would keep coming, continuing the interest in Catlett and Bigelow. Over the weekend, Gina and Drew had gone to Aspen and met with several of Catlett's oldest friends. The article was a report on their visit.

### A FOND FAREWELL

The tables at the Cloud Café in Aspen, Colorado, are covered with blue-and-green checked tablecloths, blue for the sky and green for the verdant foliage on the mountains nearby. Suspended six inches below the pressed tin ceiling is an assortment of old wooden skis and ski poles. The walls feature oversized photographs of the mountains, some snow-covered, others in full summer splendor. Running the length of the bar along the floor is a brass foot rail, and across the room, opposite the bar, is an alcove with an oblong table that can seat eight people..

At the table every Thursday, a group of men gather for lunch and conversation, which sometimes goes until mid-afternoon. Calling themselves the Cloud Club, they have been doing this for years. Sometimes, if the Denver Broncos have played an important game the day before, they meet on

Mondays as well. Thomas Sterling Catlett, known as Tomcat, has been a faithful member for many years, as have been Stan Worthington, Will Cranbrook, Norton Jamison, and Addison Sturdivant. These last four agreed to meet at the Cloud Café on a recent morning after the breakfast crowd thinned out to talk about their colleague Catlett. First off, all four said they were stunned and taken completely by surprise when they learned their friend had disappeared.

"It was our regular Thursday," said Sturdivant. "We were here, six of us, and when he didn't come we called the house but got no answer. After lunch two of us went out and saw that it was deserted, so we called Rolly, the police chief, and that's when we found out about the missing airplanes and the rest."

Patti McDonald, the waitress who regularly serves the Cloud Club, brought coffee and muffins and disappeared. We asked about Catlett. Two men answered immediately.

"Smartest man I've ever known."

"And the most unusual."

"In what way?"

"How much time do you have?"

"All day."

Worthington began, "You know, of course, that, except for Warren Buffett and a few others, he's the most successful businessman in the Midwest and the mountain states."

"What he was best known for, though, was his fairness, his business ethics."

"He lived and breathed those."

"Do you know why he left?"

The four men looked at each other. Cranbrook spoke: "We've talked about that a great deal, and we have a theory."

"Oh?"

"More about that later," said Sturdivant.

Cranbrook picked up the story. "At these lunches we talked about everything: Broncos football, Nuggets basketball, skiing, the weather, the Aspen Institute, concerts at the opera house."

"A part of all this were the trips."

"Trips?"

"He had this plane."

"We've heard."

"Several times a year during the football season, he flies a group of us to Denver to see the Broncos play."

"Before Alicia died, in the fall and the spring, they would fly twenty or so couples to Denver to hear the Colorado Symphony."

"Also art tours and theatre tours—you name it."

"Speaking of those tours, we should say a word about Alicia."

"His late wife? She died last year, we understand."

"An amazing person, just as amazing as Tomcat."

The other three nodded in agreement. Jamison continued. "Deeply involved in the Aspen Institute, the heart and soul of the Aspen Arts Festival."

"Smart as a whip, energetic, a terrific organizer."

"The outpouring at the funeral you wouldn't believe."

"Her loss affected Catlett, I'm sure."

"The whole town, but obviously him most of all. He put on a brave face, but you could tell."

"Never the same after that; we used to talk about it."

"Back to your theory of why he might have left."

After a pause, Sturdivant continued: "You have to understand that this ethics business was not something Tomcat carried on about, no soapbox oratory or harping on the subject."

"But he did come back to it again and again; it was a thread running through his thinking."

"Which was?"

"You've probably heard how he would come out at times with one word or phrase?"

"Yes."

"He had several of them: responsibility, caring and sharing, Gibbon."

"The Decline and Fall of the Roman Empire?"

"That's the one."

"He was talking about America?"

"Absolutely."

"The way he put it, we were in our own decline and fall.

The country had lost its moral compass and was in danger of losing its soul."

"His words?"

"No question."

"He said it was something insidious, invisible, that people couldn't see."

"The high point for the country, he kept saying, the great period, was the middle of the last century: the Second World War, the Marshall Plan, the GI Bill, which educated an entire generation. A perfect example of what he called 'caring and sharing.'"

"After that, without realizing it, the country began to lose its way. In his eyes, by the beginning of this century the decline was in full swing. The Iraq War with its inequities and indecencies: a war with no draft, no increase in taxes, everything off the books in the national budget. Pretending torture wasn't torture. Who was fooling whom?"

"Then the Great Recession. As he used to say, 'Millions of homes lost and lives ruined and not a single banker, mortgage broker, or stock manipulator apologizes, let alone goes to jail.'"

"More and more, the blatant denial of obvious facts: evolution, climate change, one scientific discovery after another."

"Everything's related to education, which we've downgraded to the point where we're falling behind the entire civilized world."

"It all came down to a favorite phrase of his."

"Which was?"

Two people answered at once: "Noblesse oblige."

"Those who are fortunate should share with those who are not."

"Did he think no one believed in that or practiced it?"

"Except for a few, like Buffet and Bill Gates, he would say, the entire financial and corporate elite of the country, and most of those with inherited wealth, either don't know what it is or, if they do, choose not to do anything about it. Leading the bandwagon for all of them are self-righteous, extremist politicians."

"Does this have something to do with why he left?"

The four looked at each other. Worthington spoke: "You know these people with strong feelings, the ones who say, 'If so-and-so happens, I'm leaving the country'?"

"They never do. But you think Catlett may have?"

"He wanted to make a statement, the strongest possible statement," said Jamison.

"As far as he was concerned, the 'if so-and-so happens' had already happened," added Sturdivant.

"You have to admit, this is a pretty extreme 'statement.'"

"He believed in deeds, not words. If anyone was going to take action, it was Tomcat," agreed Cranbrook.

"Obviously, he had given it a lot of thought," said Worthington.

"Been planning it for months," Cranbrook said.

"Carefully, deliberately, as he did everything," said Jamison.

"You actually think he would go this far, give up everything he has here in the United States, in Aspen, and actually do this, to let the rest of us know how he felt?"

They looked at each other, nodded, and almost as one, replied, "We do."

For several days I had been thinking about Danny's return. Once I learned that he would come to the show Monday night, I got in touch with Marshall and Leah Andrews. They were one of the couples, great friends of Dorothy's, who hadn't been able to come on opening night. I told them about Danny's return and asked if they could come the same night. If they could, I said, the four of us could have dinner at Carafini beforehand, and I would have Danny sit with them at the show. Afterwards, they could come backstage, and I would take over from there.

In the meantime, ever since Dorothy's death I had been

talking to Pierre St. Claire, the costume designer of our production. Pierre was gay, but not flamboyantly so, and he was a topflight designer whose work I had observed firsthand on the dozen or so shows we had done together through the years. In his late forties, he had a longtime partner, a very successful accountant. Pierre and I had for some time lamented Danny's involvement with Mikey, and I hoped that, when Danny returned, Pierre and his partner might be able to steer him in the right direction in the gay community.

My plan for that night was that, when the show ended and Danny had been welcomed backstage by the cast and crew, the four of us—Pierre and his partner, Danny, and I—would go out for a drink. After a short time, pleading fatigue, I would withdraw, leaving the three of them together. Happily, the plans worked out, both with the Andrewses during the show and later with Pierre and his partner. Backstage, though looking drawn and initially acting a bit tentative, Danny gradually began to warm to the welcome he received, and later, I'm pleased to say, returned to the theatre almost every night that week.

At 10:30 sharp on Tuesday morning, I appeared at the door of Binky Butterfield's apartment. I had called him on Friday only to find out he had already left for the weekend. On Monday, I called again, and when I reached him he indicated he could see me today.

His apartment was located in a building on Fifth Avenue just south of the Frick Museum, where the apartment's living room, dining room, library, and master bedroom all overlooked Central Park. I was admitted by a properly dressed manservant and shown into the living room, where I found heavy, brocaded drapes at every window, a baby grand piano with thirty or more family photographs in silver frames on top, and paintings by Childe Hassam and Winslow Homer on the walls, as well as a three-quarter length portrait by John Singer Sargent. I felt as if Edith Wharton might enter the room at any moment. I was staring at the portrait when a man entered. "My grandmother," he said.

"Stunning." I said, "Sargent at his very best, and what a lovely lady."

"She had a lot of style, especially for her day," he said. He stuck out his hand. "Binky Butterfield."

I shook hands: "Matt Johanssen."

"Peter said we should meet."

"I greatly appreciate your seeing me." Looking around, I added, "Beautiful apartment."

"Every so often a feeling sweeps over me that I should modernize, but ultimately, I resist the urge and keep it as it has always been."

"Apartments like this are becoming rarer and rarer. It's a treat to see it."

"I promised you elevenses, and I'm keeping my promise. Let's go into the breakfast room; it's a good place to talk." He indicated a door to one side. We passed through the dining room, with silver pitchers and trays everywhere, into a small, sunny room that was much more modern. With yellow-and-white striped wallpaper and sheer, light drapes at the windows, it was indeed a contrast to the rest of the house.

"Tea or coffee?" he asked.

"Tea would be wonderful. Nothing with it."

"And you must try the small croissants. No one makes them like Eloise."

There they were, with marmalade and jams alongside. Eloise, I assumed, must be the full-time cook. I took one, buttered it, added a bit of marmalade, and tasted it. "Ah. As good as any I can remember. Even in Paris."

"She will be pleased to hear it."

In addition to the breakfast table and chairs, there were two easy chairs, not overlarge, and a coffee table. He sat in one of the chairs and indicated I should take the other. Binky had on light gray slacks, a blazer, and a blue-checked shirt with a dark blue ascot at the throat. His footwear, I noticed, was a pair of embroidered Stubbs & Wootten slippers. The man himself was around six feet tall, with silver-gray hair, a ruddy complexion, a somewhat hooked nose, and large ears.

"It's about the museum murders, isn't it?"

"Yes."

"About the worst thing I can ever remember. Horrid."

"I agree."

"The only saving virtue would be if we clean things up a bit. Pay more attention to people like Sonny Beaumont. But you should ask me what you want to know."

"I know I can take this for granted, but I must say up front that this has to be absolutely, totally confidential."

"It goes without saying."

"I don't mind telling you that, from what I understand, matters are at a very delicate point just now, so any of us who discuss it cannot talk even to our closest friends and confidants."

"Understood."

265

"The person I have been asked to inquire about is Victor Arundel."

"Don't get me started."

"Peter said you had strong feelings about him. But I need to know the story of his assault on culture here in New York. When it started, how it unfolded, who the players were."

"First of all, you know he is one of these private equity guys."

"Yes."

"But the worst kind: cut every corner, slash and burn, annihilate, cheat right and left."

"That seems to be the consensus."

"As for the scene here, he had long had an apartment on the Upper East Side, but showed no interest in the cultural scene. Then, about three years ago, he met Anita Gomez, an American lady who had married a very wealthy Mexican. After the husband died, she moved to Santa Fe and became quite well known there. Arundel thought she was dynamite, and she is: lively, amusing, has a striking figure. He fell for her completely; in his eyes she had everything. In addition to the attributes I've mentioned, there was all that money. She, however, had her own agenda. She had been very active in the summer opera in Santa Fe, and from what I hear they do a very good job there. Anyway, she was on the opera board, very active, in the thick of things. He wanted desperately to marry her; more than just a trophy, for him she was a real treasure. But she had her own terms: she wanted to spread her wings, become part of the opera scene here.

"Her deal was that either he or she would join the board

of the Metropolitan Opera, and only then would she marry him. Short of that, it was no go. So Arundel, in his own 'bull in a china shop' manner, set out to accomplish that. The only thing is, he had no feel for it, none whatsoever. She might well have achieved her goal with a different partner, but with him it was hopeless from the start. In any case, he launched his campaign, a full frontal assault: hired a publicist, a public relations expert, called in every financial chit he could. He remembered Mulholland and Weatherby from the old days and got in touch with them, asked them to help, get their wives to help. They were polite but distant. After all, they had their own flanks to protect. As for the wives of those other two, not surprisingly, that was a dead end. Roxanne was as cool as Anita was hot, and Sheryl Weatherby wouldn't have been up to it even if she wanted to be. After six months or so, it was obvious to Anita that it was going nowhere. Desperate, Arundel read about the Met needing money."

"The $35 million? Peter mentioned that."

"It was more like $40 million, but never mind. He had it transferred to the Met's account. Send in the money, willy-nilly: that was Arundel's Hail Mary pass—the thing that would save the day. As far as the Met was concerned, he was not only out of his mind, he was completely out of his depth. Besides, he did this without ever telling Anita. The minute she heard, she knew it was a mistake, however well meant. You know the rest. His money was returned, and in effect he was told to get lost. Anita decamped, professing family problems with one of her daughters, and he left soon after. I thought maybe he'd gone with his tail between his legs, but I should have known better. To a man like him, this was a defeat, an indignity not to be taken lying down. If he has gone to extreme lengths to get revenge on the men he thought he could blame and on the entire arts establishment, I wouldn't be a bit surprised."

It had been quite a story. Binky obviously knew all the ins and outs, the kind of thing I felt he would make it his business to know in the smallest detail. I thanked him profusely, explained that he could see why confidentiality was so important, and expressed in the strongest terms I could, without seeming to fawn, how much I had enjoyed meeting him and being able to see his lovely home.

• • •

When I got back to the loft, I immediately called both Markham and Steinmetz. I didn't reach either one, but their assistants told me they would get back to me soon. When someone did call, it was to arrange a conference call for 3:30 p.m. When I called that afternoon, they told me that the man heading the FBI investigation, Aaron Mansfield, was joining us in the conference call, if that was all right. I said of course, and, after Mansfield and I exchanged hellos, I told them the whole story. They obviously appreciated the details that Binky had provided.

"There it is," said Mansfield when I had concluded.

"What?"

"The motive. We had an idea it might be something along these lines, but we couldn't fill in the details, the missing pieces. Now this man has. The big trick from now on will be to tidy up a few loose ends."

"More than a few," Steinmetz added.

"Yes, along with everything else, the man has to return to the States. It's supposed to be Friday, but, with him, there's no knowing," said Mansfield. "In any case, thanks, Johanssen— this information will make a real difference."

"No one would be happier than I if it did," I replied.

# CHAPTER TWENTY-FOUR

Later that day, Tuesday afternoon, I began to think about Phyllida. I had seen her on Sunday and she was coming to the show on Thursday, but that would be four days and at this point, considering my growing feeling for her, that seemed too long. So I emailed her and left a message on her cell asking if she could possibly squeeze in a brief dinner tonight, some time between 5:30 and 7:00. She called later and said it wouldn't be easy, there was a full-court press at the magazine. I told her there was a Pret A Manger near her office; we could get a pick-up meal there and I would at least have a few moments with her. She said she would call me back shortly, and she did, saying OK, but it would have to be on the run.

I met her in the lobby of her office, rushed her off to Pret A Manger and had the satisfaction of being with her, if only for a short time. We both ordered quickly, and I asked her how things were going at *Vanity Fair*. She said they finally had the story on the patron affair nailed down. They were going with an idea similar to my original idea—"the impeccable past"—focusing on women trustees who had the right pedigree and experience, writing profiles of one or two from each of the major museums or performing arts groups and, of course, taking elegant photos of each one wearing designer clothes. There was also going to be a second, smaller piece, about generations: women who were second- and third-generation board members, carrying on a family tradition. The publication of my friend Sonny Beaufort, she said, had been invaluable. The newest issue was coming out soon, and one of the editors had obtained an advance copy.

She asked how the show was going. I told her briefly about Danny having been there the night before, and the plan I had arranged. Monaghan, with his wife and niece, were coming tomorrow night, and Dorothy's daughter, Annie, and her husband on Saturday. "And who's coming on Thursday?" she asked.

"The best of all, you, if you can still make it." She said it wouldn't be easy, but she had told the magazine about this commitment over a week ago; besides, she was working overtime to get her part of the story completed, so she felt sure she could make it. At this point I had to rush her back to her office, and had no time to waste getting to the theatre.

• • •

Wednesday morning, the first issue of Sonny Beaufort's magazine *Arts View* since the two museum murders came out. There was a tribute to Dorothy on a full-framed page that included an attractive picture of her with the playwright and the director at an early rehearsal of *The Unwitting Executor*. Someone else, a man named Reginald Simon, wrote an article about arts subsidies that repeated the oft-cited fact that, unlike the United States, in Europe and elsewhere governments make large annual contributions to arts institutions. The National Theatre in London and the Comédie-Français in Paris, for example, each receive upwards of $30 million a year.

Another article provided an in-depth profile of board members of the seven most prestigious art and cultural institutions in New York. There were breakdowns in several categories: How many on a given board were longtime New Yorkers, and how many were recent arrivals? Where had the fortunes of trustees come from: was it inherited wealth or new wealth? How many were men, and how many women? What was the age breakdown? How many had had any real exposure to the discipline of their museum or performing arts group, and how many had not? The results were offered in a series of charts, one for each of the seven institutions. Needless to say, the results were quite eye-opening.

In addition to the signed articles, incoming emails, text messages, letters, and phone calls to the magazine were so voluminous that Sonny devoted eight entire pages to reprinting differing views and observations on the issues raised by the two museum murders. Needless to say, they ranged all over the place. Some advocated that arts organizations take money from wherever it was offered. If it was tainted, or the source was suspect, take it anyway: the arts needed all the help they could get. Others were more on the purist's side: arts organizations should not take any questionable donations, even if they had to curtail their activities. And there were a certain number of comments about the responsibilities of trustees, the dumbing down of the arts, and the pernicious influence of cell phones.

Sonny himself wrote a thoughtful editorial focusing on boards and the naming of buildings. His position was that institutions should be extremely wary of naming any large bit of real estate for an individual who was not strongly identified with the arts as well as being above reproach in his or her business and private life. A theatre or a major wing in a museum are there, presumably, forever, and though it is tempting to jump at a huge offer of money, ethically, it may come at much too high a price.

• • •

That Wednesday evening Monaghan came to the show with his wife, Florence, and niece, Yvette. After the performance, they came backstage, and I got the impression that both Kevin and his wife were much more caught up in the evening than they had expected to be. Yvette, the aspiring actress, was clearly thrilled to be in the presence of real actors, especially ones she had just seen on stage. After I changed, I took the three of them to Joe Allen's for a drink. I knew I was expected to impart some advice if not wisdom to Yvette. She was young, of course, and, if not glamorous, she was attractive and had considerable poise for her age. It turned out that she was a sophomore at Hunter College.

My advice to her was to stay where she was and finish college, not go chasing after Juilliard or Yale, where the odds were against anyone who was not somehow noticeably different. If she wanted to get theatre training in the meantime, she should seek out a good summer program. I did tell her, however, that on the basis of meeting and talking to her, she might have a chance to succeed, depending, of course, on both her talent and her willingness to work extremely hard. It was the kind of encouragement I had given to many aspiring young people, and I felt it was vague enough not to be disingenuous.

• • •

The next day, Thursday, I had lunch with Monaghan. We had planned this a few days before, chiefly so I could get his take on what was likely to unfold in the Tremayne case. Before we got to that, however, he thanked me for the previous evening. "My wife and I enjoyed seeing the show much more than we thought we would."

"I'm glad to hear you were pleasantly surprised."

"And I especially want to thank you for being so kind to my niece."

"She looks like she has better prospects than most young ladies I meet. Mind you, she's chosen a tough path, trying to make a go of it in the theatre, especially as an actress."

"We know that, and her parents do, too, but at this point there's no dissuading her."

"I can't tell you how many times I've heard that. But— about Warren—what do you think is going to happen?"

"I can't say with certainty, but my best guess is that the charge against Warren will be reduced from first-degree to second-degree murder on the basis that his deadly assault on his ex–wife was not premeditated or carried out with malice aforethought. Even so, he would be charged with murder and almost certainly convicted. There's too much evidence against him

—the upside-down prints on the wine bottle and Mikey's eyewitness testimony, for starters. He'll spend much of the rest of his life behind bars. They may work something out so that he goes to one of those white-collar prisons, but it will be incarceration none the less.

"As for Mikey, he will no doubt spend time locked away. Just how much depends on his silver-haired lawyer and the fact that he is a cooperating witness against Warren—the chief witness, in fact. The young man, Stuart, is a different story entirely. He had nothing to do with the murder, and if his story of total ignorance is believed, he may possibly get a short time away, and possibly even a suspended sentence."

• • •

Thursday was the night Phyllida was coming to the show for the first time. If I said I wasn't nervous, I would be lying. I realized I cared very much how she reacted to the play, but even more to my performance. I tried to pretend it was just another night, but it wasn't. It's odd, no matter how many years you have been doing this, there still come particular nights when the old nerves from the past kick in.

It turned out I need not have worried. After the performance, she came back to the dressing room. "It's my kind of theatre," she said. "I was around during the days when there was lots of avant-garde stuff, confrontation with audience members—that sort of thing. Never my cup of tea. I'm not against cutting-edge art, but sometimes, especially in theatre, it's pretentious as hell."

"Ours is a traditional piece," I said.

"And a marvelous example," she replied. "I was beginning to think this kind of theatre was going to disappear from the face of the earth."

"It almost has." I continued to change clothes, getting out of my costume and putting on a jacket and tie for dinner.

"Not quite. Your friends, and Dorothy's friends, must love it."

"Fortunately, they do."

We headed for the restaurant. I had asked her to pick the place, and she had chosen a seafood restaurant on the East Side: Le Voyage. The décor, not surprisingly, had a nautical theme: portholes around the walls, large photographs of sailboats skimming across blue seas—altogether, an appealing and inviting atmosphere. This being a seafood restaurant, after we ordered a bottle of white wine, Phyllida chose branzino for her main course and I ordered sea bass. She had lots of questions about the production: How old was the playwright? What else had he written? Were there problems during rehearsals? Did we make changes? She told me her favorites among the actors, which ones were engaging for the audience, which ones seemed less authentic. Not surprisingly, she asked about my role. How did I feel about this character who was both real and unreal? Was that hard to play?

After I answered as well as I could, I told her it was my turn. How were things coming at the magazine? "We're all under the gun," she said, "as you might imagine. But if we keep at it, we can make our deadline of midnight tomorrow."

Unfortunately, she said, that meant she could not linger

tonight. She still had work to do on her part of the coverage to lock things in. And so, after lingering till past midnight, we hailed a taxi, and I took her to her house in Murray Hill. On the way she explained that the house was left to her by an uncle, the brother of her mother, who had no children and always said she was his favorite among his nieces and nephews. She lived on the first two floors and rented out the top two. At the house I asked the taxi to wait and took her to the door.

"I'm sorry I had to make an early night of it."

"Midnight is not exactly early," I said.

"Still."

"Sunday is only three days away," I said. "We can relax and be together all day if we want."

"Scout's honor?"

I didn't answer but kissed her—twice. The taxi driver honked. I touched her cheek and left.

• • •

On Friday night, after I returned from the theatre, among my emails was one from Tracy Gammage, Steinmetz's assistant, telling me that I should check the news on television first thing Saturday morning, which I did. There, on every channel, I saw news anchors excitedly proclaiming that the suspected mastermind in the so-called patron murders had been arrested. Sometime after midnight, they said, the FBI had carried out multiple arrests in a number of places in the eastern United States. Three computer geeks were arrested in Minneapolis, and half a dozen men in places like Little Rock, Amarillo, and Wheeling had been taken into custody, as well as a man in New York, Francis Kopec, a self-appointed know-it-all who posted gossipy blogs on music and art. The center of all this, however, was a man named Victor Arundel, who was arrested at his home on his eighty-acre estate near the Virginia–West Virginia border. Arundel, a volatile private equity giant, was alleged to be the person who conceived, planned, and ordered the two sensational murders. More details would be given later when more information was available.

• • •

In the days and weeks following the arrests, it was revealed how the enterprise had unfolded. Arundel, who himself had hoped to snag a trusteeship on a prestigious arts board, had become insanely jealous of the two victims, knowing that each one had corporate skeletons in his closet. A man known to have a volcanic temper, he set about planning his revenge. He already had in place many of the tools with which to do this. The three computer techies in Minneapolis, whom he had often used for corporate spying, particularly on companies he felt were takeover targets, had been on his payroll for some time. This was the crew that had hacked into the computers of the two museums.

The men arrested at various places around the South and Midwest were part of a team Arundel's lieutenant, Hank Herkimer, had recruited and trained to engage in corporate espionage and other nefarious activities. The cadre was made up of a half-dozen ex-cons and renegade Special Forces men, for whom Arundel had built a large wooden lodge, with a number outbuildings, at a secret location fifteen miles from his home. This was the place where these men would gather to get their instructions from Herkimer, just before an operation was initiated, for activities such as pilfering emails, confidential memos, and secret balance sheets. In some cases, it was alleged, they had actually roughed up individuals who Arundel felt were withholding important information. These men, of course, were also the ones who had carried out the missions at the two museums.

As for Kopec, he had been hired by Arundel as someone who knew all the dirt in the arts world as well as plans for such things as galas and art openings. Kopec, it was thought, had helped Arundel identify and plan the locations and scheduling of the crimes. In every case, it was made clear that Arundel had paid handsomely for these services; each person involved, it was alleged, had received spot payments or annual salaries many times what they would otherwise have earned.

Despite this, even the rich rewards could not outweigh the threat of going to jail, perhaps for a long, long time. And so, when the case began to unfold, the three computer geeks and the arts blogger turned against Arundel. In each case they claimed, probably correctly, that they had been told this was all a prank: that Arundel simply wanted to play a trick on these men and embarrass them in a very public way. They were horrified, they said, that the outcome actually ended in murder.

Arundel hired a battery of very expensive lawyers, but it seemed unlikely that they could successfully counter the evidence mounting against their client. He had contributed, it was thought, to his own downfall—first, by having such a prodigious, uncontrollable temper, and second, by his massive ego, which led him to believe he was in some way invincible. He had lulled himself into complacency, especially when he became convinced that law enforcement would never suspect him as long as they had Bigelow and Catlett in their sights.

• • •

On Friday, six days after the arrest of Arundel and his operatives, the following article appeared in the *New York Times* under the byline of Georgina Fleming and Andrew Considine:

> The nation of Cape Verde consists of an archipelago of ten islands in the Atlantic Ocean roughly 350 miles west of the coast of West Africa. The islands vary in size and topography, with the larger ones home to most activities, such as the country's four international airports, the capital, and its luxury hotels. It was to Cape Verde that Thomas Catlett moved at a time that coincided with the second of the so-called Patron Murders. The timing of the move, together with the fact that Cape Verde has no extradition treaty with the United States, gave rise to the suspicion that Mr. Catlett might have been a suspect in the case. Since that is no longer the case, an interview with Mr. Catlett was obtained by the New York Times through the office of his attorney, Mr. Seth McFarland of Denver.
>
> In conversations with Mr. McFarland several facts were established. The first was that Catlett's leaving Aspen was not sudden or precipitous but had been long planned. The second was that the timing of his departure coinciding with one of the patron murders astonished Mr. Catlett as much as anyone else. And the third was that he had wanted to go public with the facts from the beginning but was persuaded by the FBI to delay

any announcement until the actual culprit was in custody.

Mr. Catlett's new home is on one of the medium-sized islands: a sprawling structure of rough, beige stucco walls, a red tile roof, and floor-to-ceiling windows with wooden slat blinds. Inside is a spacious living room; seven oversize bedrooms, each with its own bath; a state-of-the-art kitchen; and a makeshift office with books and cartons strewn on all sides. In the front is a wide veranda facing a stretch of lush, green lawn and a broad sand beach along the Atlantic Ocean. A series of verdant mountains rise in the distance behind the house. The compound also includes a number of outbuildings of the same stucco with tile roofs as the main house, an oversize swimming pool, gardens, and a helicopter pad.

His visitors were invited to join Mr. Catlett in his new office, a large space equipped with all the latest in computers and communication, but still somewhat in disarray due to the files and books that had not yet been shelved or put in cabinets. Making way for his visitors by pushing a few cartons aside and bringing a spare chair from the living room, he invited questions. A lean, seemingly fit man about five feet ten, he has red hair streaked here and there with a bit of gray. Though he has penetrating blue-green eyes, a sharp nose, and a firm chin, his face nevertheless was warm and welcoming, and he occasionally broke into a mischievous smile. He asked what we wanted to know.

There were two questions, his visitors said, the first probably easier to answer than the second: "Why Cape Verde as a place to retire?"

"I first came here," he began, "a little over a year ago and was quite impressed. I had come because I'd made a sizeable investment in a firm that produced turbines for the wind farms Cape Verde is developing. Right now, 25 percent of the electricity for these islands is created by wind power, and in less than ten years the figure will be 50 percent. I'm also interested in helping the country get into solar panels and other non-carbon-producing energy initiatives. You'd be amazed: this place has an opportunity to become a showcase, a lab for the whole world, as far as cutting back on carbon emissions goes.

"But there was more," he continued. "The country has an

unbelievably moderate year-round temperature and great music—have you heard it?"

"Not yet."

"You've got a treat in store. Beyond that, though, the place is a thriving young democracy, and has wonderful people."

"Sounds ideal."

"It is. But you had a second question."

"Are you really leaving the U.S. for good?" he was asked.

"Absolutely," he replied.

"Renouncing your citizenship?"

"We haven't gotten that far."

"When did this idea about leaving take shape?"

"Some time in the late '90s, I noticed an insidious, creeping infection and immorality among financiers, business leaders, and politicians. It was a breakdown in ethics that people never mentioned and pretended not to see. It was like a person with a deadly disease that no one, including the patient, admits is there. Then one day they perform a CT scan or an MRI, and it not only turns out to be terminal, it has invaded the whole body."

"Can you be more specific?" he was asked.

"Take finance," he said. "Over the past twenty years, there has been a snowstorm, a veritable blizzard of new investment techniques—structured products, derivatives, high frequency trading—that have one thing in common. They are so maddeningly technical and highly secretive that no one can understand them. Actually, they have two things in common: they invariably benefit the few at the expense of the many."

"Your friends at the Cloud Club said that your favorite phrase was noblesse oblige."

"With rare exceptions, for today's billionaires those words are not only a foreign term, they are a foreign concept. I'm not speaking of blatant crooks engaging in Ponzi schemes or out-and-out fraud. I'm speaking of the so-called 'good guys,' upstanding CEOs of admired corporations, major bank presidents, Silicon Valley gurus, hedge fund managers. Instead of noblesse oblige, their standard is: 'Everybody's doing it.' Take the salaries of CEOs, which have become more and more inflated every year to a point where they are beyond all reason or justification. Board finance committees always justify such outrages by saying, 'So and so's CEO makes $32 million a year and ours only $12 million. What's wrong with us?' Whereupon they up their man's annual salary to a ridiculous, entirely unnecessary figure. Believe me, I know what it takes to live a luxurious life—four houses, let's say, a private plane, and the rest—and it's not $32 million. A couple of million a year will do very nicely, thank you."

"Are there no bright spots?"

"You tell me. Look at education. Day by day the United States is falling further and further behind the rest of the civilized world. Even now, half the adult population doesn't believe in the reality of either evolution or climate change. How retro is that?"

"In your mind, is it really that dire, that bleak?"

"Right now" he replied, "America is like an ocean liner of a hundred years ago, the Titanic or the Mauretania. Like those ships, our boat has three classes. In first class are the billionaires, the .001 percent; in second, the reasonably well-off; and in third, everyone else. The ship has long since sailed, blindingly hoping to land on some enchanted shore where life is idyllic. The ship, however, had hardly left port when the first-class passengers were demanding more and more perks—and getting them. At the expense, I might add, of those in second and third. Those in second class, not to be outdone, were forcing some of their fellow passengers with little clout to move down to third, where both food and space were becoming scarcer and scarcer.

"And because the custodians of this vessel had long since given up any idea of maintenance or investing in the future, suddenly, when the ship was far out at sea, in the middle of nowhere, the rudders malfunctioned, making it impossible to steer the ship. Not long after, the radar went out, and then all satellite communication. There it was, this vast luxury liner, adrift in the middle of the limitless ocean, headed for who knows where, and time fast running out."

"So you see no hope for the country?"

"At the moment, no—at least, not in my lifetime."

# CHAPTER TWENTY-FIVE

These events were in the future, the Catlett interview a week away and the trial of Arundel many weeks after that. As for the present—the Saturday morning after Arundel and his cronies were apprehended—I was in my loft preparing to grab a bite before heading off for the matinee when suddenly the buzzer rang. Having no idea who it could be, I pushed the intercom and heard Phyllida's voice.

"Sliced chicken or tuna?' she asked.

"Phyllida?"

"I have one of each. You can have your pick if you let me come up."

"I'll come down."

"Just push the buzzer."

A few moments later, she got off the elevator with the two sandwiches, as well as various items like pâté, cheese, and crackers, and a bottle of wine.

"To what do I owe this vision: a lady bearing gifts?"

"Come on, Matt, surely you can guess. The news spread all over TV."

"Something, isn't it?"

She moved into the kitchen, where she began to open cupboards, pulling out plates and cutlery. "For God's sake," she said, "open the wine."

"I've got two shows today. Remember?"

"One glass won't hurt you, even two."

We made our way into the living room, put the plates on the coffee table, and sat down. I was ready to take her in my arms when she put up her hand. "First we eat a bite, then I hear about these cases and your involvement."

"I was hoping you had come to see me."

"*Ça va sans dire.*"

I poured a glass of wine for each of us, and we dived into the hors d'oeuvres.

"The Tremayne affair first," she said. "How involved were you?"

"As you know, I had known them for fifteen, twenty years, and was extremely fond of Dorothy."

"Were you two ever romantically involved?"

"I think keeping that out of the equation allowed us to be that much closer. Anyway, I did get involved in that case, so involved that I found myself one day in the loft here being confronted by the son's boyfriend with a gun in his hand aimed straight at me. I don't think he meant to kill me, but he was so wired, so on edge, he could easily have shot me accidentally. Fortunately, Detective Monaghan appeared just in time to get me out of it."

"Jesus," she said.

"In the museum murders, there was nothing remotely like that. It was 98 percent the FBI, tracking down those people all over the country."

"Even so."

"Please, Phyllida, don't get carried away."

"I will if I want to." After a moment, "It's ironic, isn't it?'

"What do you mean?"

"Those two trustees were killed not by someone who believed as Sonny Beaufort does, as we all do, that rich people shouldn't be able to buy their way onto boards, but by someone who believed just the opposite, that you should be able to buy whatever you want, including being a trustee on a major arts board."

By this time we had finished eating. I put my hands on her shoulders, looked at her, and said, "A wonderful insight. You're absolutely right, but suddenly, right now, my mind is on something else."

"What is that, pray tell?"

I kissed her and pulled her down on the sofa. We held each other; she touched my face; I held her breast. We kissed again. This went on with increasing intensity for some time. We were lost in the moment when she abruptly pulled away. "Don't you have a matinee?" she asked.

I looked at the clock on the wall. "Oh, my God . . . I barely have time to make half-hour."

"Love interruptus," she said.

"God, what a time to have to leave."

"Go, go," she said, and started to pick up the dishes.

"Leave everything," I said, "and thanks for a marvelous lunch."

• • •

Saturday night Annie and Curtis were coming to see the show. They had arrived from Boston on Friday, and we met for supper before they came to the theatre. Afterwards they came back to the dressing room, and everyone gathered on stage where we had arranged a wine-and-cheese reception. The playwright was there, as well as the director and Ardith and Freddie from the CTG. It was one of those occasions that was both happy and sad. Annie and Danny had recently lost their mother, and their father would soon go to jail. At the same time, the show was going very well. The outlying press and TV, in New Jersey and Connecticut, had been excellent, and word-of-mouth was enthusiastic. We were playing to full houses every weekend as well as a few weeknights. At the reception, people stayed much longer than I would have expected, which I was happy to see, especially for Annie, Curtis, and Danny.

• • •

On Sunday Phyllida and I met at the Morgan Library at 37th and Madison. After all that had gone before, we had silently agreed that there would be no talk of my show, of the museum murders, or of her magazine articles. So we became regular museum visitors, looking at the main exhibit that was on: watercolors, engravings, illustrations, and poems by William Blake. The draftsmanship was extraordinary; some colors vivid, others subdued, and the mystical and religious subjects haunting and evanescent. After the exhibit we had lunch in the museum's small, tasteful dining room, but skipped dessert and coffee. Phyllida said we could have them at her place.

We walked the short distance to her brownstone on 38th near Park. Once inside the house, we entered the living room—a large, comfortable space that was a combination of contemporary and traditional: an abstract painting, for instance, hung over a richly textured antique chest. The room was striking for its total lack of artifice or pretension; rather, it had a comfortable, settled feeling. The kitchen was clearly modern, with black granite counters and the latest in appliances. She didn't even mention dessert and coffee, but took a bottle of wine from the fridge and gave it to me, along with a corkscrew. "Open it," she said, "while I get the glasses."

Bottle in hand, I followed her to the staircase. Neither of us spoke. At the top of the stairs, we entered her bedroom. She put the glasses down, took the bottle and poured a small amount in each glass, gave me one, raised hers, and said, "Cheers."

"Cheers," I said.

After one sip she put her glass down and began to undress. I did the same. When I had taken everything off, I looked up. She was standing there with nothing on, and I noticed two things right away: one was the confirmation that the arresting auburn hair on her head was absolutely authentic; the other was that she had the most beautiful breasts I'd ever seen. She went to the bed, threw back the covers, and held out her hand. We got in bed, held each other, and went from there.

When it was over, I said, "That was quick."

"What do you mean? We took our own sweet time, and I enjoyed every minute of it."

"I don't mean the lovemaking; that was as good as it gets—I would even say the best. I meant our getting to this point."

She pulled back and looked at me. "We were almost there a week ago, and yesterday we would have been there except for that damned matinee."

"That would have been even quicker."

"Quick, quicker. My God, would you just relax?"

"You're right," I said and took her in my arms again. We held each other for some time. Eventually, as she lay on her back looking at the ceiling, she said, "The way I see it, any man who, in a matter of days, solves three murders and opens in a Broadway show is entitled to a little R and R."

It was going to be a long, lazy afternoon.